Gillian Slovo is the author of eleven novels, including *Red Dust*, which was made into a film starring Hilary Swank and Chiwetel Ejiofor and *Ice Road* which was shortlisted for the 2004 Orange Prize for Fiction. Her family memoir, *Every Secret Thing*, was an international bestseller. Her play, *Guantanamo*, co-written for the Tricycle Theatre, has played in theatres around the world, including New York and Washington DC.

'Captivating . . . Character traits and societal pressures are never distinct from each other in *Black Orchids*; they interweave into a nuanced and moving narrative. But in addition to this being an astute look at racism and belonging, this is also a roller coaster of a narrative which combines startling surprises with painfully inevitable moments. Slovo knows how to pace a story, and how to make you care about the fates of characters you may not even like' *Guardian*

'An epic narrative is driven by a commitment to profound and contemporary issues. The novel pledges itself to a noble ethic, showing at each moment the folly, cruelty and ubiquity of the toxins of racial prejudice . . . Provocative and original' *Independent*

'Immensely absorbing and poignant . . . [Slovo's] themes are consistent with her earlier work and just as potent: race, class, the tumultuous politics of identity and belonging, and a dogged refusal to let her characters forget the consequences of their actions' Ceridwen Dovey, *Financial Times*

'Gillian Slovo's tightly paced novel doesn't just offer a social history of ethnicity in a changing England; it's an examination of the often indivisible link between personal weakness and social prejudice. And in refusing to let characters off the hook, it's a study in the politics of belonging that's much more than skin deep' *Metro*

Nörling

Black Orchids

GILLIAN SLOVO

virago

VIRAGO

First published in Great Britain in 2008 by Virago Press
This paperback edition published in 2009 by Virago Press

A CIP catalogue record for this book
is available from the British Library.

ISBN 978-1-84408-313-8

Typeset in Garamond by M Rules
Printed and bound in Great Britain by
Clays Ltd, St Ives plc

Papers used by Virago are natural, renewable and
recyclable products sourced from well-managed forests and certified
in accordance with the rules of the Forest Stewardship Council.

Mixed Sources
Product group from well-managed
forests and other controlled sources
www.fsc.org Cert no. SGS-COC-004081
© 1996 Forest Stewardship Council

Virago Press
An imprint of
Little, Brown Book Group
100 Victoria Embankment
London EC4Y 0DY

An Hachette UK Company
www.hachette.co.uk

www.virago.co.uk

To Ronald Segal

for a friendship that crossed generations

1946

Ceylon

When Evelyn looked at the toddy tapper, he looked away.

With her wavy blonde hair, pale skin and height, Evelyn was used to being stared at by Ceylonese men. Her sister always maintained that she somehow must encourage this attention. But she didn't. Absolutely not. It stopped her from looking as she would want to. And yet, as the toddy tapper's lids flickered up once more to set her in his sights, she conceded the point to Marjorie. If the attention were to end, she might miss it. She smiled.

The man did not smile back.

Embarrassed, Evelyn looked beyond him.

A rising wind had begun to sway the branches of the coconut palm and to send clouds scudding across a darkening stretch of sky. The warm, cloying damp air pressed against her.

'Must you always stray?' Evelyn's sister, Marjorie, often addressed her as if she were one of the three dogs their mother kept and an undisciplined member of the pack at that who never would respond to any bidding.

Marjorie was standing at the red-brown sanded verge of the narrow road. Having, as ever, refused to remove a single item of clothing including her white cotton jacket that was buttoned up over her long-sleeved yellow frock, she was so hot her mouse-brown hair made dark clumped tracks down her thin neck. Her face was also reddened by the heat and by the ignominy of having to wait in front of all these natives, a circumstance that, since she never could bring herself to criticise the fiancé whose car had broken down, she now attempted to take out on Evelyn. 'And must you stare so?'

Sighing, Evelyn looked across the road. There railway tracks led in one direction to Colombo and, in the other, to the island's southernmost tip. Two sari-clad women were walking down the middle of the tracks, closely followed by a Buddhist monk in saffron robes, his upheld umbrella shielding his shaven head as he daintily over-stepped the timbers on which the rails rested. Such a peaceful sight. Evelyn was seized by an impulse to cross the road and the railway tracks and keep on going until she got to the rubber trees beyond, there to dig a groove and watch the oozing out of that thick, white mucus which, hitting air, would congeal elastic. But if she did, she'd miss the moment she'd been awaiting.

Having agreed to chaperon Marjorie and Gordon on their day trip down south, Evelyn had wished and wished that they would pass this knot of palms in time for the toddy tapping, and wished again (because she knew Marjorie would say no) that they could stop and watch. And then just as they were passing, Gordon's Austin had snorted and banged, emitting acrid fumes, and had ground to a stop and, by the look of the growing cluster of men, their heads tucked under the raised bonnet, there was not going to be any quick way of getting the car back on the road. Evelyn was in luck.

She was exhilarated. It happened increasingly these days.

She would be possessed by an excitement whose source she did not quite understand. Her mother said it was her age, her sister that it was her way of getting attention, and her ayah that it was all the changes about to take place. But Evelyn thought there was something much more mysterious at play. A premonition; no, it wasn't just a premonition it was more a certainty that something good was about to happen.

That early morning as she had lain in bed listening to the rhythmic thwack of the ceiling fan beating its giant arms through the muggy thickness of the air, she had been possessed by this same certainty. Still dark although the household would soon begin to stir. First the kitchen staff rising and washing themselves outside before putting on the pots to boil. Then the sound that had run right through Evelyn's childhood, the rhythmic scraping of a grater against coconut to produce tiny flakes to thicken and add taste to sambols and curries beloved of the staff (and Evelyn as well). These along with the moist squares of kiri bath rice or paper-thin scooped hoppers were exotic accompaniment to the boarders' English breakfast.

Evelyn had been bursting with expectation of the day to come and gripped by a conviction that her life, directionless since she had left school, was about to open up even if she didn't know how.

Her wooden shutters were propped half open. There was no glass to stop her peering out beyond the intricate iron fretwork to breathe in the egg-yolk closeness of the pre-dawn dark. A neighbour's dog began to bark, setting off another. In the garden her mother's latest rescued stray lifted up his head to sniff the air.

It was already airless and stifling hot. Going through the curtain that separated her bedroom from the corridor, Evelyn had come upon Minrada stretched out on her bedroll. Although Minrada, always a light sleeper, must have known that Evelyn was there, she had kept her eyes tight shut even when Evelyn had leaned down to whisper in her ear, 'I'm only going out for air.' She tucked a stray strand of Minrada's still glossy black hair behind her ear before kissing the old woman gently on the forehead and moving on.

Down the long teak-lined corridor, her passing stirring up the curtains that served as partition to her mother's bedroom and her sister's, the rustle of this fabric a gentle counterpoint to the snores that penetrated the doors behind which the lodgers upstairs lay.

Evelyn had picked her way past the lounge's three-piece suite that, bequeathed by her mother's mother, was jammed up against the rattan chairs and love seats that had come with the house.

She had been happy, on the point of singing out. How wonderful to have possession of this place without the hindrance of its daytime bustle, scrubbings and gratings and washings and cookings, the monotonous cycle of a household that survived by renting out rooms to English ex-servicemen who administered this soon to be cast off colony.

The other servants would all still be asleep in the back room that adjoined the kitchen. Evelyn left the house, as she rarely did, through the front door. She stepped out to air thick with moisture. Pulling the door shut, she had considered walking along the veranda that ran the whole length of this front part of the house. But as this might wake her mother and Marjorie, she had climbed down the wooden steps and into the garden.

A half-suppressed yip from the new dog. The other two merely had sniffed and licked her outstretched hand before slumping back down, conserving their energy for the day.

Standing, waiting for the darkness to differentiate, Evelyn had begun to see the outlines of the wide stretch of lawn and beyond it, the high bushes that lined the garden fence. That moment before dawn was filled with sounds that her bedroom fan had filtered out, the rustling of frogs and palm squirrels in the undergrowth, the trundle of a rickshaw on the dirt street, the clop of a horse-drawn cart and, spiking above these, the percussive chatter of fruit bats coming in to roost on the branches of the towering tree next door. The high snarling of the already settled rose up into the fading night, escalating to an abrasive screech as they were jolted by the crash landings of clumsy newcomers.

By dawn the bats would all have roosted, soft tattered lumps of dark cloth clinging with their feet to the topmost branches, their long finger wings furled around their bodies and occasionally fanning out. And if the bats were almost all back, then somewhere soon the red fireball of the sun would rise. Not that Evelyn would be able to watch the sunrise, their rented house having been constructed in such a way that day followed night and night day without any of the fireworks that should attend them.

Which, Evelyn had thought, said much about their life, and their place, in this Ceylon.

'Dreaming again?'

For once Evelyn had reason to be grateful for her sister's scolding. It would not do to miss the first moment of the climb. As Marjorie, having distributed another morsel of her considerable reserves of spite, moved off, Evelyn looked back to the knot of palm trees.

The toddy tapper was double-hitching up his sarong and tying it at the waist so as to free himself of restraint. His shirt gaped open. She could see the outline of shadowed ribs beneath.

Behind him and running up the serrated trunk of the palm was a succession of knotted pieces of rope that were to be his ladder. The tree had been bent by years of driving winds so that even as it stretched up into the changeable sky it leaned towards the ocean. Such a giant of strength with its long trunk, drooping fronds and thick high spray burst of orange coconut flowers. A tree to match the inge-nuity of its human allies, the tappers who, high up, had attached three rope guide-lines – two for the legs, and one for the hands – running them through the air to a second tree some ten feet away and on again on to the next to produce, between these seven differently sized palms, a roped gangway.

The tapper took up his thick leather working belt and slung it low around his waist. Into the deep, dark brown wooden box that hung off the belt he slotted a flat-bladed knife for the cutting away of branches, a broad, curved knife for the slashing open of coconut flowers and a bulb-shaped wooden tapping tool. He moved the box until he could easily stretch back his long arm and pull out any implement. He bent again, this time to pick up a rope which he coiled, so fast she could barely catch the movement of his hands, before securing it to his belt. Lastly, he tied on the bowl that was the kernel of a browned and dried labu fruit.

Then across his lined face, thin to match his wiry body, there passed an expression she couldn't quite decipher. Doubt, she thought, as the expression settled – he has forgotten something. As if in confirmation, his bony hands dropped to his belt, his tapered fingers checking what he had. Finding everything in place, however, he did not start his climb. He moved, instead, over to another man and they began an earnest conversation, their heads almost touching except for the moments when one or other of them would look up, suddenly, at the sky.

She was too far away to hear what they were saying and even if she had been closer her rudimentary Sinhala would have let her down. But she knew they were worried about the wind.

She also looked up. It wasn't going to rain, she was convinced of it. It was only threatening to. And it wasn't even that windy.

Her luck, her magic, had brought them to this place specifically so she could watch him climbing. That's how it should work. What she, Evelyn Elizabeth Dorothy Williams wished for, is what she should get. And yes, she saw him nodding, and then she saw him waiting as the barrel man rolled some shredded tobacco mixed with limestone paste into a betel leaf. He handed the pellet to the toddy tapper, who chewed for a moment before letting out a stream of red spit and then moving back to the tree.

Victory. He was going to climb. An exhilaration, similar to the one that had visited her that early morning, returned.

But the toddy tapper seemed once more to hesitate. Go on, she willed, go on. He turned, suddenly, to look in her direction.

His gaze was straight and clear, unusual coming as it did from a Sinhalese stranger. And something else, something shivering underneath this inspection. Not curiosity at this white missie who had come to watch his prowess. Not derision either. Something deeper, darker and sadder. Resignation, that was what she was looking at and with this realisation there came a thought – that he was going to fall.

The man wiggled his head in that Ceylonese way, his neck moving from side to side as he gave a small elliptical nod, his recognition of her interest acknowledged and topped by a sudden smile. As his expression cleared, she read in his face the truth of what Marjorie was always telling her she did – dramatising situations to suit her own needs. The toddy tapper was mocking her.

He turned and began to climb. His knees he kept bent and open as he glided up the trunk. He was fast and he was light, a thing seemingly constructed not from skin and bones and muscles but from air. Having reached the point, way above her, where the first branch joined the trunk he hauled himself up and there, for a moment, stood. A tall man, he looked tiny on the crest of that enormous tree whose branches were waving in the wind.

A dark bird, a black crow, flew past the tree, so close that, from Evelyn's point of view, it seemed to graze his head. Taking no notice of the bird, the toddy tapper shifted closer to the place where the branch joined the trunk. There spathes gave way to a mass of flower buds from which was hung a second bowl. He poured its liquid contents into the bowl on his belt before using his broad knife to chop at the point where a spray of palm flowers was bound, cutting through the sheath to expose a fresh surface of buds.

Now Evelyn must step away or else be hit by fragments of coconut cork that came spinning through the air, catching the light as they fell, landing on the hard and dusty ground and scattering. She picked up one small, round, faded yellow piece. Held it to her nose, breathing in that faint damp of coconut and bark, a foretaste of the thick, sweet and slightly soured toddy that would be the first product of its fermentation.

The man was already on the move. Both hands circled the top rope and pushed forward as his feet, out-turned like a ballet dancer's, glided along the two lower ropes. Even in motion he was half crouched, his knees angled, the sinews of his legs straining against the ropes that bent a little to his weight. Such an odd posture. Despite the flexion he achieved he looked less like a ballet dancer than a man-sized praying mantis, those long toes gripping and sliding along the tightrope, moving him upwards (the next tree in the sequence being higher) until, securely on that trunk, he poured more gathered liquid into his pot.

The pot now being full, he let drop one end of his long rope. After it had touched ground, he tied the pot to the other end. He let go, the unencumbered end rising up as mirror to the falling of the heavy pot that twisted and spun its way down until it could be caught by the man on the ground. She could see the clouded grey liquid topped by a thick white foam from which there issued a pungent smell that grew more rank as the man poured it into the barrel.

Having reeled up the empty pot, the toddy tapper hacked out another opening before turning towards the third of the seven trees. It was higher than the one he was on so he must swing his leg over a branch in order to put out a foot. As he did, the wind picked up. It moved the ropes laterally so that he had one foot on the trunk and the other heading down to the place where a rope should have been but wasn't.

He is . . . Evelyn thought, holding her breath, seeing him floundering in space, trying to make contact with a rope that a fresh gust of wind swung even further away . . . he is going to fall; this thought seemingly occurring to the man, who darted back his head. But the ropes behind him were also wildly swinging. Still holding firmly to the trunk he turned to face frontward. He drew himself up.

Don't, she thought.

The man was tall and he was strong. And so alive, she thought. She spoke to herself in Marjorie's sensible voice. He won't fall, is what she told herself. He knows that danger. He'll be careful.

His foot stretched out to lock in the rope as simultaneously he took hold of the guide-line and then he was safely on both ropes, pushing down in the wind so that he bounced a little as if on a trampoline, that strong stick insect of a man moving through space as three things happened.

The first, the return of the bird, or one just like it, flying close to him, registered its jarring caw as she heard a second sound. A train – she could hear its throaty whistle. She turned briefly to see a steam engine pulling four dark red carriages. Back again and up she looked. Which was when there came the third intrusion. Another new arrival. Someone driving full throttle on a motorcycle. All these events Evelyn registered and was to remember registering for all her life, those three unrelated happenings stuck in memory because of what happened next.

The toddy tapper was moving over the last few inches of the rope. One hand holding on to the rope, he reached with the other for the trunk. The wind was swinging him but no more violently than before. And then there came the bird, the train and the motorcycle, none of which he probably noticed, and none he would probably ever notice again, for he was already falling.

From the moment he had lost his grip he must have known that he was lost. And yet, arms flailing, he grappled for a rope that was no longer in grappling distance. A gust of wind sent a cloud skittering away, and the sun shining, bright on that thin and blackened figure as it fell. That thin, double-jointed scarecrow of a man tumbling down to earth. Legs furiously pedalling at hard angles to each other as if, should he exert himself enough, he might fly up, and this even as he was twisted down, agonisingly slowly to the beating of her heart, and far too fast for the ending of his life which came, she was sure it had, when his body hit.

And there at the red point of the spat-out betel leaf lay a jumble of fragmented skin, and bones that once had been a man.

Evelyn could hear, but distantly, the sound of Marjorie's screaming. I should go to her, she thought. She looked across at the toddy tapper's partner, equally motionless by the barrel. Somebody must, she thought . . . somebody must . . . and then somebody did.

A man striding past. Without breaking pace his hand plucking something off his head and flinging it away. She could not bring herself to look down and see what it was. Her eyes were too concentrated on the stranger as he came abreast of the fallen man and crouched down and reached out and, without hesitation, touched the dead.

The heap moved and it groaned.

The stranger turned. For a moment he seemed to be looking in her direction and in that moment she thought, he knows that it's my fault. He knows I willed this into being. But his gaze had already shifted past her as he barked out some instructions.

He was a man clearly accustomed to being obeyed. Wheels cracked over stones as a rickshaw was dragged up. Then men picked up their injured comrade and laid him in the rickshaw and hauled him off.

The stranger rose and kicked the ground. Covering the

blood, she thought. He turned and this time there was no denying that she was the focus of his scrutiny.

He sees – her thought – he sees what I have done.

The thought filled her with shame. And something, some sense of excitement, that embarrassed her.

She forced herself to meet his gaze full on. She saw a slight, wiry man with delicate features, brown eyes so dark they were almost black, thick black eyelashes and smooth honey brown skin. She also saw the strength of his resolve, an assessment reinforced by his refusal to turn away. She was the one to flinch and to blink and to look down.

There was a sprinkling of red-brown dust on her wedged brown pumps and the line of one of her nylons was twisted above the shoe. I should straighten it, she thought, but not in public, and then she thought that she would far rather take off the nylons and her shoes as well, and walk barefoot into the sea, immersing herself, and that way obliterate the image of the man who kept spinning down in memory just as the cork he had hacked out had spun.

The new arrival was suddenly close to her and bending down. For a moment she thought he might have come to straighten her nylons but instead he picked up the goggles he had earlier discarded and smiled at her. It must have been his motorcycle, she thought, remembering the sound.

There was something so familiar in his smile. She looked away, quickly, and as she did she also seemed to hear his voice; *Nice ankles* is what she seemed to hear him saying.

Surely not. A man had fallen, had almost certainly lost his life and she was thinking about this stranger's admiration for her ankles. She was appalled by her own callousness.

'Come.' One of his hands holding hers, and the other under her elbow. 'Come.' She could feel the heat of him as he half carried her over to a tree stump where he helped her sit. She closed her eyes. She felt his hand again, this time on the back of her head – pressure, although gentle, she could not resist.

'Wait until the dizziness passes.'

He was right, she was terribly dizzy, and her head so heavy. She let it drop. And there she sat, and sitting, didn't move.

She was conscious of the pressure of his hand and of a roaring sound. Not the vengeful sea but her blood pumping furiously in her ears, this noise gradually diminishing, until other things – the beat of the hot sun and the wind picking up, the cry of a bird and the rustling of palm branches, and, underpinning these, the thundering call of the waves – began to claim her attention.

'Better?' He was kneeling.

She nodded. And yes, truly she was better.

'Take your time.'

She felt her breath constrict.

'The wind was too strong. He should not have risked it. These people,' he shrugged, 'have their minds too focused on their next meal. Yesterday it rained so they didn't climb. Today, it appears, that foolish toddy tapper was determined. Or else his master was.'

Of course. It hadn't been her fault. She said, 'Will he . . . ?'

'He was fortunate. Some bones broken but with luck he will survive.' And she, despite her memory of the tumbled and bloodied heap, wanted to believe him. He's that kind of man, she thought, who makes you want to believe.

17

'Evelyn.' Marjorie's voice.

'My sister . . .'

'Is over there by the car. Are you strong enough to walk to her?'

A whirlwind of charm and confidence, the stranger introduced himself as Emil. So sure was he of being accepted that he had little trouble overcoming Marjorie's suspicions when he asked, and obtained, her gracious permission for him to send someone from his estate (of course, Evelyn thought, the fact that he was Sinhalese ruling class, and rich, and educated was evident in the precision of his English, his shining motorbike, and his brisk air of command) who would see to Gordon's Austin. And after that, he said, they could continue on their way.

He's going to get back on his motorcycle, Evelyn thought, and drive off, and without a further thought, found herself saying, 'I want to go home.'

'Yes.' This from Marjorie. 'Weren't you listening? We will go home. As soon as the car is mended.'

'I want to go home.' Feeling his curious gaze on her. 'I want to go now.'

Which is how she ended up riding pillion.

He steadied her as she sat side saddle before, as per instruction, swinging one leg over and swivelling to face frontward. She felt the motorcycle shake as he hefted himself on. His hands went up to his head, straightening the goggles until they lay flat across his black hair, and then he turned to tell her where to place her feet. As she rested them on the chrome bars, she couldn't help noticing him looking at them.

'Hold me tight around the waist.' He turned away.

She wrapped her arms against the hard flat of a stomach that contracted as he kicked down. A roar and they were off.

Her first time on a motorcycle and she loved it. She loved that glorious sensation of freedom and of speed, the wind pulling back on her hair as she nestled close up to his billowing white shirt. She could feel his muscular back, hard against her, a strange feeling that she made herself swallow down.

He drove down the middle of the dirt road swerving expertly to avoid the potholes. Remembering the roar of his arrival (and with that the bird, and train as well) she knew he must be driving more slowly because of her. She couldn't help wishing he'd go faster.

The muscles in his upper arms contracted as he turned the throttle. As the motorcycle shot forward, she felt the increased push of him against her.

Looking up, she watched the flashing past of high cables that ran beside the road and noticed that, hanging off them, were fried and slithered scraps of tattered black. Bats that had been electrocuted, she thought. She remembered the sound of the fruit bats landing that early morning. She swayed.

He braked and stopped. 'Was that too fast?'

She shook her head. 'No, not too fast.' She could feel tears blearing. 'Something in my eye,' she said, hoping he would believe her.

He acted as if he did. Almost. He took out a pressed white handkerchief. For a moment as it lay there in his brown hand she thought he was going to use it as a mother might dab her daughter's eyes. What he did instead was hand the handkerchief to her. She wiped her eyes, before returning it. 'Thank you, that's much better.'

He pulled his goggles off and offered them to her.

'Oh no, I wouldn't hear of it.'

He got off the motorcycle and put them on her, walking then to adjust them at the back. And then he climbed back on and kicked down and they were off.

Soon afterwards, he steered the motorcycle away from the main road. Now she must clasp him tightly as, weaving through a grove of rubber trees, the motorcycle bounced across the rutted dirt. The goggles pressed against her eyes, and his hair against her skin. The hair was thick and sleek and black and it smelt like . . . like an orchid, she thought, although it had not occurred to her until that moment that orchids even had a special scent.

The plantation through which they were passing was peopled, although it took Evelyn a while to spot the men and women collecting sap. She knew that they must long since have registered her presence and, if called upon, would afterwards be able to describe exactly how close to him she had been, as well as the manner in which she had been disarrayed, the skirt of her white frock flaring from her waist. She saw how they nodded at Emil, some of them going as far as to tip their hats, and after they had passed, she felt curious eyes boring into her back.

The undergrowth grew increasingly more dense and the air that was displaced by the surge forward of the motorcycle felt hot and thick. She could see a bright orange festival of flowers, the topmost branches of a jungle fire tree that towered over the dark green under-pull. Were they heading straight into the jungle?

As the engine strained up a long incline, she turned to look back. They were high enough for her to see beyond the rubber plantation to the road that led back to Marjorie and to Gordon and her life. For a moment she was frightened, fear making her loosen her grip.

He instantly responded, pressing one of his hands on top of hers, shouting over his shoulder, 'We don't have far to go.'

And soon, too soon it felt, he made a sharp right hand turn and the jungle seemed magically to retreat. They were out in the open now, careering up a long dirt driveway that led past a clipped and rolling lawn up to a large house. He stopped the bike, swinging himself off.

'I'll go and call the PD.'

She put her feet on the ground but did not climb down. She was too busy staring.

The house was monumental and two storeyed and white and it stood at the apex of a vast, open garden, its long sloping roofs of green tin glimmering in the sunlight. Running along the whole of the first floor was a wide, pillared and segmented balcony. Below this, on ground level, was a gabled and shaded wrap-around veranda. She counted, and counted again to make sure, and yes there were at least ten grand windows on each level at either side of the square entrance which, marked out by two thick white pillars, was partially concealed by tall bamboo.

A voice sounding in her ear, 'Madam.'

She hadn't noticed two people, a diminutive woman in a sari and a man in a long white shirt and white sarong, approaching. Now, holding her palms up and together and dipping forward in a gesture of respect and welcome, the woman said, 'Madam. My *lamanthani* says that you best be quickly coming in from the sun.'

Looking to the front door, Evelyn saw a second woman, also sari clad, although hers, a soft, pale pink, glittered with fine threads. This must be Emil's mother, she thought, although she couldn't help thinking that the woman, with her dark framed glasses, close-cut black hair and ferocious scowl had little of her son's elegance or his charm. A woman to be reckoned with.

'Thank you. That's very kind of your mistress.'

The man unfurled a tasselled parasol that he held up to shield her from the sun. She walked with him on one side and the woman on the other, nervous about meeting Emil's mother (how familiar his name already was), but by the time they got to the front door, the woman had gone.

'This way please, madam.' She was shown through the vast entrance hall into a drawing room whose proportions conjured up for her the contrasting image of the shabby, overcrowded lounge in the house that her mother didn't even own. Below an inlaid teak ceiling was a vast parquet floor dotted by fine woven rugs. Around these were artfully arranged sets of matching upright chairs and sofas, their light, mahogany carved arms and feet a contrast to the dark polished corner cabinets. Such a stately room, like the calm epi-centre of the social whirl of the high caste *goyigama* which, thinking about the estate she had just passed through, it probably was.

'Madam, please to sit.'

She sat where indicated, and chose from the offerings on an ornate silver tray, a glass of wood apple juice. It was thick and sweet and cold. Sipping it, she was cooled by one of the room's many fans.

The maid slipped quietly from the room, leaving Evelyn to its tranquillity. In other rooms, she knew, would be other members of the family, and their guests, and the scores of servants necessary for the preservation of such sedate luxury. But in here not one unnecessary or unwanted sound would ever penetrate.

What it must be to be mistress of the house, she thought, remembering herself and her expectations that early morn-ing. Today, she had thought, today it will begin. By which she had meant that this thing, unnameable and unknow-able but that she would surely recognise when it happened, this thing of which her whole nineteen years had been lived in expectation, this moment when she would make the first step into becoming the person that she had always known she would become, would this day unfold. She thought of the impression of Emil's back against her body, his hair against her face, his hand in hers.

'No.' She said the word out loud and shook her head. Marjorie was right. Her daydreaming, when she gave rein to it, always led her into dreadful trouble.

She put down her glass, and with it her dreams, to sit and wait. Patiently at first then with growing irritation.

She was revving up this indignation, when the door opened. She saw him – Emil – standing there. She saw how he was smiling.

'I was wondering where they'd hidden you. I've sent somebody to repair your sister's car. We can be off. Ready?'

She got up thinking yes, she was more than ready.

She had to hurry to keep up as he led her through the entrance hall. He was walking so fast that she wondered whether he might be running away from something. Or from somebody, she thought, and, sure enough, before they reached the door, she heard 'Emil.' She turned to see Emil's mother.

She felt Emil stiffen and she knew (just like her, she thought) that he would rather have ignored the summons. But this woman could not easily be ignored. Short and squat and fierce, she held out her hand. 'Miss Williams, I trust my son took good care of you?'

'Yes.' Evelyn felt how firm was the grip. 'Thank you. And thank you for the cold drink.'

'No need to thank.' A curt smile. 'You are heading off home?' It sounded much more like an instruction than a question.

'Yes I am. Your son has been kind enough to offer me a lift on his motorcycle.'

'I see.' Even from behind the thick lenses of her spectacles, the displeasure she was sending to her son was evident. 'Don't you think that Miss Williams might be more comfortable in the car, Emil?'

A measured pause before Emil, the dutiful son he obviously reluctantly was, turned to Evelyn. 'My mother is right. The car will be more comfortable. Shall I not call the driver?' to which, she knew without a single doubt, there could be only one answer – yes – and one that every young woman in her position would give.

'I would prefer the motorcycle.' Dazzled by her own daring as she looked straight at him: 'if that wouldn't be too great an inconvenience?' seeing out of the corner of her eyes how startled was his mother, but also his expression of delight.

'No inconvenience whatsoever.' He opened the door for her saying 'I'll see you later,' leaving his mother no choice but to nod, grimly, after which her son, grinning, confirmed Evelyn in her conviction that, like her, he did not care what other people thought.

There was something, he told her, he wanted her to see, and she held on as he revved the motorcycle over the rough terrain and deeper into the jungle. At first she found the ride uncomfortable but soon she had adapted and even begun to enjoy the sensation.

After the heat and grit of the main road it was dark and cool under the dense canopy of trees. Dappled light kept breaking through, washing everything, including the arms that she had wrapped around him, with green. She wished that whatever it was that he wanted to show her would be very far away. But soon they came to a small clearing.

They were close to a banyan tree, from whose vast branches hung a gnarled and trailing lace-work of external roots. He couldn't have brought me here for this, she thought, for she'd already told him how she had been born and lived her whole life in this country where banyan trees were commonplace.

She climbed down to stand in the lush, green cool, looking up at that dome of dark green that was broken sporadically by the spiked flywheels of palms. The sight reminded her of the toddy tapper. It came to her that Emil certainly must have lied. No one could have survived such a fall.

The *kick-kick* of a honey bird, and the long whistle of a magpie broke her thought as did his, 'Look.' His hand was up-stretched and aimed at a nearby tree.

All she could see were branches like all the rest, and many leaves. She looked at him a question.

He took sudden possession of her hand and led her over.

'Up there.' Now she realised that he was pointing at a set of thickened grey stems out of which blossomed a profusion of pale, pastel flower heads. Orchids. She remembered the scent of them on him.

'Aren't they exquisite?'

And they were, of course that was the right word for them, they were exquisite.

'I used to come here as a boy. This tree was my favourite – look how easy it is to climb – and I climbed it without regard, as boys must do. One day I nearly fell' . . .

. . . and she, seeing in her mind's eye an echo of that other's flailing, falling body . . .

'To break my fall, I grabbed those stems. I was clumsy. They broke off. Which brought me to myself. I felt the hurt I had inflicted.'

She heard his voice, strangely sober.

'I'd always loved orchids,' he said. 'I kept coming back in the hope that the damage I had inflicted would somehow be repaired. And so I was privileged to watch the stems growing back and from them, eventually, came this incredible blossoming. Many more flowers than before. My clumsiness had

actually helped the plant. Look –' turning away to point at
the tree – 'how she hangs, air rooted like the banyan and yet,
unlike the banyan, so alluring.'

And only now did he turn to look at her. His face so very
serious.

'That man,' she said, 'the toddy tapper.'

'Yes?'

'He won't survive, will he?'

'No.' His head shaking. 'Probably not.'

'But you said . . .'

'I told you what you needed to know in that moment.'

What was she doing, alone, with a man who had no compunction about telling her what he thought was necessary,
even if it was a lie? She didn't know where to look.

'Come.' His voice suddenly full of energy: 'come and see
for yourself –' stretching up and grabbing hold of a low
branch, bracing his legs against the trunk so that he could, in
one smooth motion, swing himself up. And there he sat,
smiling down on her. 'Do you have the strength?'

It was a challenge she knew she should resist. 'Of course
I do.' She took hold of his outstretched hand and, bracing her
feet against the trunk, let him pull her up which he did,
easily.

The two of them side by side. The linen of his black
trousers against her white frock. She felt – no heat this time.
She felt calm.

'The man who fell. It was his time.'

'What? His time to die?'

'Perhaps. His karma made it so.'

'You believe that?'

'Not necessarily. But he would have. As would those closest to him. This was not his first climb, nor would it by any means have been the first death over which that palm has presided. The man was a member of the *durawa* caste – to them falling is an occupational hazard. Part of life and, if necessary, part of death.'

'Is that supposed to make me feel better?'

'No. But then is any of what happened to do with you?'

Yes it was, she thought, thinking that it was she who had forced the man to climb. But, catching the thought and hearing how nonsensical it was, she held it back. She didn't anyway have to supply him with an answer. She didn't have to do anything. She could sit like this, comfortable in his company.

'Look.' He reached out to take gentle hold of a pink orchid blossom, turning it to reveal the delicate veins that ran across the waxy surface of its pale blushed petal. 'There are over 170 species of orchids on this island and although many are endangered, all of them seem absolutely fragile. But try pulling one,' he gave a tug, 'and you'll find out how very strong it is. Orchids grow almost out of nothing – some moss, no soil. They are the proof that those who defy convention can be the most successful.'

She thought at first that he was talking about himself and about the way he had disobeyed his mother, unusual for a Sinhalese. Then it occurred to her that perhaps he was talking about her.

He leaned over and kissed her gently on the cheek. Before she had time to even think about responding, he had laughed as if it had all been a joke and jumped down, standing under the tree holding up his arms to catch her. There he held her for a moment, so she could get her balance, and then he let her go.

She asked him to drop her off in Pettah some half a mile from where she lived. The excuse she gave was that she had to do some shopping. Not that she needed an excuse. He must have known that she was sparing them both the fuss that would certainly attend her arrival home on the back of a motorcycle driven by the kind of boy against whom Minrada was always warning her.

She smoothed down her skirt. 'Thank you.' She handed him back his goggles. 'And thank you for rescuing me.'

'My pleasure.' He smiled so infectiously that she did too.

To hide her smile, she looked down at the motorcycle. Trembling with the force of its running engine, it seemed almost alive. Like an animal waiting for its master. It would be a pity if she never rode on it again.

'I see you're admiring my Silver Star.' He ran his hand along the curved leather of its seat. 'She's old and she's slow but she is beautiful, isn't she? I'll buy the new model when finally it comes off the production line but I don't hold out much hope that dreary post-war prudence will produce any-thing even half as dazzling as this 1939.'

'I expect it won't.' She wondered what it must be like to plan, so carelessly, the purchase of the latest version while still in possession of one that was so serviceable.

'Well,' he said.

Her thinking, well . . .

'I hope our paths cross again, Evelyn Williams.' He leaped on to his motorcycle, lifting it up to release it from its support and then was off.

It was already mid-afternoon and the sun was hammering down on dusty streets that shimmered in the noise and heat. Rickshaw coolies stripped to the waist, loose shirts flapping over khaki shorts flip-flopped their bare feet, stirring up the dust as they weaved past ponderous bullocks pulling palm thatched carts, all of them caught up in an unequal contest with a queue of cars.

She joined the stream of pedestrians that was continually shifting, men (for it was mostly men) peeling off as new-comers arrived. She could hear that low murmur of conversation that rose up into the heat along with other, much more strident sounds, the jingling of bells from passing trams, the blare of horns, the cry of a street hawker and from the makeshift shops that lined the road, boastful descriptions of the qualities of shimmering silks and brightly coloured saris.

She felt herself to be invisible or, if not invisible, then a sight to be noted and skipped over. No matter that Colombo, and Ceylon, was the place where she had been born and lived her entire nineteen years. Since she was neither Sinhalese nor Tamil nor Muslim, nor even

Burgher, she would always be other. A stranger. Forever an Englishwoman. Nothing, and certainly not the political changes about to rock this country, would change that.

Except with Emil in the jungle. Then she hadn't felt a stranger. With him, what she had felt was right.

Past roadside barbers and their customers she went, past men crouched down waiting to be shaved as white-clad moneylenders did brisk business from makeshift kiosks. On and on, past groups of men, their long hair knotted in place by tortoiseshell combs, squatting in the shade, laughing as they threw down cards. She stopped to buy a sugar snap. Such a familiar sensation, licking sugar granules off her lips as daily after school she had used to buy a whole bag of the soft round pastries all of which, despite her best resolve, she was sure to have wolfed down before getting home.

She loved this country. So much. It held so many memories.

But soon memories was all they'd ever be.

Two more monsoon seasons and then, in early 1948, King George's emissary, the Duke of Gloucester, would open the first session of a fully native Parliament. So long anticipated was this moment that the plans were already far advanced. There was to be a huge shaded hangar built and decorated, traditional style, with strips of tender coconut leaves and festoons of paper on which flat-hatted and wide-pantalooned Kandyan drummers would drum away the end of English rule. While Evelyn . . .

She didn't know what she was going to do.

She left behind the hubbub of Pettah and walked down a calm street that was lined with yellow flowering Suriyas. Almost home. Almost returned to her own skin.

It was a meaningless kiss, she decided.

She pushed through the gate, pressing down to stop it from squeaking, hoping that way to slip in unobserved. But no sooner had she committed herself to this route than she caught sight of Tommy Patterson.

Tommy, who was by a flowerbed and turning over the soil, had his back to her. If she were quick and quiet she could perhaps turn tail and go in the other way. She could even, since she badly wanted to avoid attention, use the door into the bottom bathroom that only the Tamil lav cleaner ever used.

But as she was about to make good this escape, Tommy, who always seemed to sense her presence, turned. 'Oh Evelyn.' Brushing dirt from his hands on to his trousers, he rose. 'I didn't . . . I didn't expect you back so soon.'

He's blushing, she thought, but since Tommy was the kind of Englishman whom even a touch of sun turned red and who also must be flushed from his exertion, she dismissed the thought.

'You said you were going to be gone the whole day.' His hint of accusation underlined something she had previously noticed, that Tommy always paid careful attention to her plans and seemed put out by any changes.

'The car broke down.' Why did she feel the need to justify her behaviour? 'Marjorie and Gordon decided to press on after it was fixed . . .' and also it seemed, to tell him only a partial truth? 'But by then I'd had enough.'

'Oh, I am sorry.'

His commiseration sounded so sincere she regretted her lack of candour.

'I expect you're tired.'

How characteristically kind of him to have spotted this. She *was* tired. She looked across at him. She saw his shirt rolled up to the elbows, and a thin film of perspiration overlaying his forearm's downy blond hair.

His colour deepened. He dropped his spade, hurrying over to the garden table, all the while rolling down his sleeves and threading through his cuff links so that by the time he reached the table, he was able to take his jacket from the back of a chair and slip it on. And there he stood, properly suited in the sweltering heat.

She couldn't help smiling. Tommy and his awkward manners always did make her smile.

She thought about the first time she had laid eyes on him. He was a greenhorn then who, immediately post demob, had been sent to help administer the last days of this British colony. He had come to them from Colombo jetty after one quick stop at Cargills where he'd been outfitted with that standard Assistant Government Agent's complement of black shoes, khaki shorts, white shirts and, most importantly, the Britisher's favoured pith helmet, the ubiquitous topee. Seeing him then, so diffident and so shy, she had immediately taken a liking to him. But she also remembered thinking, give him a month with a peon to guide and flatter him and a bevy of servants to smooth his path, and he'll be as arrogant as all the rest of the civil service chummery. Except this isn't what had happened. After his first circuit, when Tommy came back to Colombo, an increased physical assurance seemed to be his only visible change.

Now, pointing to the flowerbed, he said, 'I was longing for some exercise.' In contrast to the other boarders who never lifted a finger, Tommy always found ways to help while simultaneously pretending that everything he did was not for them, but for himself.

'That's kind.' Smiling, she turned, intent on going in.

'Would you . . . ?'

She stopped.

'Would you care to join me in some exercise?'

Frowning, 'Do you mean would I like to do some digging?'

'No. Hardly.' His blush flaring to crimson. 'I wondered whether you might like to take a walk with me.'

Her first thought, no, I certainly would not. Then the thought that followed, that what she most wanted to do was go to her room and there be left alone to think of . . . But that is exactly what she had resolved she would not do.

'A walk,' she said. 'What a good idea. After I've had a rest if you don't mind,' the perfect thing to say to Tommy in whose universe all ladies must continually take rests.

'Of course and shall we ask . . . ?' He let the sentence hang.

'Ask . . . ?'

'Your mother.'

'You want my mother to walk with us?'

'No, no.' His head shaking madly. 'Of course not,' and

then just as frantically nodding, 'I mean, yes of course. Of course if she'd like that. But what I had meant to say was, shall we not ask her permission?'

Which was just like Tommy. His chivalry came, if not from another century then certainly from another ethos. Such a contrast to that man off whose motorcycle she had just clambered. 'If you want to, then do,' thinking that it would please her mother to find a man who was so respectful to her headstrong younger daughter.

She hadn't meant to keep Tommy waiting. Once she reached her bedroom, however, she found herself overcome by a debilitating exhaustion. It was the shock of the witnessed fall, she told herself, and the ride that had followed. Combined with her early rising, all three events catching up on her.

Without bothering to take off her frock she pulled over the bed covers, closing her eyes in expectation of the instantaneous descent of sleep. But instead a mental picture – that stick figure of a downward-spinning man – drove out this possibility.

Her eyes snapped open. She sat up. Got out of bed to plump up the pillows against the bed board and smooth down the coverlet, doing this until the jolt of adrenalin had drained away. Then she lay down again, her gaze tracing the run of wooden ceiling rafters from one side of the room to the other and back again. Looking up at the blackened arms of the fan circling space, she thought about how everything was soon to change.

This house would not be home for long. They would be moving. To England, the country Evelyn had never even visited. There Marjorie would marry Gordon while their mother, whose lifeline supply of English lodgers were already beginning to reduce, would take up a housekeeper's post in Surrey. As for Evelyn . . . Well, if she didn't find a suitable alternative, she would be going with her mother.

To live in someone else's house! On someone else's terms! To watch her mother bowing and scraping to another, richer woman. The prospect filled her with despair. The only way she could damp it down was by scrunching shut her eyes. Which is when, just as she had thought she would never get to sleep, she sank into unconsciousness.

Someone shaking her.

All she wanted to do was to keep on sleeping. She tried to shift over to the furthest end of her bed and out of grabbing distance but the hand already had hold of her and it was too determined. It pulled her back. 'Wake up Missie Evelyn. Wake up.' Minrada's voice.

Opening her eyes, Evelyn saw light filtering through the unglazed window. Had she slept the whole night through?

'What is it?'

'You must get up before the pacing *hamuduruwo* wears a deep hole in the corridor.'

Tommy. Which meant she hadn't slept that long. 'Please tell him I'm sorry and that I'll soon be with him.'

She watched as Minrada walked slowly through the curtain. Seeing the bent curve of her beloved ayah's shoulders she thought, how can I live without Minrada – and in England?

Her head was thick with heat and sleep. She went over to the basin that Minrada had just refilled. She sank her hands into the warm water before splashing some on her face, waiting as it evaporated and cooled her down. She pulled off her crumpled frock, changing it for another and then another, a simple, pale blue dropped-waist dress. A quick twirl in front of the mirror having told her that her hourglass figure was now showing to its best advantage, she left the room. Smoothed down her blonde hair as she went to the lounge where her mother was on the sofa embroidering a cushion cover.

Tommy was there as well. He was standing by the window and he was looking out.

'Ah there you are, darling.'

At the sound of her mother's voice, Tommy turned, his rising colour matched to her mother's approving 'You look lovely.'

Her mother, in contrast, looked tiny. And somehow defenceless.

Evelyn knew that this apparent fragility concealed the indomitable nature of a woman who, having been left a pauper by the unexpected death of her husband had, by dint of hard work, managed not only to keep the bailiffs out but also to keep herself and her daughters. And all of this without much help from me, the thought provoking her to say, 'Would you like to come with us, Mummy?'

'Thank you. That's kind of you but I have altogether too much to do.' Although the refusal was gently voiced, Evelyn couldn't help registering how tired her mother looked, and, although she was always pale, how much paler than usual.

'Shouldn't I stay and help?'

'No, dear.' Her mother was uncharacteristically sharp as if what Evelyn had said was an annoyance. 'I already have plenty of help.' She rose and walked to the door, turning in the doorway to say, 'Have a lovely time dears,' before going out.

'Well.' Tommy's cough was delicate for a man's. 'Shall we?'

'Yes, let's.' Of course her mother was as tired as anybody who was contemplating the imminent packing up of an entire life would be. And besides, a small interior voice chided, worrying about her mother was most likely a way of trying to put off the moment when Tommy and she stepped out, a strange thought to have, since stepping out for a walk was something they had done together dozens of times before. She linked her arms to his. 'What a good idea this was,' she said, walking with him into the garden and out.

The men who rented rooms from Mrs Williams always took their evening meal together, their manly company leavened by the presence of the three Williams women. This practice made Mrs Williams's boarding-house much sought after and therefore something on which she continued to insist. No matter that Evelyn was often there on sufferance (she would much rather have shared the staff meal). What Mrs Williams, in her quiet fashion, wanted, Mrs Williams got. And if the price to be paid for her edict was her younger daughter's atypical hush, well perhaps Mrs Williams regarded this as no price at all.

That evening, Evelyn sat at table and wished the meal over. The conversation was led, as most often it was, by Marjorie's fiancé Gordon and it featured, as ever, the incompetence of the native population. Delaying the passage of a neatly cut morsel of beef into his mouth Gordon was saying, 'As my old GA always used to maintain, better a man who has walked the streets of London than a Ceylonese.' Popping in his forkful, Gordon looked about, checking that the assembled company had heard, and that they also all agreed.

As murmurs of assent accompanied the sequential nodding of heads, Evelyn gazed down at her meat and brown gravy and roast potatoes. She thought longingly about the sharp, hot curries that the kitchen staff would soon be consuming.

'The new civil service is a shambles,' one of the other lodgers was saying, 'As for their MPs! Well, I wouldn't put most of them in charge of a tea party, never mind a country.'

'Absolutely.' Gordon laid down his fork. 'Only the other day one of my chappies treated me to his whole political philosophy. Full of "Magna Cartas this" and "Magna Cartas that", it was. I let him run on for a while before pointing out that universal suffrage in Britain took hundreds of years to evolve and Magna Carta was only ever for the Barons. That took the wind out of his sails, I can tell you.'

A collective chuckle punctuated by Marjorie's looking across at her fiancé with such blind admiration that Evelyn was overcome by a desire to reach over and slap her sister, an impulse which it is possible their mother picked up, because she said, suddenly and very brightly, 'Can I help anyone to more roast?'

'Thank you.' A plate up-held as Gordon said, 'I blame Donoughmore.'

Not Donoughmore again. Evelyn's heart dropped. The Donoughmore Commission – which had laid the ground for the Ceylonese take-over of Parliament and the civil service – had been the subject of choice every supper-time for longer than she could bear to remember. Gordon was, in fact, so fixated by Donoughmore, he'd probably want to talk about it on his wedding night.

'It's all very well for Donoughmore to parachute in . . .' he was saying.

Passing the plate on to her mother, Evelyn sighed.

'He didn't stick around to see the consequences of his grand sounding recommendations . . .'

If leaving for England meant that there'd be a change of topic, Evelyn thought, well then maybe going wasn't such a bad idea.

But then, she thought, if she left she would never see Galle Face Green again and neither would she ever luxuriate in the ferocity of a sudden monsoon outburst.

She thought about how it had been that early evening standing with Tommy on the Green. She had been content to look up at three kites – bright red, orange and purple – their long fish whipped, violently, by the wind. Three vivid slashes of colour snapping across the slate of the sky when, suddenly and with a loud crack, the skin of the sky had ruptured. Warm, thick rain had come splashing down, hard enough to soak her. Not that she had minded. She had opened her arms wide open as the torrent of water knocked the kites out of the sky and almost knocked her over as well. She had tilted her head back, welcoming in the flooding of that bracken water and, like the small boys on the Green and that group of loudly shrieking women in long, mauve-white dresses, she had stood luxuriating in the downpour.

'Over there.' Tommy had pointed urgently towards shelter but she had wanted to stay just as she was, and revel in that sensation of being utterly saturated by sheets of falling water so powerful that, having hit the ground, they also splashed up.

'We better make a run for it.'

The water curtained vision, the promenade having been almost completely submerged by fast gushing streams of rainwater that flowed and lapped over her feet. She had tried to ignore Tommy's attempts at rescue, standing there and remembering how earlier she had been almost overtaken by an impulse to soak her feet. Which is what she then had done, had taken off her shoes so as to luxuriate in the warmth of the water feathering through her toes.

'Darling?'

Shaking herself out of the reverie into which she often disappeared at supper-time, she saw her mother holding up a freshly replenished plate.

'Sorry.' She passed the plate on to Gordon who used his pivotal position in the relaying of second helpings to say, 'Mark my words, Ceylon is heading straight for rack and ruin.'

'How about you, Tommy?' This from Evelyn's mother. 'Can I help you to more?' In reply to which Tommy (one of whose saving graces at supper was that he never threw his tuppence into the gleeful and unvarying forecasting of doom) shook his head. 'Thank you, Mrs Williams, but I have eaten more than enough.'

Maybe Tommy, Evelyn thought, would, like her, have preferred to eat in the kitchen. But no, she saw how he (such a good boy) had polished off his food before laying together his knife and fork on his plate.

'The largest portion of blame is naturally to be laid at the door of your average Sinhalese,' she heard Gordon saying and it was all she could do to stop herself from groaning out loud.

46

This was Gordon's second-favourite conversational furrow – a contemptuous division of the population of Ceylon into 'your Sinhalese' (who, the supper coterie had long since agreed, were so fixated on land they would rob their own grandmothers for it), 'your Tamil' (always a good worker) and 'your Muslims' (or 'bearded Johnnies' as Gordon liked to call them). And sure enough:

'Because your Sinhalese has not the faintest idea what it is to do a proper day's work,' Gordon was saying. 'Not like your Tamil,' pausing so that agreement could wind its murmuring way round the table. 'I have one chap in my department – Sinhalese of course – jobs only for the boys these days. He's as charming as can be. Give him a carefully worked out report to approve and he will sign it – with the most magnificent flourish, I'll grant you – but without bothering to read the damn thing.'

'Just like you.' Evelyn didn't stop to think how her criticism would be received.

'I beg your pardon?' This from a taken-aback Gordon as her mother issued a warning, 'Evelyn.'

As mildly as her mother had pitched her tone, there was no doubt she was telling Evelyn to let the conversation sink back to its comfortable norm. Which Evelyn knew was what she ought to do.

'When you first started,' she said, 'you didn't write your own reports.'

Another, 'I beg your pardon?' Something comical in the repetition accompanied as it was by the outraged rising of Gordon's eyebrows.

'Wasn't everything you signed prepared for you by your peons?'

'Really, Evelyn . . .' Gordon deliberately lowered his brows, visibly gathering himself up in preparation for the setting right of Marjorie's errant sister who, knowing that nothing would now stop Gordon from telling her precisely why she was so wrong, regretted her small piece of conversational mischief. But before Gordon had time to launch his rebuttal, Tommy jumped in. 'Mine were.'

The assembled company, Evelyn included, looked at Tommy. He was grinning with the embarrassment of joining the conversation, something he normally never did. Yet, good for him, he now continued, 'The only sentence of the letters I signed during my first rotation and that I actually understood, was the closing sentence. You know the, "I have the honour to be, sir, your obedient servant".'

She shot him a grateful look as Gordon blustered, 'Well yes. But . . .'

Gordon's 'but' was sure to lead to one of his other favourite conversational gambits – the rapidity with which he had found his feet in his first jungle post – and Evelyn knew, even without her mother's soft and prompting cough to reinforce this knowledge, that she should let it go there. At the same time some inner devil drove her, not only to continue but also to raise her voice: 'It's only common sense that if you stop people from learning the ropes, they won't know how to run things when you do an about-turn and give them back their country.'

'*Their* country?'

'Well it is theirs, isn't it? Isn't that why we're leaving?'

'Yes, strictly speaking – in the most narrow definition of terms – it may possibly be said to be theirs.' Gordon's eyes narrowed. 'But I think you might take note, young lady, that we are bequeathing to them a very different country from the one we first encountered. Before we arrived, there were no tea estates. Not a single one. Look now at the area surrounding Nuwara Eliya – it is quite literally carpeted by tea. What was once jungle has become a veritable gold mine. And all because of us.'

'Because of the efforts of Tamil labourers, you mean. They did the work.'

'Well yes, they did the physical labour. But without us, there would have been no tea.'

Which Evelyn knew was true, even as she said, 'We didn't exactly do it for them though, did we?' seeing astonishment in Gordon's face and sharing it.

She could hardly believe that this was she who was speaking out so boldly and that, even hearing her mother's 'That's enough dear' and knowing that her mother was right, and that she should stop, she was driven on to say, 'I don't know why you expect them to be grateful. We've got much more from the tea estates than they ever have,' hearing, but distantly, the shocked silence into which her mother's, 'Do you really believe any of this, dear?' intruded and thinking she didn't actually know whether she did believe it. The words had come to her almost as if some stranger had deposited them in her mouth.

Part of her was as alarmed at her own daring as her mother was. Another part was enjoying itself. Her revenge. For all these interminable evenings of having to listen to Gordon and his ilk drone on about their important jobs, and their lazy underlings, and their unselfish and unstinting efforts to put this country on a sound footing, along with their battle-hardened accounts of drinking at their precious clubs and their exclusive watering-holes from which she, by virtue of her gender and her mother's genteel poverty, had effectively been excluded. And now she had found the courage to express sentiments she hadn't even realised she felt, but that sounded so impressively lucid. This is such fun, she thought, revving up for the delivery of one final caustic sentence of condemnation except that her mother's 'Yes Minrada?' cut through what she had been about to say.

Minrada?

She turned to find that not only had Minrada come into the dining room without her hearing, but that she was standing close.

'Yes, what is it, Minrada?'

'A person is asking for Missie Evelyn.' The disapproval in Minrada's voice was, Evelyn knew, not a result of her cheekiness (to which Minrada, thankfully, had not been witness) but at this infraction of normal custom that held supper sacrosanct. And one other thing Evelyn also knew and this without a doubt – she knew who had come for her.

She got up, excitedly turning away, only almost immediately to look back to ask her mother, 'Do you mind if I . . . ?' then to be released by her mother's weary, 'Yes, Evelyn, by all means. Do go and see who it is.'

The stretching out of the silence as she walked to the door told her that all eyes were fixed on her. She wouldn't let that bother her. He had come. She wanted to skip and to jump and to hurry along the moment of seeing him again even as she knew that she must not. She drew herself up tall, and slowed herself down, aware of the accompanying swishing of her skirt. She was conscious, also, of what they would be seeing, her limbs loose and long, and her waist small, her blonde hair luminous against the soft blue of her frock, and the skin of her swan neck a flawless porcelain so that even Gordon, she knew it must be so, would be watching in admiration as she left the room and turned towards the front door.

'No, missie, not that way. He's waiting at the back.'

Of course – she turned in the opposite direction. Emil was nothing like those stuffed shirts who would always insist on proper ceremony. He was rich and confident enough never to have to worry about doing the right thing.

And soon she would see him again. She was walking fast, making straight for him, ignoring Minrada's insistent, 'Who is this boy, missie? And what does he want from you?' knowing how much trouble it was for the crippled Minrada to keep up but not bothering to slow down until, that is, she heard Minrada say, 'I told him to come later, but he said his master had ordered him to wait for your reply.'

She felt a moment's dull disappointment and then, feeling Minrada's hot breath on her shoulder, she made herself let go of it.

A man like Emil would naturally have sent a messenger. Better, anyway. It gave her time to prepare for the fact that he was going to rescue her from the boredom of her life.

Flickering torchlight played along the steel chains that had been dug into the mountain to help pilgrims haul themselves up this, the steepest section of the climb. But Evelyn would not be amongst them. She was far too exhausted.

Of all their many secret expeditions, of all the foolish risks she and Emil had run, this one was by far the craziest. Was it for such a rout that she had lied to her mother and her sister, pretending to be with a friend who didn't even know she was Evelyn's alibi? Only now to find herself facing the humiliation of being halfway up a mountain and defeated by it?

She dropped her head. 'I can't.' Emil was wrong in his insistence that she should not leave Ceylon without first having climbed Adam's Peak. Hardly any of the other English had done the climb and they were leaving without as much as a backward glance.

'Here.' He lifted up a thermos.

She took a grateful sip of hot, sweet, spicy, ginger tea before he popped in something from the Tiffin box as if she were a baby bird. 'Suck it.'

It was jaggery, its rich sunburst filling her mouth.

'Better?'

'Not really.' It didn't matter how much jaggery she ate. 'I can't.'

'You will.'

What gave this man the audacity to tell her what she would, or would not, do? Look at him. He was a stranger with those black stones of eyes staring from out of a darkened face.

'I'll wait for you here.'

'But you've almost made it.'

She didn't care if she had. She wanted him away. She shook her head.

She thought that he was going to try and pull her up and that, if he did, she would scream, but all he had been doing was reaching for a torch. Now he clicked it on and held it under his chin so as to illuminate his face. She could see his part affectionate, part teasing smile that the last few weeks had made familiar. 'We're nearly at the top.'

'You said that an hour ago.'

'To encourage you. But this time it happens to be true. I promise you, Evelyn Williams, this is the last stretch. You have already come all this way. You will make it to the top,' and seeing his rich red brown skin shining in the yellowed light she couldn't help thinking that this man could convince her of almost anything, including the fact that he was right, and that she would make it.

The summit was surprisingly small and it was also very crowded. She saw how small darted threads of torchlight were weaving in and out like fireflies flitting above water. An icy wind cut through the thin blanket someone had put around her shoulders. Shivering, she pulled it closer.

It was so dark. As if it might never be light again. And sombre as well despite the way (or perhaps because of it) that inside the walled-in unroofed interior of the shrine a bell rang out once for each new arrival and once again for each time the new arrival had previously been up this Sri Pada, this mountain of the holy footstep, and so many other names – Lanka, Svargarohanam, Samantkuta, and Adam's Peak.

She could hear pilgrims chanting, some of them paying tribute at the shrine of the god Samanta. Others were kneeling, palms closed and to their chests as they leaned over to touch their heads against the wooden enclosure, their prayers directed at the stone where, legend said, Buddha's footstep had been imprinted.

'Although, according to the Hindus of southern India, it's Shiva's footstep,' Emil had told her, 'or Pwan-ko's if you are Chinese, or the Devil's if you believe Moses of Chorene, or Adam's. That's why Adam's Peak. Legend has it that, in falling from Paradise, Adam landed here. Trying to expiate his disobedience, he stood for so long he left the impression of his foot embedded in the stone.'

'Adam's but not Eve's?'

'Good point. Eve was probably too light of foot to leave an indent.' She saw the flash of his white teeth. 'But the land around here is jam-packed with gems. With rubies, sapphires, garnets, topaz and so on. Legend says these are the crystallisation of the tears Adam and Eve shed after the Fall. Perhaps we must assume that it is in this display, rather than in the matter of a dull footprint, that Eve has left her mark.'

As she returned his smile, it came to her that even though the night was almost over and she had not yet slept, she was no longer the slightest bit tired. Gone were all her regrets about the lies she'd told to her mother. She had made it up Adam's Peak. Surely this was worth any lie?

'It's almost time.' Emil gently steered her round until, like all the other people on the summit, she was facing eastwards.

Her first impression was that the sun seemed rapidly to shoot up into the sky even though later, thinking back on it, she could remember each separate moment of its rising. First there appeared a rim of astonishingly bright scarlet and, after that, a flaring of orange that compacted and deepened as the flaming red ball of the sun rose and softened, turning yellow in its bloodied sky. There was chanting that grew louder as waves of blue-tipped cloud filled the vast space between the rim of Adam's Peak and the peak opposite. Land shaped and yet ethereal, the heavens hovering almost as if they could be touched.

She wanted to stand for ever and drink it in.

But Emil's hands were on her shoulders once more to turn her, this time to face her to the west. His soft, hot breath in her ear. 'Look –' and there it was, the sight for which Adam's Peak was famed.

First she saw the red of the sky softening from saffron to peach and gradually to blue, and the green of land glimmering through the grey-blue clouds. And after that, astonishingly, and etched clearly in this sea of cloud and mist and land, she could see the perfect outline of a grey-blued conical pyramid, an exact shadow of Adam's Peak.

Magic. Real magic, so powerful it belied the certainty she sometimes experienced that she could make her own fate. Now what she felt was simply human, unable even to hold on to this enchantment. The image of the peak was already fading, the mist burning away to reveal the earth as lush as any Paradise and as over-brimming with life. She saw how the bright green of man-made tea plantations carpeted the land only, in the far distance, to give way to the dark green of a jungle that had once been everywhere. Beyond all this were other mountain tops, crimsoned and purpled and browned by a changing sky and, even further out, some shining blue, as if it was actually possible to look across the island and to the sea.

She would remember this sight long after she had left Ceylon. She was grateful to Emil for bringing her here and for forcing her to make it to the top. She gave one long, regretful sigh.

'It is wondrous, isn't it?'

When she turned to Emil, she found herself blinking away tears she hadn't known were welling.

'I come here every year,' he said.

'While this is my first time. And my last.'

'How so?'

'We're leaving soon.' Which he already knew.

She seemed to see his expression shifting. Like a decision forming.

'You could not go.'

'How?' She laughed. No matter how much she loved this country, she knew she could not stay.

'You could if . . .' one hand seemed stuck in the air just as the thing he was trying to say was likewise sticking, 'if . . .'

During all the time they had spent together, Emil had never been anything less than completely self-assured. Now, however, she saw an almost imperceptible shifting in his body, as the sun had shifted in its heavens. He's going to kneel, she thought. He's going to propose.

'Evelyn,' he said. 'Evelyn . . .'

She swallowed. 'Wait . . .'

Which is all it took. His expression changing. Odd. She saw disappointment there, but she also thought she saw relief.

'You have dust on your shoes, Evelyn.' Having brushed one of her shoes, he rose, so easily that she might have imagined everything that had gone before, a thought reinforced by his careless, 'We should start our descent before it gets too hot.'

Had the residents of the Williams household been asked whether there was anything different about Evelyn, they would have answered that she seemed much the same as ever. Yes, granted, she was dreamy, but hadn't she always been dreamy? And if, come to think of it, she *was* a little more moody than usual and showing an even greater inclination to keep herself to herself, the explanation must surely lie in the strain of her impending departure. As for her mysterious comings and goings – they were neither regular nor frequent enough to have been remarked on. Only Minrada, the bearer of Emil's messages, knew anything was up and Minrada had long since learned to keep her knowledge, and her opinions, of her charge strictly to herself.

If Minrada had demanded of Evelyn why she was mixing, and in secret, with such a dangerous boy, Evelyn would not have known what to say. Not because she would have wanted deliberately to withhold the truth, but because she didn't know where it lay.

Her days she divided into three. The times when she was with Emil, and those much longer periods of 'the before' and 'the aftermath'.

While the times with him were the best, their immediate aftermath would find her joyously reliving each moment of their time together. Soon, however, and far too soon, she would find herself returned to her skin and engaged in the minute inspection of her own behaviour. What earlier had seemed natural, hindsight now made peculiar. She would worry that she had been too stand-offish or too friendly, too loud or too shy, too distant or too familiar. She couldn't seem to stop herself from repeating this ritual, over and over again until, in the place of remembered pleasure, there slipped a kind of fearful anticipation – the beginning of her tormented 'before'. Then she would start fretting that Emil would never again make contact and, once he had, worrying whether she was right to have agreed once more to meet him.

She loved him.

Or at least she thought she loved him.

What she knew, for sure, was that never had a man taken her to so many interesting places or brought her so many thoughtful presents or made her laugh so much. And he was a man who, like her, refused to live by other people's rules or care what they might think. He was, she sometimes thought, her perfect match – so much so that it frightened her.

Yet was this truly love? Having not previously experienced its like, she had no way of knowing. Even having to ask herself the question seemed to fuel her doubts. No good, she would tell herself, could come from their liaison. Their backgrounds were too different and at the same time they themselves were too much the same. And although there was no doubt that she felt desire for him, this was sometimes counterbalanced by a puzzling sensation that edged closer to aversion. Not to him. Never to him. He was the most beautiful man she had ever met. Perhaps her difficulties sprang precisely from her desire. There was, and she couldn't stop herself from thinking this, something wicked in her. Something that was altogether too much at odds with convention.

Yet had she – she couldn't keep back this contradictory thought – so summarily put him off (that he had been on the brink of proposing was not in doubt) because of the colour of his skin? Or was it because his proposal had been too casual? Was he too arrogant?

Tortured by these thoughts, she lay on her bed at the same time telling herself that all her questions were a waste of time. He had not been in touch. Not since Adam's Peak.

She had shamed him. Had put him off. Or, and this was more likely, had saved him from himself. He could have anyone he wanted. Why would he choose her? He was bound to be entangled now with someone else, and congratulating himself on his narrow escape. So did she tell herself, all the while waiting for Minrada to announce that another message had been delivered.

She heard Minrada's soft footfall.

She sat up. Smoothed down her skirt. Composed herself so that although she was still smiling, she would not look too deliriously happy.

Minrada pushed through the curtain. 'Your mother asks to speak with you.'

When Evelyn stepped into the lounge, the speed and synchronicity with which both her mother and her sister looked up told her that they had been waiting for her. They had been sitting in silence, with neither books nor embroidery to keep them occupied, a clue, just as Minrada's practically pushing her down the corridor and into the room had also been a clue. And in addition, her mother looked so very serious, while Marjorie visibly was gloating. Trouble? Evelyn stood in the doorway, trying to work out what she might have done.

Nothing she could think of, save for her meetings with Emil, about which they did not know. Unless . . . was it possible that Minrada had betrayed her? But no, Minrada had been smiling, beaming in fact, as she had hurried Evelyn down the corridor.

Perhaps, Evelyn thought, hope rising, perhaps her mother had changed her mind and would not be leaving Ceylon. Or, and she found herself warming to this theme, perhaps Mummy has come into a little nest egg and so, although we'll still be leaving, we'll be able to afford our own house in England, this prospect filling her with foolish expectation.

'There you are, dear.' Her mother's mild greeting was chased out by Marjorie's accusing, 'You took your time.'

'Marjorie!' her mother said in reply to which Marjorie, oddly, instead of protesting, said, 'Of course', adding as she hastily exited the room, 'I'll leave you two alone', which, given how much Marjorie hated being left out of anything, was even odder.

'Come, dear.' Her mother patted the sofa. 'Come and sit by me.'

As Evelyn began to lower herself down, her mother said, 'Tommy asked if he might speak to you', so abruptly that Evelyn immediately got up again.

'Tommy? You mean Tommy Patterson?'

'Is there another Tommy?'

'No. He's the only one.' She wondered why Tommy needed permission to speak to her.

'Do sit down, Evelyn.' Her mother's voice was uncharacteristically sharp. 'My neck is beginning to lock.'

She sat.

'That's better.' Though her mother's pale blue eyes were now sharply focused on Evelyn, she did not go on with what she had to say.

They sat in a silence that soon seemed to weigh as heavily as the heat. Evelyn could hear pots banging in the kitchen, and the tramp of someone (Tommy?) pacing up above, and the snip of a gardener's shears, the trundling of a lorry and, cutting through these, the *whip-whip* of some calling birds, and all the while that she sat, apparently preoccupied by these sounds, she knew, of course she did, what it was that Tommy wanted. He wanted to ask her for her hand in marriage. 'He's going to propose,' she said, her mother's answering nod provoking from her an indignant, 'To propose to me?'

'Yes, dear. Who else?'

'Well then why did he ask you first?'

Her mother laughed. 'Don't you think Tommy might have thought it would go easier on him if you were forewarned?'

'So he talked to you? And to Marjorie?'

'No, just to me. Marjorie accidentally overheard.' Which was just like Marjorie although in Evelyn's opinion her sister's eavesdropping was never accidental. 'It's a serious proposal,' her mother said. 'Tommy loves you.'

But I don't love him. The thought welled up so fiercely in Evelyn that she thought she might actually have brought it out to air, but no, her mother was just looking at her sadly, and fondly as well.

'Strange how children can be so different,' her mother said. 'Take the two of you. Marjorie is so sensible – so immensely practical – and she was ever thus. Whereas you . . . well you were always impulsive, Evelyn, even as a child.' She reached across to take hold of one of Evelyn's hands. Looking down at it fondly, she squeezed the hand.

With her answering squeeze, Evelyn couldn't help noticing the purpled-blue veins that ran across the dry parchment of her mother's skin and the way that skin, once so delicate and white, had been coarsened by hard work.

'But your impulsiveness can make you difficult.'

'I know.' She felt so sorry for the trouble she knew she caused her mother. 'I do make too much fuss.'

'That you do.' Her mother let go of her hand. 'But I trust you also know how very much you mean to me?'

Such uncharacteristic forthrightness wrung from Evelyn a 'Yes' that seemed to crack from deep within her throat. Out of nowhere there came that old, stabbing grief that she usually managed to keep down and with it the realisation that her mother had, for the past nine years, been both mother and father to her daughters and, despite her own grief, had never failed them.

'I would not have you different.' Such a wonderful thing to say although the effect was partly ruined by her mother's dropping gaze. 'But now,' as if she couldn't quite bring herself to keep looking, 'our circumstances have changed. While these changes might not be of our making, we must find a way of adjusting to them. Foremost of these adjustments is that we can no longer live in Ceylon. This you know.'

'Yes.'

Her mother's returning gaze was as resolute as was her voice. 'Which is why I am asking you, please, to listen to what Tommy has to say – for this once, if you can, without interrupting. He is a good man. He will look after you.'

And yes, Evelyn thought, Tommy would. Except . . . she didn't want to be looked after. She wanted . . . she wanted to be loved. And to love.

'Will you listen to him, Evelyn?' There was an urgency to her mother's voice that Evelyn didn't understand. 'Will you do that for me?'

Evelyn nodded.

The springs on the old sofa shifting, 'I'll tell him you're waiting,' as her mother got up

64

'Mummy?'

'Yes, dear?'

'Do you think I should marry Tommy?'

In that moment, her mother no longer seemed that same, calm, unflustered woman on whom Evelyn had always depended. She seemed different. Much more tired, and much more hardened, as was her voice when she said, 'You expect me to tell you what I want is for you to be happy. Which is indeed what I do most reverently desire. But life has taught me to value financial security. Tommy is a nice boy and he is steady, he will never leave you in need . . .'

. . . as my father left you, Evelyn thought.

'I married your father out of love,' her mother said, 'only later to discover that he was not the most practical of men. You know as well as I do, the terrible impact of our financial tangle after his death. So there is something to be said for choosing, as Marjorie has done, a man who will provide for his family.' And with that, her mother left.

Two proposals, Evelyn thought, and in as many weeks. How hilarious. Nineteen years old and already two proposals – well, Emil has as good as, she decided – and nothing she had done to elicit them. Not like her sister who, having set her sights on Gordon, had reeled him in so hard that the poor dope had no other option but to propose. No wonder Marjorie was miffed.

A delicate cough. Tommy was already in the room. And, she saw, already blushing. He really was quite lovable.

'Tommy,' she said hearing his reply, 'Your mother . . .'

No, she would not have a proposal begun with mention of her mother. 'Why don't we go into the garden?'

Once they were outside, words seemed to abandon Tommy. When she looked at him, he averted his gaze. She knew he was going to propose and she knew she was going to accept. To distract herself from this terrifying imminence, she made herself imagine what her life would soon be.

When they were younger, and also better friends, the two Williams sisters often had liked to imagine themselves in the England their parents' photographs and fragmented memories had helped conjure up. The house they'd imagined was a picture-book cottage in an English village, its low front framed by roses and honeysuckle and watered by the kind of soft English rain, in contrast to the ferocity of the monsoon, that their mother longingly used to describe. There, they would promise each other, they would lounge in the cool of an English summer eating scones and strawberries and cream, or in winter toast crumpets over roaring log fires while pillows of soft, white snow nestled against dimpled window panes. Food was a major feature of this make-believe, in particular the rich aroma of roast meat that they, confident housewives with smart aprons, proudly would bring to table.

Such a satisfying fantasy – except that the adult Evelyn now knew that in England the meat would be accompanied by the tasteless white and brown sauces their lodgers loved, and afterwards by tapioca or sticky toffee puddings and . . . and how could, she suddenly thought, how could she marry Tommy?

'Evelyn . . .'

How characteristic that this is when Tommy found his voice. If she accepted him, it would be ever thus.

'Evelyn . . .'

'Do you mind, Tommy?' She went over to the gate.

Her mother had told her to listen. Yet what could Tommy say to deny what she knew, that if she married him he would disappoint, and that when this happened, she would turn on him? She stood seeing not the colourful road in front of her, but a great big blank the like of which would take over her life if she agreed to marry him.

Tommy never would haul her up a tree. Or kiss her when

she wasn't expecting him to. Or persuade her to flout convention by climbing Adam's Peak. He was too respectable and too respectful. And Tommy, whose prospects were limited (and no matter how mercenary this made her feel, she had to admit that it was important to her), would also never be able to lift her out of this life of 'making do' she so detested.

She and Tommy had such different ambitions. And as well she wasn't nice like him. He would try and give her what she wanted but would never manage. He would love her. And she would make him unhappy. Not that he would complain. He was far too nice for that. He would always cede his quiet ways to her flamboyant ones which, she knew, would only make things worse. This is why she couldn't marry him.

A memory of the gusto with which he ladled those horrible sauces on to his food was what had convinced her. Not that it was a question of food. But food was emblematic. What was at stake was their different tastes. If she married him, she would be discontented and, because of that, she would make his life a misery. And so, before she could change her mind, she turned to look at him and say, 'I could never make you happy, Tommy,' and saying this, she knew it for the truth.

Tommy, having blushed and stuttered out his thanks for her kind consideration of his offer, turned tail and hurried in.

Watching the slumped curve of his retreat, Evelyn was filled with remorse. He was such a nice man. He had shown her nothing but kindness and admiration. And now she had summarily knocked him back. Is this, she wondered, why her mother had warned her against her precipitous nature? Should she call him back and ask for more time so she could talk it over with her mother?

From where she was standing, she could see the dining room where the servants were laying the last of the condiments on the sideboard. Soon afterwards she also heard the ringing of the handbell, her mother summoning their guests to supper. She shifted out of sight into the furthest reaches of the garden and as she did she remembered how, as Tommy earnestly had pronounced her name, the sight that had preoccupied her was not his open and eager face but his wrists on which nervousness had made fine blond hairs bristle, and his pale hands with their sprinkling of freckles. Those same hands that would soon be bringing out a ring. It was then that she had seemed to see that other rich, velvet smoothness of Emil's skin and the dark pools of Emil's pupils and the feathery blackness of his long, thick eyelashes, all these filling her with desire. Not for Tommy. Never for him. For Emil.

She went over to a bench. Things grew so fast here. Although the bench had been in this shaded position for less than a month, still she had to push away thick tendrils of a vine that, hanging down from a nearby tree, had begun to wind themselves around the fretwork. The gardener should have done this, but with her mother preoccupied, the staff grew increasingly more slipshod.

She yanked a section of the vine, breaking it off. She was left holding a piece of the stem that was pulpy and oozing a milky liquid. Discarding it, she sat with her face in her upturned hands, which way she continued to sit, eyes closed, as the faint clattering of cutlery against plates and the murmur of conversation issued from the house.

'Are you all right?'

Startled, she looked up to find Marjorie standing close.

'May I?'

Not like her sister to ask permission. Evelyn made room for her and then when Marjorie was seated the question, 'How's Tommy?' that she knew she must not ask, popped out.

'He didn't come down to eat.'

Stupid boy. Evelyn wondered how long he would keep himself upstairs. Perhaps he would starve himself for the love of her, a prospect she might once have considered romantic but which now just felt irritating.

'What happened?'

'He proposed.'

'And?'

'And I refused him.' She said it defiantly in anticipation of what she knew was bound to ensue: that Marjorie, who liked Tommy and would consider him a catch, was going to describe to Evelyn just how selfish she always was. 'I couldn't marry him. Not without loving him.'

Marjorie merely nodded. 'Well then, of course you couldn't accept him.' Even more surprisingly, she put an arm around Evelyn.

Such unexpected kindness made the lump in Evelyn's throat rise up and with it, despite the fact that she rarely cried, came tears. Soundless, dripping down her cheeks as Marjorie hugged her and Evelyn, sobbing, thinking that their childish daydreams had once involved countless offers of marriage and subsequent refusals followed by the breaking of men's hearts. This aspect of the coming into womanhood from afar had seemed such jolly good fun. But Tommy's crestfallen face, and Emil's absence, had turned out to be no fun at all. She felt so guilty about having led on both men and dashing their hopes, something of which she was sure this newly sympathetic Marjorie would soon accuse her. And Marjorie would be right. Not only could Evelyn not stop thinking about marrying Emil, there had also been a time when she had played, secretly, with the prospect of marrying Tommy.

'There, there.' Marjorie tucked a strand of hair behind her ear. 'There, there.'

'It's all such a mess.'

'What is?'

The sympathy in Marjorie's voice almost had Evelyn blurting out the story of Emil's driving her into the jungle, and their subsequent assignations, and the way she had lied to Marjorie and her mother in order to go up Adam's Peak. But even as distraught as she was, she knew this for the mistake it would turn out to be. The sisters had not been particularly close even before their father's death had left them locked up in their separate miseries, and besides, Marjorie was not as free thinking as Evelyn. When she looked at a man like Emil, she wouldn't see his charm, or his quick humour, or that hint of danger that made him so exciting to Evelyn; what she would see was that he was different. Sinhalese. Black.

And there was something else, and something more disturbing, that troubled Evelyn.

'What is it?'

Evelyn wiped a hand across her cheek. 'It's Mummy.'

She felt the sudden rigidity of Marjorie's arms. 'What do you mean, Mummy?'

'I think she was hoping that I'd say yes.'

'Why? Did she tell you to?'

'Not in so many words. But I think she was meaning to tell me without actually saying it.'

When Marjorie turned away, Evelyn had to look at her in profile.

'There is something.'

Something?

'It's going to be hard for Mummy to keep you with her,' Marjorie said. 'Even if you're willing to help out – and who's to say that Mrs Crawford needs more help – another bedroom would have to be set aside for you. Either that or you will have to share Mummy's. And Mrs Crawford would also be obliged to feed you, and have you there, a stranger and not an employee, in her house. Can't you see how difficult that might make things?'

And yes, Evelyn thought, now Marjorie put it like that, she did see that it might be difficult. But why hadn't her mother said so? 'Has Mummy talked to you about this?'

Marjorie's old impatience came bursting out. Her 'Oh why do you always have to be told everything, Evelyn?' drove Marjorie off the bench. 'Can't you ever see anything for your-self?' She stood staring down on Evelyn.

On any other occasion Evelyn would have fought back. She would have reminded Marjorie of the times when it had been Evelyn who'd had to set Marjorie right. But now the fight seemed to have gone out of her. She dropped her gaze, and with it her head, saying, 'I'm sorry. I don't mean to be so . . .' not knowing how to finish the sentence because there were so many things she hadn't meant to have done. Like hurting Tommy, or causing her mother such terrible worry, or . . .

'Ssshhh.' Marjorie's hand on her shoulder. 'Sssh,' and Marjorie's voice shushing out her tears. 'It's I who should apologise. I shouldn't have snapped. I didn't mean to. What I meant to say was that you don't have to worry. I'll talk it over with Gordon. I am certain – he's such an understanding man – that he will be more than content for you to come and live with us.'

A snapshot. Two sisters who, as their mother had recently remarked, always had been so very unalike. The one, filled with the good feelings her selfless generosity had evoked in her, walked into the house to break the news of her generous offer to her intended.

The other's bewilderment seemed to have nailed her to the bench. Although her eyes were open all she could see was her future panning out. A future that she now knew would be filled by Gordon's anti-Donoughmore complaints and by his wife's regression to her custom of constantly correcting her sister. And she, the gooseberry in that jam, her presence blighting their marriage while her junior spinster status ruined her prospects.

But if not that, she thought, what else is there for me to do?

Sitting under a ceiling fan that stirred at the veranda's thick-ened midday heat, Emil was comfortable in a rattan armchair. Agreeably tired from a lunch well taken and almost on the point of drifting off to sleep when a question – *what kind of madness?* – jolted him awake.

He turned his attention to the garden. He breathed in the sweet flavoured scent of jasmine and of the *pansal mal,* the yellow frangipani flowers, his mother picked each early evening to take to the temple. Such a still day. It seemed to shimmer with heat, bright light making blackened silhou-ettes out of the estate girls who were going about their business at the garden's end. As he took another sip of a cold drink, Emil watched them.

One in particular he picked out. By the coquettish flick of her plait that ran all the way down to her pert bottom, he could tell that she was conscious that he was looking. And not for the first time. He'd taken note of her before.

Most of the estate's Tamil girls would be happy to dally with one of the master's sons but this girl seemed to hold out the promise of being especially free with her favours. She was different from the others, made even more interesting by her sharp tongue and apparent fearlessness. The first time he noticed her, he'd been passing as the superintendent, Vidu, was berating her for dawdling. Not an unusual occurrence. It was her quick response that had made Emil stop. 'Bite my cunt,' he had heard her saying, 'and drink my menstrual fluid,' to the accompaniment of the sucked-in breath of her fellow rubber tappers and her superintendent's loud disgust.

That sort of cheek should have sealed her fate. Yet even though the reddening of the superintendent's face, and his bluster, had lasted for some time, he did not turn her out. Which suggested that there was something between those two. The kind of something that the married Vidu would rather his wife did not unearth. And if the girl had lain with Vidu how much more likely she would be to offer herself to one of the boss's sons albeit even the youngest, and relatively low in the pecking order.

Emil, who was already twenty-four, was no saint. He had toyed with the prospect. It would be a diversion for them both. Except in the end he had kept away from her. It wasn't only that – as his mother was always saying, the lion does not eat grass – it was that he was no longer interested in casual sex. He wanted something more. He wanted . . . he wanted Evelyn.

There again – *what kind of madness?* – this time more insistent.

Once again he played out the whole damn thing. His incredulity that he had so nearly humiliated himself by asking a woman, who would never consent, to marry him, followed by his wondering why he had not carried through with the proposal. He kept going over this same ground and it was beginning to get him down. He wanted rid of it. Perhaps, he thought, if I face the question. Answer it. Perhaps then it will go away.

He sat on the veranda seeming to look out but now what he was seeing was not this lush garden but that high and distant place. Adam's Peak.

He hadn't intended going down on one knee. It hadn't even crossed his mind. Well – that was not entirely true. It might have flitted across his mind only to be instantly discarded. She was, after all, English. Or to put it another way, she was white. Not that this would present much of a problem to his peers. To them, she'd seem a prize wife. But his mother had made clear what she thought of his even offering Evelyn a lift into town, and, at heart, he knew that his mother was right.

Evelyn was not a girl one dallied with. One was either serious or one left her kind alone. And while she might have fitted snugly enough into his enlightened circle, there were other things to consider. Her place in general society, for example. Her responsibility as the wife of a master's son. Not only the duties his wife would have to his family and especially to his elders, but also her duties to the workforce.

It didn't matter how eager to set up home Evelyn was (and he had a notion that she wasn't the domestic type), this would not make her one of them. She had not been brought up, as every well-bred Sinhalese girl had, to fit into his type of oriental set-up. The odds of having such a splendid blonde beauty sitting on the lawn and gossiping with the other women as they groomed each other told him how absurd it was – the very idea made him want to laugh louder than at endless crude talk of cunts and menstrual flow.

Yet on Adam's Peak he had found himself on the point of asking for her hand in marriage. Only the faintest hint of her rejection, which hindsight had made him doubt, had stopped him. But every time he had thought of her since, the urge had anyway returned.

So many things that fascinated. Her staggering determination, for one – he had never thought she'd make it to the top of Adam's Peak – and her conduct was so absolutely up to the minute, even ahead of her times. She did things that others in her position would never dream of doing. Plus, and he couldn't deny that this also was a factor, there was the way she reminded him of a beautiful princess from a well-loved if long-discarded story book.

But what really had set the seal on his desire was her expression of enchantment as she had stood on Sri Pada watching the dawn. In that moment, he had wanted her more than he could ever remember wanting anything.

The impossibility of her ever being his was clearly understood. In reinforcement of this he had seemed to hear an echo of his father's accusation that the trouble with him and the other useless chaps was their assumption that nothing should be forbidden them. His father was wrong. He had known, from the very beginning, that Evelyn was forbidden. Yet despite this, a sly, sibilant voice had insinuated itself into his psyche, urging him forward to a proposal of marriage. This voice it was that drove him to that sentence with its hanging if . . . the sentence that, if he hadn't been aware of how imminent was her refusal (imagined or not), he would certainly have completed.

Such forbidden fruit. It was the devil in him that made him consider reaching out for it. Which must mean that it was a god (in whom he wasn't sure he actually believed) who had stayed his tongue.

Thank God then or thank his common sense for the fact that he hadn't fallen into the trap of making a bloody fool of himself. Evelyn and he could never make·a go of it. She was too young, too impetuous, and simultaneously too naïve. She wasn't right for him.

Knowing this, he had still continued to feel the pull of her. Which is why he had decided never to see her again, a decision, he kept telling himself, that would get easier as time went on.

'*Hamu* Emil.'

One of the house servants had come on to the veranda and was standing close by his chair, and must have been for God knows how long, trying to attract his attention.

'Yes. What is it?'

'There is a Mistress Evelyn on the telephone. She is asking if she might have a word with you.'

As soon he felt her hands around his waist, Emil opened up the throttle. The engine roared and jumped forward. He lowered his body until he was slanting low. The road was empty and would soon be full of potholes, some of them only partially visible. With a warm wind brushing against him, he steered down its centre.

The reflection of rows of banana trees that lined its banks had turned the surface of the sluggish river a startling emerald green. Beyond this grove of dusty and jagged fronds, light glittered against the brown sheened skins of the water buffaloes standing at the end of the paddy fields.

He was driving slowly, enjoying the press of Evelyn's body against his back when a remembered question, *Where do you think you are going?* made him further rev the engine. He felt the surprised tightening of her hands as the motorcycle shot forward. He was reminded of the time of their first driving-off and how cautiously he then had reined back on his speed, this a result of his idea of her as a cosseted blonde beauty most suited, he had assumed, to the muffled cotton wool of genteel English society. Now, knowing her better, he knew that she was almost as fearless as he was, this thought, somehow, letting back in the sound of his own defiant, *Out. I am going out,* which is how he had answered his father's question.

He had wrenched open the front door of their house, hoping to put an end to the encounter.

Are you going to see that girl again?

And, *Yes.* The encounter yawning open, *I am going to see that girl who, as it happens, has a name; Evelyn,* remembering the sensation of standing, defiantly, against the onslaught of his father's, *Did your mother not speak to you? She promised that she would.*

Emil twisted the throttle and the engine roared, his beloved motorcycle a live thing beneath him. It gave a hard surging movement in response to which he could feel the further tightening of her grip, and the intake of her warm breath against his ear. Apart from that, she made no sound. She was, he thought, as he pressed himself forward, bracing them both against the onslaught of the wind, the most unusual girl.

She is an English girl, Emil.

He had resisted raising his hand against his father as he had wheeled round. Had walked off accompanied by his father's parting, *You cannot seriously be contemplating marriage to such a girl, Emil. She is not our type.* And his father's fading voice, *Loyalty. That's all I ask of you, my boy. Loyalty to who we are . . .*

On the motorcycle Emil came to in time, but almost too late, to see the deep, wide hole in the road ahead.

Tightening his grip on the handlebars he hauled as hard to the left as he could, simultaneously bending his body

81

almost too late, and certainly too late for Evelyn to respond, so that the motorcycle swerved, sharply, as it also started up, high into the air and then reared back. Only the concentrated forward press of his weight, one foot stamped down on the brake while the other he flung out as tripod and extra brake, stopped them from tipping over. Even so, the motorcycle skidded, its wheels locking, and juddered to a halt. Instinctually he grabbed hold of Evelyn and pulled her free of the machine which, with their weight removed, keeled over. It thudded down, the impact causing a sheet of reddened dust to rise.

A thought – that his carelessness might have killed them both, or if not killed, certainly badly injured them – drained away what was left of his energy. Standing limply and saying, just as limply, 'I am sorry', he turned to look at her.

He saw how she was pushing a strand of hair from her face. She seemed calm enough, although her hand continued to brush at the selfsame place where there now was nothing to brush away. She must be in shock.

'It was unforgivably careless of me.'

'We're neither of us hurt.' She didn't seem that shocked. 'Come.'

It was he who had been turned stupid by the accident and who couldn't figure out what she wanted.

'Come.' She led him to a clearing. It was a quiet place and cool, nestling below a canopy of green. The harsh light of day flickered through leaves that, plumped by recent rain, hung slack. Amongst all this stippled, shadowy green, he could see a spray of dark red bougainvillaea, technicolour bright, that trailed down from a high branch.

'There.' She pointed to the place where a fallen tree had made a natural seat. 'Why don't you sit,' and, following her suggestion, and going to sit he couldn't help remembering how, on their first meeting, he likewise had seated her.

She sat at his feet. He saw her blonde hair shining as she bent her head. It was all he could do to stop himself from reaching out and stroking it.

She touched his leg. Patted down his calf and then took off his shoe before gently, gently rolling down his sock. He looked down and only then did he understand what she was doing. She was exposing his calf's deep, copiously bleeding graze.

'Poor you.' Her quick gaze up was cool and unafraid.

'It's not so bad.' Was he trying to convince himself? 'Looks worse than it feels.'

'Even so.' She sprung up, gracefully, to her feet. 'We need something to staunch the blood. I know . . .' She turned.

He watched as she bent forward. Even from behind he could see that what she was doing was lifting her skirt and taking hold of her petticoat. A shaft of light shone through the trees, illuminating her legs.

He could not tear his eyes away. Knowing that he must, he concentrated his gaze on watching the muscles in her neck moving as she worked at the material until at last she managed to tear off a strip of petticoat.

'There,' she whirled round, smiling triumphantly at her brilliance but, seeing him swallowing, she looked quickly away. 'You weren't supposed to look.'

'Wasn't I?'

Another woman might have played the coquette. Evelyn

didn't. Her blue eyes regarded his brown ones with such daring it was all he could do to hold her gaze until mercifully, although only after a moment's long pause, she lowered herself down.

She lifted his injured leg. With one hand supporting his foot, she used the other to wind the strip of petticoat around the wound. She let go of his leg so she could pull the material tighter.

'Ouch.'

'No more than you deserve.' She pulled harder before tying the ends together. 'There. It should hold until we get back.' She made as if to rise.

He stretched out a hand.

All she had needed was this one, gentle touch and she became quite still. He feathered the tips of the fingers of both hands along her neck. She shivered. He moved his fingers. Pausing at the tip of her clavicle, he could feel the jut of bone under her soft skin, and the faint jumping of a pulse. She seemed to shift almost imperceptibly against his touch.

He felt her swallowing, and then he felt something else. Was it possible? He put his hands on her shoulder and applied a gentle pressure until she was facing him.

Yes, it was possible. She was crying. 'Why?'

She lifted a hand to wipe away her tears. 'I don't know.' She shrugged. 'Because it's almost over?'

He reached across for her hand. A frozen moment, the two looking at each other, before he said the thing that he knew, without a doubt, he meant. 'I don't want you to go.'

Strange how fast everything could change. The house in which Evelyn had lived since her father's death, all the lodgers gone, and all their possessions boxed, no longer felt familiar. It even smelt different, she thought, as she walked, for the last time, from what had been her bedroom to the lounge.

The photographs that once had lined this hallway had all been packed away. Passing each yellow-rimmed space, she tried to reconstruct in her mind's eye images of what had once hung there. To her great surprise she found that, in several instances, she was no longer sure she could remember. Also, and again to her surprise, it didn't seem to matter.

The stripping out of the house had helped free her from doubt. The more it had emptied, the stronger had grown her conviction that it always had been more a source of income than a proper home. A place of compromise and privation. Not like the home that she would soon possess. The one that she and Emil would make together.

She and Emil.

Emil and her.

Evelyn and Emil.

No matter what the order, the pairing had a proper ring to it. She'd made the right decision. She was sure of it. Yes, there were problems – his family was threatening to disown him, and hers was leaving – but, as they kept telling each other, they were all the family either of them would ever need. Remembering the touch of his hand against her cheek as he had whispered this, she blushed.

This was, she was sure of it, this was love. Real love. Passionate love. Not only was she in love, she was also in love with being in love. She gave a little skip of joy just as she heard Marjorie saying, 'You have to tell her', this injunction followed by her mother's, 'Do I?'

Tiptoeing over to the half-open door, Evelyn saw her mother and her sister standing in the middle of an empty room.

'If you don't,' Marjorie was saying, 'she'll be the one to suffer.'

'I'm tired, Marjorie.'

It was true. Her mother did look tired. Not that this stopped Marjorie from a determined and repetitive, 'You have to tell her, Mummy. You have to.'

Her mother swept out her hand to encompass the room. 'Packing all this has worn me out. I can't continue to fight. I haven't the strength.'

'I know it's difficult. But you *are* her mother.'

'Yes, Marjorie –' her mother gave an unamused little chortle – 'I am aware of that.'

'You owe it to her.'

'Is it your opinion that a mother must always owe her children? Even when they are grown up? Even unto death?'

'No but . . .'

'You know what Evelyn's like. Once she has set herself on a particular course, there is no holding her back. She'll marry him and they'll settle here. It's all decided. And perhaps, given the circumstances, it's for the best.'

'But Mummy . . .'

'Enough.' Her mother sounded so extremely weary that, pushing herself into motion, Evelyn walked into the lounge, saying breezily, 'What's for the best?'

A beat, her mother and her sister exchanging a quick glance, and then, 'We were talking about your marriage to Emil,' her mother said, which, this having been the main, almost the only, topic of conversation since Evelyn had announced the engagement, was an unnecessary explanation. 'Were we not, Marjorie?'

Marjorie's sullen, 'Yes, that's right we were', she followed by looking away.

Evelyn had already written off Marjorie's carping as jealousy at the way Evelyn's glittering engagement had made Marjorie's pale. But now she thought that Marjorie didn't look so much jealous as sad. Was it possible – surely not? – that Marjorie was upset at the prospect of their imminent separation? Perhaps – was it possible – Marjorie was going to miss Evelyn. Perhaps – and this thought almost made Evelyn retch – Marjorie had been looking forward to living with Evelyn, something which, Evelyn had to admit it, if she had been about to marry Gordon she would certainly have wished for.

'They'll soon be here,' her mother said. 'Why not check your room, Marjorie? Just in case.'

That was what Evelyn had been hoping for – the last few remaining moments alone with her mother. But after Marjorie had left, she found herself oddly discomforted, a feeling apparently mirrored by her mother's rather tentative, 'Well . . .'

Despite her determination not to reopen the subject, Evelyn spoke awkwardly: 'I do love him.'

'Yes.' Her mother's expression seemed to soften. 'I can see you do,' although there was still something not quite right in her mother's smile.

Telling herself that her mother was having to leave not only her but also her chosen country, Evelyn thought she understood her mother's sadness.

'We'll see each other soon,' she said. 'Emil promised – any time you want to visit, any time at all, he'll send a ticket,' thinking then about the exhausting few months her mother had just spent packing. 'Or if that feels too much, we'll come and visit you.'

'That will be nice.' Her mother's smile stretched wider.

'We'll probably end up settling in England. We're already talking about it,' in response to which her mother repeated the sentence, 'That will be nice.'

'Is something the matter, Mummy?'

Her mother blinked. 'No, darling. Why?'

'You sounded . . . I don't know . . . you sounded unsure.'

'Did I?' Her mother looked at Evelyn properly. Swallowed, and intently, as if making up her mind about something, said, 'I was thinking, I suppose, about your children. I was thinking that this is not an easy world for those who don't conform. That Britain is not an easy place for people who are . . . who are . . .'

So that's what Marjorie had been egging her mother on to say. 'Who are half-caste, you mean?'

'Yes, I suppose, if you must put it so baldly, that is what I mean.'

Marjorie's grievance made manifest. Doing little to hide her indignation, Evelyn said, 'Didn't you teach us that it is what a person does, and not the colour of their skin, that matters?'

'I taught you that everybody deserves equal courtesy', her mother said, 'but that doesn't mean that you should . . . that you should . . .'

Marry one, Evelyn thought as her mother continued,

'. . . flout convention. Or if you do insist on flouting it, then you must understand, darling, that some of the consequences may be visited not on you, but on your children.'

Evelyn bit her lip. Her mother did not normally talk like this: she must be very hurt by Evelyn's decision. Half Evelyn's life had been spent dreaming about the kind of all-embracing love she felt for Emil. Never had it occurred to her that this same love would be delivered on an undercurrent of so much pain. She said, whispering, 'I'm sorry.'

Her mother, pale grey eyes shining more brightly than usual. 'Don't be sorry, Evelyn. The world is not always of our making but we must make the best of it we can.' She twisted something from her left hand. 'Here.'

In her mother's outstretched hand was a diamond, glint ing. It was her mother's engagement ring, the only piece of value that she had not sold during the days of penury that followed her husband's death.

'I want you to have it.'

'But . . .'

89

'No buts, darling. You know I can't be here for the wedding. I'd lose the job if I was. So instead, as some small compensation, you should keep this.'

'Won't Marjorie mind?'

'Marjorie will have me in England. Please, Evelyn.' Her mother put the ring in Evelyn's hand and afterwards gently closed the hand. 'Not another word.'

As she stood waiting for Emil, Evelyn kept turning the ring, and that way pushing away the things her mother had said.

Her mother and Marjorie were both wrong – Marjorie because she was prejudiced and her mother because she was old fashioned. She had come to adulthood in a different time, her perspective shaped by the solidity of empire and not by the reality of empire's imminent end into which Evelyn had grown. This had to be the explanation for her mother's uncharacteristic display of prejudice. And this also was why, Evelyn told herself, her mother's 'You're doing the right thing,' at the last had sounded more like a question than conviction. And then her mother had reached up to gently stroke away the tears on Evelyn's face, and whispered, 'I love you,' coaxing out a smile.

It was that smile and not the tears that must persist. Today was the first day of Evelyn's new life.

Her back to the sea she peered down the road. She wished Emil would hurry. No matter that she was much earlier than she'd said she'd be (she had not been able to bring herself to watch as the tug carried them to the ship), she needed him. Be here, she thought, Be here, and heard the roaring of his motorcycle.

He drew up. Lightly jumped off, a breeze fluttering at his new white shirt. He smoothed back his hair and she saw that he was smiling, as he always was when he was with her. He loves me, she thought, and that's all that matters.

He moved decisively and quickly to her side and put his arms around her.

She could feel the strength of him. He was so attuned to her needs. Through touch he had read how the parting from her mother had been, and had guessed correctly that he must hold her, but not close enough to make her feel that she was being suffocated.

No room, any longer, for her doubts. No reason either. She had chosen him. She loved him.

She felt herself relax.

Close to land the sea was greyed by foam but as it got deeper, it looked greener, the far distant sheen being almost emerald against the light, bright blue of the morning sky. And there, on either side, a grove of dark green palms to frame this picture of her paradise.

1950

Once scores of young Englishmen had stood eagerly on deck as their ships steamed east. Now, as the political tide began to turn, it pulled people back to places that some had once called home, and others had only ever imagined. Amongst these was Evelyn.

Only four more hours to go, she thought, before we reach Tilbury.

Four, an appropriate number. It summed up all those other fours. Four hours. Four months. Four years.

The first, the hours before she was due to see Emil again. The second, the months since he had left Ceylon to set up house in London. The third, the years that had elapsed since she had last seen her sister or her mother. Her mother whom Evelyn would never see again for her mother had died in her ninth month in England, the advanced stage of Evelyn's pregnancy having prevented her from attending either the sick-bed or the funeral.

The boat's forward motion was made visible only by the striking of waves against the bow, foam and spray stirred up as the boat ploughed through water that seemed, despite the cold, to be furiously boiling. The seascape was a monotonous shade of grey that perfectly matched the overhanging sky, presenting Evelyn with a vast, blank canvas without, seemingly, even a horizon. Such a contrast from earlier sights. From the purpled flying fish that had used their folded tails as lift-off and their fins to glide them up, or the small, fat, snouted black porpoises that had kept occasional pace with the ship, or the miraculous gleaming of phosphorescence that flashed up from the inky blackness of the depths.

Shivering, she pulled her new lined linen coat tighter. Ludicrously heavy in Colombo, here it felt almost threadbare.

She thought about her wedding. About her long white satin frock and about Emil, handsome in his tailored black suit, waiting beneath the bower of orchids that only his indefatigable persistence could have organised. It hadn't mattered that neither of them had any family present – that hers were too far away and his had refused to attend. They had each other, which was more than enough. Then she thought about the red outfit she had worn, to return not to her mother's house as custom dictated, but to the sweet dwelling that Emil had organised for them in Colombo. There she had established herself as mistress of the household, her old ayah Minrada being all the reassurance she needed to step into this role. And thus had begun her very own fairy tale.

So many changes for which she was continually giving thanks. How wonderful, firstly, no longer to have to scrimp and save. And how fortunate to have a husband as generous, and demonstratively loving, as Emil. She was soon the beneficiary of all manner of privileges from which her mother's poverty had excluded her. Attendance in Nuwara Eliya for example, not just in the season but in the small season as well. There Emil would laugh raucously every time the money she bet was lost. And later he named a racehorse after their son.

Evelyn had become a mother.

In her darkest hours after hearing of her own mother's death, she had thought nothing would ever make up for her loss. But when at last she had looked down on her newborn son's wrinkled, brown face, the love she had felt for him seemed to connect her to her mother by a thread that would never be broken. Almost every day after Milton's birth, she would catch herself counting her blessings. And if Emil had seemed a little jealous of the new arrival (only natural, Minrada said), there was still nothing he wouldn't do for his wife. Everything Evelyn wanted, everything she asked for, everything that was in his power to give, she was given. Including at last that most precious of her desires – this relocation.

She had only gingerly broached the subject and Emil, who had never anyway forgiven his parents their refusal to acknowledge his wife, immediately agreed to move. And not only that. He had even swallowed his pride, giving up on his determination never to visit his family home unless Evelyn was also welcome, so as to talk his father into providing the funds.

How he had made her laugh when he had stood, legs astride, in the middle of their lounge in imitation of the pompous, 'Glad you have stopped making such a foofaraw out of our disagreement, my boy' with which his father had greeted his request. And how she had continued to rock with laughter as he had gone on to quote his father's, 'and that you have also come to understand that, only two years after independence, we are already in a position to reverse the balance of power,' after which his father had expanded on his conviction that, with his money and Emil's entrepreneurial skills, they could set up the first outpost of their very own rubber empire. 'All we need now,' his father had concluded, 'is a bloody good war.' Which, Emil had told her, was not just his father's natural gift for hyperbole. War, you see, was always good for rubber producers.

And war – in Korea – is what they had got, a reality brought home to Evelyn when her ship had passed through Suez. Then, as the high banks of the canal seemed to drift by, she saw the fluttering sails of Arab dhows dwarfed by fat American troop ships on their way to Korea, tangible evidence of Emil's boasts about his booming business and the eager partners he had found. All of which meant that everything of which she had begun to dream since Milton's birth, and especially that Milton should have, as his birthright, the key to his grand-mother's country, was coming true. She should be beaming.

She shivered as she looked out on the watery gloom.

'Cold enough for you?' John Davidson, fellow passenger and husband to Catherine (who had been so kind to Evelyn during the journey) came to stand beside her. 'Penny for your thoughts.'

'Oh I don't know.' She smiled. 'I suppose I was thinking how bleached of colour everything is.'

'That's it exactly. The further north one goes, the more

white the world becomes. Peculiar, isn't it? But you know what's even more peculiar?' John paused as if waiting for her to say, that yes, she would certainly love to know. But, having shared his table three times a day and for as many weeks, she'd grown accustomed to John's habit of answering his own questions, and sure enough, 'Well I'll tell you what's more peculiar. I have a clear memory of standing at these same rails (well in a manner of speaking, they were the rails of the boat on which we took passage out) as the sky got bluer, and the days warmer. And I remember remarking to Catherine how fortunate we were to be leaving behind fog-bound old Blighty. But do you know what?' Another pause. 'Well I'll tell you what. The grey and the cold, and the damp are amongst the things I most missed. They can keep their sun, and their bright light – and incidentally their foot rot and their heat rashes and their biting insects. None of those can match the joy of a good old coal fire and the rain tapping at the window panes, and the comforting smell of crumpets,' and as John said this, Evelyn couldn't help remembering how her mother had also used to talk of sitting rooms with fires, and of the melting of butter into crevasses of toasted crumpets. All of which – she felt a smile spreading – would soon be part of her life.

'Where's the little chap?'

'The purser took him down to the engine room. The sailors are all so kind. They let him push buttons to his heart's content.'

'Yes well.' John returned her smile. 'He's such a jolly roly-poly little fellow.'

John was right, the three-year-old Milton had spurted up during the journey and also widened. Something to do, she supposed, with all the jam and custard and bread puddings into which he had so enthusiastically tucked.

'Would you like that?' she heard John saying.

'I'm sorry, John. What did you say?'

'I was enquiring as to how you planned to travel into London, because if it is to be by train, Catherine and I would be more than happy to escort you. Show you the ropes and so on.'

'That's kind of you but my husband is to meet us by car. He has a new one of which he is particularly proud.'

'I see.' A surprised pause. 'Your husband must be a well connected and enterprising sort of chap,' and surprise also written on John's expression. 'Cars are rather in short supply.'

And yes, Evelyn thought, Emil was an enterprising chap.

'Well then . . .' John's tail-off reminded her of her manners. 'Perhaps we could offer you both a lift?' in reply to which John's 'That's very kind of you' was delivered with alacrity. 'Only if you have space,' he said. 'And now, if you don't mind I should go and see how Catherine's faring with the repacking of the final bits and bobs.'

Cloud hung like damp smoke as the ship slid through the greasy swell. Past Southend, past miles of mud and through a landscape wreathed in grey.

Standing at the rails with Milton in her arms, Evelyn could feel him shivering. She knew it would have been better to keep him inside but she hadn't wanted to miss a single moment of her journey's end. She pulled the child closer, hoping that way to transfer her body's warmth to him.

'Here.' Catherine helped Evelyn put a rug around Milton, wrapping it so tight that he had no choice but to stop his wriggling.

'Thank you, Catherine.'

'It's a pleasure. I expect you can't wait to see your husband.'

And yes, Evelyn's heart was beating faster at the prospect of being with Emil again. She was also on tenterhooks as she waited to catch her first glimpse of this, her new country.

Such a different vista, so far, from the one she had imagined. She wondered whether everything else would also be so utterly different. So utterly . . .

'Dreary, isn't it?'

And yes, dreary was the word that sprung to mind, what with the outline of mean houses huddled together and the barnacled ribs of encrusted wooden barges sticking up through the blackened mud, and the sun that finally had pushed a sufficient hole in the clouds to streak the horizon a dirty yellow – all of it was terribly dreary.

'As if someone arranged it deliberately to fool foreigners into passing by.' John sounded so extremely cheerful.

The ship's horn sounded as they moved closer into dock, and as it did, the haze seemed suddenly to lighten. Now Evelyn could see how the high tilted black stripes were in fact cranes placed at regular intervals along the line of the shore, while those other, lower smudges of dark were buildings.

'For the storage of cargo.' John's words were accompanied by his wife's, 'Home sweet home.'

Evelyn ruffled Milton's curly hair. 'Home,' she whispered. 'We're going to see Daddy,' hearing how Milton echoed her last word – 'Daddy' – but ritualistically and without much enthusiasm. Four months was a long time in such a little boy's life. Although she had tried to keep the memory of Emil alive, she wouldn't be surprised if Milton, a late talker who'd not yet had a word for Emil before he left, didn't think that 'Daddy' was the black and white photograph of a grinning man his mother was always showing him.

'Quite a reception,' John said, which told Evelyn that the faint high-pitched calling she had taken for the cry of seagulls was coming from the dock where a grey mass of people had gathered. There were so many of them crammed together and roped in before the gangplank that she, who had imagined immediately spotting Emil and running into his arms, now thought she was going to have trouble picking him out of the crowd.

Except of course she had no trouble.

His was the only brown arm raised in that sea of grey and white, and his the only brown face beaming. His lips parted and he seemed to jump up, high in the air, arms waving (there was something brown in one of them), and she thought she could hear, even over all those other hurrahs, the sound of her name, and she was also about to lift her arm and wave back calling 'Emil' when . . .

'Look at that chap, over there, making such a frightful scene. You'd think he'd have had some manners drummed into him by now.'

It crossed her mind to pretend she hadn't heard, or that if she had, she didn't know who was the object of John's derision. But that, it felt, would be a betrayal of her husband. And so she turned to look at John. In time to catch Catherine's reproachful look, followed by the dipping of her head in Milton's direction as if her husband might actually be too stupid to have understood her meaning.

As Emil helped her into the splendid fur coat he had brought with him, she couldn't help noticing how his hands were more cracked than she remembered them, while that glori ously honey brown skin seemed to have been discoloured by that same greyness that hung over everything she had so far seen. Was it possible that he had changed so much? Surely not; it had only been four months.

'All right, darling?'

'Yes, of course. And thank you, Emil, the coat is beauti-ful . . .' she stroked down the lines of fur, shifting from side to side to watch it following her every twist and turn, 'and it's so warm,' knowing that the change she thought she had seen in Emil was only a trick of the light. Must be, for she was accustomed to seeing him under blue skies and in bright sunshine. And besides, how could she be judging him when, after so many weeks at sea, she also must look a shadow of her former self?

'Let's get you into the warm.' He picked up her travelling case. 'This way,' meaning to link his other arm to hers. But she reached down for Milton, who was still wrapped in Catherine's rug.

'Isn't he old enough to be on his own two legs?'

'It's too crowded. He'll get trodden on.'

'Of course.' When Emil smiled she was warmed by his affectionate familiarity. 'Come. Let's take you both away from this crush.'

He walked ahead to clear the way. She followed carrying their son who was wrapped up so well that only the tip of his nose was peeking out.

Milton, after first contact with his father, had shut his mouth so tightly that his lips had started to quiver. He had not said a word since Emil had lifted Evelyn off the ground and hugged her. 'He's just shy of you,' she had told Emil, 'and cold, he'll warm up soon.' Now she whispered into Milton's muffled ear. 'When we get to the car you must tell Daddy how much we've missed him.'

The boy gave no sign that he had heard. She was thinking of repeating the instruction when a shrill 'Excuse me' intruded.

'Excuse me, my good man.'

A white-haired woman, also fur clad, was blocking Emil's path. She looked angry as if he had offended her.

'Are you talking to me, madam?'

'Naturally I am. Who else would I be talking to?'

'Well then,' Emil gave a little bow, 'how may I be of assistance?'

'After you have settled this lady,' the woman said, 'you may come back for my suitcases.'

Evelyn freezing. Standing at her husband's side, staring into the woman's parchment grey face and darting out a silent thought: how dare you? How dare you treat my husband – and this despite the fact that he isn't even dressed in porter's uniform – as if he were at your disposal?

'Certainly, madam,' she heard Emil saying, without a moment's hesitation. 'If you wait here, I'll be back in the merest jiffy.'

Having deposited Milton in the back, Emil held open the front door.

She looked at him. 'Aren't you going to . . . ?'

'To what?'

For a moment she wondered if she need remind him of his promise to the woman but then she saw those tell-tale signs – his quivering lips, and the faint movement in the laugh lines that ran to the side of his dark eyes, and the slight juddering of his neck – and, knowing that he was struggling to keep a straight face, her smile burst out, releasing his.

Which meant, she realised as she started laughing, he hadn't really changed. He was the same man – a jokester, undaunted and undauntable and defiant of the niceties of convention – that she loved.

'You never know, that good lady might be an heiress in search of a likely heir,' he said. 'You think I should go back and make the most of her largesse?'

She cuffed him lightly on the arm, the burden of her worries dropping away. Despite the greyness, she thought, it's going to be all right.

'How about getting in?'

'In a moment, darling.' She took in the smooth curve of the maroon door he was holding open. 'It's nice.'

He smiled. 'She's a beauty, isn't she?' He stroked the paintwork. 'The very latest Lancaster 6.'

'Some friends from the boat thought you must be very well connected to have a brand new car.'

'Not so much connected as Ceylonese. The war has almost brought this country to its knees. To wit, the government's new slogan, "Export or die." Which means that I, with my foreign passport, can be included in the category of persons buying export goods and, bingo, the car is mine.'

'But don't people mind?'

'People?'

'You know. English people. Don't they mind that you can buy one when they can't?'

'Oh, don't worry about that,' he said. 'They might take me for a porter when they see a suitcase in my hand, but as soon as I get into the driving seat, I am immediately elevated to the status of foreign dignitary. An exotic Maharaja is my guess. You'd be amazed how often my passing is saluted, not only by commissionaires, but even in some instances by English

106

bobbies.' He smiled again, his expression lighting up. 'But where are your friends?'

'My friends?'

'From the boat. We could give them a lift.'

Strange how fast things could change. 'Let's not bother, darling.' She tiptoed up so as to kiss him. 'I'd much rather be alone with you. And besides, my so-called friends have turned out to be the most frightful snobs.'

As Emil drove to their new home that he promised 'would astound', she watched what seemed to be unending dilapidation and decay passing by.

A dulled landscape was drawn in greys and dingy reds over which man had heaped his own defeats. Jangled telephone wires and electric cables littering unkempt but tarred streets. Kerchiefed women scrubbing wearily at dingy front steps that would never come clean. Bruised-kneed children playing in the rubble of houses long since destroyed while adults, grey skinned, scurried with lowered heads past the bombed-out buildings.

It was so ugly. Her precious Ceylon (precious now that she had fled its shores) had been sketched out in all the glory of its technicolour tumultuousness while this, her mother, seemed tired, and old, and drained by war. As if Evelyn had missed her step and instead of touching ground had sunk down under a sea of sticky fluid that muted sound and dulled colour and had her struggling for her every breath.

'It's the fog,' Emil said. 'You'll get used to it,' while she, looking out endlessly through the window, doubted she would ever get used to this rolling cityscape so overdeveloped that even if you were to turn a score, a hundred, perhaps even a thousand, corners there would be no new sight to see. No glorious clashing of greens. No glint of sun. No blue sky from which to shade your eyes. No laughter. None of that. Only more of the same.

It will be better tomorrow, she thought.

'What's that?'

She hadn't realised that she had spoken her thoughts. 'I said tomorrow will be brighter.'

'I wouldn't count on it.'

She watched him driving so masterfully through this strange terrain. 'The first thing you learn about this country,' he said, 'is that the weather is going to continue to be unremittingly foul. But there are plenty of compensations. Opportunities to be grabbed. Particularly if you haven't been brought up to doff the cap.'

He smiled at her and she smiled back, but uneasily. She had been so certain that this relocation was what she wanted, and what her son needed, that she had even left behind her beloved Minrada (who had refused, point blank, to come with them). And now, she thought, have I made a mistake by persuading him to bring us here?

'Evelyn.' He was waiting at the bottom of the stairs. 'Come down.'

She stirred herself into motion, her descent marked by the rustling of her gown. It was the most glorious concoction, low busted and tight waisted, with a long flowing skirt and a grey taffeta underlay that stiffened the topmost folds of grey-blue satined silk. To buy it she had gone, not to a dressmaker as she would have done at home but, on Emil's insistence ('*I told you war would be good for business*'), to the smartest shop she had ever seen there to sit, nervously, alongside peeresses, ambassadresses and even, or so it was rumoured, the Queen's agent, as mannequins paraded a succession of flowing evening gowns one of which, regardless of cost, Emil had insisted that she buy.

'You look beautiful.'

And yes, she did feel beautiful.

'For you.' He was a magician, unfurling his palm to reveal a small package.

'What is it?'

'Only one way to find out.'

Laid out on a royal blue velvet lining she saw a necklace

of cornflower-blue sapphires. The stones caught hold of the light from the chandelier and reflected it back as if, she thought, she had been enfolded in the flashing brilliance of the country she had left behind. It was so exquisite, it almost brought her to tears. She tried to thank him saying, 'It's . . . it's . . .' but couldn't find words to describe how beautiful it was. 'It's . . .'

'Yes, it certainly is, isn't it?' Gently he laid the necklace around her neck. 'It was made for this dress –' doing up the catch – 'and for your eyes. And for your skin.'

She was filled with love for him. For his generosity and his thoughtfulness. So much so that she was almost shaking with her strength of feeling. She turned away to try and hide this (it would not do to let go, not now, before the party) and caught sight of Milton.

He was standing in the doorway. Her little son, all spick and span and scrubbed from his bath and clad in pyjamas, his big dark eyes widening at the sight of his mother in such finery and his father coming round to kiss her.

'Like it?' She did a little twirl especially for Milton, laughing at his furiously nodding head.

'A boy with taste.' Taking her by the arm, Emil led her into the lounge.

They were all three sitting together when the bell rang.

'It's not time, is it?'

'No need to be scared. It's a party, not an execution.' Emil got up. 'But no, it's not yet time. It must be Marjorie and Gordon. A chance for them to meet the boy.'

Oh, of course. How could she have forgotten? It's only nerves, she told herself as she heard the housekeeper opening the door and, following that, Marjorie's once familiar babble as, handing in her wrap, she commented loudly on the size of the hall and the brightness of the hanging chandelier before the door swung open and there they stood – Marjorie and Gordon. Her sister and her sister's husband.

A beat. Four adults frozen. Two sisters and two husbands facing each other across the room and united by a single thought – how very different they had always been. How different they still were. Then Emil bestirred himself, making his way over saying, 'Marjorie. Gordon, at long last,' in such a welcoming manner that his voice unfroze the others, including the unexpectedly shy Evelyn who crossed the room, going up to her sister and kissing her, but gingerly, just as Marjorie tentatively returned the kiss.

No avoiding the awkward contrast between Evelyn's sapphires and her low-cut sweeping beauty of a dress, and Marjorie's unadorned and faded floral day frock or, having registered this, noticing how, when Marjorie smiled, her lips turned down into an expression of such petulant dissatisfaction that two new channels ran from each corner of her mouth all the way to her chin. And as for Marjorie's hand that went up, nervously, to her mouth – well it was roughened as her complexion also had been chapped, both of them presumably by the rigours of the English winters.

'Isn't it wonderful to be together again?' Emil sounded strangely hearty. 'This, Milton, is your aunt and uncle.' His tension betrayed in a barked-out 'Please get up quickly and say hello.'

After an encouraging nod from Evelyn, Milton inched his way towards Marjorie.

'My, my, you are a big boy, aren't you?' Marjorie delivered this with such a tight pinch of her voice that Milton, over-tired and confused by his mother's failure to speak, seemed to shrink back.

'Long past your bedtime, my boy.' Emil shushed Milton into the arms of the waiting housekeeper, before turning his attention to their guests. 'What can I get you to drink? Gordon? What would you say to one of my finest malts?' Emil who rarely took alcohol was nevertheless an expert on all manner of drinks. 'And Marjorie, I think you'd appreciate the sherry I've recently acquired.'

Marjorie and Gordon nodded like marionettes. Evelyn, who also found herself stupidly nodding, couldn't help feeling grateful to Emil for covering over the general awkwardness.

'Come,' Emil was saying. 'We don't stand on ceremony here. Sit. Sit.' He handed them their drinks.

'So tell us –' He patted the space beside him to indicate that Evelyn should likewise sit. 'How are things?'

Emil's interest seemed so genuine that Marjorie, after a little more prompting, began to comment on how peculiar it was that fate, which had once separated them, had now reunited them and in England. Although, Marjorie continued, Gordon's job (*'He has been moved up another civil servant rung, you know'*) naturally meant that they couldn't be based so very centrally, and apart from that, they did have to live more modestly. After which Marjorie (having been the recipient of Gordon's quick, reproving glance) made haste to say that it was actually a very nice house and in a respectable street, they had a garden back and front, both of them requiring some updating, but she would soon get round to that . . . all of this and more egged on by Emil's animated nodding and his helpful questions. On and on Marjorie gushed as Evelyn, who once had disliked the way her sister's conversation was peppered by so many different irrelevancies as well as by all the things that always had to be said, now wished Marjorie would never stop while simultaneously she couldn't help noting the unusual transformation in Gordon's behaviour. He remained uncharacteristically silent. Either the home civil service whose virtues he unendingly used to praise had managed to tame the opinions out of him or else he was too uneasy at being Emil's guest to speak. That would certainly be true of the old Gordon.

'Well.' Emil looked at her. It was her task, as hostess, now to take over.

She couldn't think of anything to say and neither, it seemed, could Marjorie.

How odd that they, who had spent nineteen years together and only five apart, had become such strangers. But with their mother (who had always bridged the gap between them) dead almost everything had changed. Not only the continents they both had breached and the longitudes and latitudes they'd shifted, but both were now married (neither having been at the other's wedding).

'Marjorie might like to see the house,' Emil suggested, to the obvious relief of Marjorie who replied, enthusiastically, that yes, there was nothing she would rather do.

*

Was it her eagerness to keep conversation at bay that had Evelyn conducting her sister on a tour so comprehensive it even included the kitchen ornaments? Certainly she was at pains to highlight every single one of Emil's multifarious and up-to-the-minute acquisitions. The special sink heater that ensured a constant flow of hot water into a stainless steel sink, for example, or the fat Frigidaire that allowed the former pantry to house the new electric washing machine, or the Formica-covered built-in counters which were absolutely the latest trend.

She led Marjorie through the dining room with its polished mahogany table large enough to accommodate the set of twelve – genuine, she was at pains to say – Louis XV chairs. Next the hall and up the stairs, where she swept her sister through bathrooms and spare bedrooms (for more children, she gaily heard herself telling the childless Marjorie). Flinging open the door to the main bedroom she pointed out the large mahogany bedstead on either side of which were two octagonal tables carved in traditional style (very pricey, as she was sure Marjorie must remember). And there, in pride of place, she made sure that Marjorie remarked on it, was the knee-high elephant of royal ebony. It was so heavy, Evelyn told her sister, it took four strong men to carry it upstairs, never mind what it must have cost to acquire and ship from Ceylon.

Given how impoverished both Marjorie and Gordon looked, there might have been some sadism involved. And yet might it be instead that, in all her boastful showing off, the person Evelyn was really trying to convince was not Marjorie but herself? Perhaps. For when she took Marjorie over to the window to say, unnecessarily, 'and there's the garden. It's big, they say, at least big for an English garden. Not much yet to see. Emil has had the whole thing uprooted in order to replant it,' she was uncomfortably conscious of her boastful twitting and her tweeting even as she was driven on to say, 'You know what Emil's like – extravagance is his middle name. Of course we're fortunate to be able to afford his little . . .' giving, then, a deprecating little giggle, 'or, his not so little, luxuries,' which was when it occurred to her that the person most discomforted by this ostentatious display of wealth might be her.

Strange to have these thoughts, now, just before her party.

In buying her this house, Emil had demonstrated both his generosity and his penchant for extravagant display. So was it disloyal, she wondered, to think that it might have gone easier for her if, instead of a vast whiteness of a building, he had chosen a smaller house in a less isolated area?

'Look to the bottom of the garden,' her words spoken deliberately to deny this unease, 'there's an orchid house there,' and then, her voice unexpectedly dropping, 'I am so lucky.'

Perhaps it was this change in tone with its undercurrent of uncertainty that nudged Marjorie into saying, loudly, that yes, Evelyn had indeed been fortunate and although the night had been made so very dark by fog (dreadfully hard, Marjorie said, to get used to this English weather) she could appreciate what a big garden it must be. And then, for some reason that neither woman could have articulated, Marjorie's approval allowed the sisters to stand for a moment in a more comfortable, and relieving, silence that stretched on, eventually to be broken by Marjorie's soft, 'Towards the end, she liked nothing better than to look out on the garden. She would sit for hours.'

Evelyn could not trust herself to speak.

'Sometimes she would look so hard her eyes seemed to have lost focus. I don't believe she was even seeing Mrs Crawford's garden. I think she was seeing ours. I mean the one we had.'

And yes, Evelyn thought, their mother had always loved her garden.

'It was hard on her,' Marjorie said, 'dying so far from home.' A pause. 'She missed you terribly.'

'I would have come.' Evelyn's tone sounded more strident than she had intended. 'If I'd been told in time.'

'I know you would have, but she wouldn't let me tell you.' And Evelyn remembered how she had walked in, that last day, on her mother and Marjorie arguing.

'Was she sick? Before she left Ceylon, I mean?'

Marjorie looked away.

'She was, wasn't she?'

'She wouldn't let me tell you,' Marjorie said 'She thought things were hard enough without the news ruining the first days of your marriage. She wanted so much for you to be happy.'

For the first time since Marjorie had arrived, a kind of peacefulness descended. As they stood looking out, they seemed like their mother to be seeing not the darkness but the past that they had shared. In that moment, Evelyn thought of other things she might still share with her sister. Not just the grief she still felt for their mother, or her regret at not having been present at the end, but also her feelings of anxiety that here, in this country, she would never fit. Or the way the distance between Emil and Milton didn't seem to shorten. Or . . . But no, she severed the possibility. Telling Marjorie, who'd never approved of Emil, would be an act of disloyalty. As for the questions she might have asked Marjorie, like whether Gordon had become permanently silent and disappointed, or whether Marjorie was managing financially, or whether her chapped skin came from the cold or too much housework – all the topics she could have broached seemed so laden with difficulty that the ringing of the doorbell came as considerable relief.

Hearing its long, hard, distinctive pealing, she said, 'That must be Yuri. He always leans on the bell,' and sure enough, she could hear Yuri's booming voice. 'A lovely man. Come – let's go and say hello.'

Yuri half lifted Evelyn off the ground, his thick brown beard tickling as he kissed each cheek in turn and then a third time before Emil laughingly instructed him to 'unhand my wife or risk my wrath at the ruination of her frock'. At which point the bell rang and after that kept on ringing, more and more people flooding in until the lounge was packed.

Yuri took charge of Gordon and Marjorie. Every time Evelyn looked in their direction she saw them caught up in animation as Yuri shared with them potted histories of each new arrival. Seemed like her husband's lovely Russian partner could talk to almost anyone. At one point she even saw him pulling off the seemingly impossible feat of making Gordon laugh.

Evelyn meanwhile moved through the press of people all of whom already seemed to be such intimates that it began to feel as if she, Marjorie and Gordon were the only strangers present. Sternly she told herself that this was her house and her party and then, her courage up, she tossed her pretty head at her guests' pretty compliments, the skirt of her gown swirling and her laughter tinkling, and the light burnishing her blonde hair, and oh, to her great surprise, she was a picture of confidence and joy. Until, that is, Marjorie came to whisper that they should be off, and thank you they'd had such a lovely time, and although they had stayed for a respectable period, their abrupt departure left Evelyn deflated.

Emil was weaving through the throng. Catching her eye, he gestured for her to join him. She felt suddenly too shy. She shook her head, smiling to indicate that she wanted to take a break from this unending chatter and went to stand in the corner where Marjorie and Gordon had spent most of their time.

From this sideline she watched as Emil continued on his jovially weaving rounds. How very much himself he was. Loud and hospitable, filling glasses and cracking jokes. How easily he found it, she thought, to make people laugh. And how at ease he was in this group of well off, confident people.

Not like her. The more she stood, the more she found herself wondering whether she would ever fit in. Her shyness kept growing and she might have remained alone for the whole duration if not for the man whose, 'They put on quite a show,' sounded in her ear.

A tall man, a stranger, handsome, fair-haired and blue eyed, was standing close, smiling as he continued looking into the fray. 'As different as they are, they both equally draw the eye.'

The 'they' must be her husband and Yuri. Following his gaze, she saw that he was right. Although Emil was slight and Yuri a big bear of a man, they shared a vibrancy and a will to connect that meant that no matter where they were, they drew the eye. And, as well, the ear.

'It's quite a gift.' The stranger turned to smile at her, fondly, as if they were already friends although, in contradiction of this, he said 'I don't believe we've been introduced,' proffering then, his name – 'I'm Charles' – confidently as if she naturally would know who Charles was. And so she said, 'Oh yes, of course, Charles,' as if she did know. She held out one of her white-gloved hands as she had seen other women do.

He lifted the hand quickly to his lips and kissed it, a liberty taken with a soft grace that both surprised and enchanted her. Then reluctantly, or so it seemed to her, he let go of her hand. 'You've not got the foggiest idea who I am, have you?'

He was looking at her keenly. 'I'm afraid not.'

'I'm another of your husband's partners – the junior partner.' She looked away, embarrassed.

'I'm fairly new on board as well as pretty unimportant. I wouldn't have expected Emil to mention me. He never stops talking about you, though. Given his proclivity for hyperbole, I took what he said with a pinch of salt. But now,' the skin by his sharp blue eyes crinkled, 'I see that, far from embellishing your beauty, he actually understated it.' The compliment was delivered with such easy charm that it warmed her. Only for a moment though, because it dawned on Evelyn that this stranger was acting as if he was an old and cherished friend. Perhaps this kind of familiarity was normal for this smart English set but she couldn't stop her face from burning. She swallowed.

121

'I'm sorry,' he said. 'I have an irritating habit of always saying the wrong thing.' He frowned and looked about as if searching out something that might put her back at ease. 'Quite a crowd,' is what he came up with.

She nodded.

'I expect they are all congratulating themselves for their bravery at being amongst such foreign outlandishness.'

Sharply she looked at him. She found his gaze not, as she'd assumed, on Emil or Yuri but scanning the crowd, slowly and deliberately, as his frown gathered. 'They're like a pack of jackals', he said.

She had not the slightest idea how to respond to that. Once more that feeling that she was the stranger here.

'We're an insular people,' she heard him saying, musingly, as if taking for granted that she was perfectly at ease. 'Most of our time and energy is spent ensuring that everything and everybody keeps to their proper place. It's all nonsense of course, but then, I'm afraid, that's the English for you.' He smiled, sadly, and she wondered whether he was including himself in that description. 'But stuffy as we are,' he continued, 'we sometimes experience an inclination to break out of our isolation. That's why there are so many people here. What a lark to be part of Emil's circle! It makes us feel interesting. And courageous,' and so saying, he seemed to shudder.

It was an almost imperceptible movement that she might have imagined if not for the fact that he then shook himself, visibly, from reverie. He looked at her, his lips parting as if he were about to say something but then, with noticeable resolution, shut his mouth.

122

And now, in place of the sadness she thought she had detected, was only a perfectly blank, smiling politeness. 'I am so pleased to have met you, Evelyn. But much as I would like to keep you here with me, I know I mustn't be so selfish.' He shifted backwards, giving a little bow, sweeping his arm, Walter-Raleigh-like. And so, although she might rather have stayed with this puzzling man, leave she did.

She could feel the touch of his gaze on her bare shoulders as she walked away. She tried not to look back. Tried to forget that he was even there. And she might have managed if the things he had said about this crowd hadn't changed the way she viewed it.

There was a kind of braying quality to her guests' laughter as if they really were a pack (even if not of jackals). Which they were – a pack of English gentlefolk with shared histories. They were bound to find the same things funny. Yet, with Charles's words resounding, she began to see hands raised to lips after her husband had passed by, and she seemed to overhear comments that were not intended for her ears. A wave of snickering and a sniggering that combined with exclamatory shards she also overheard – 'Isn't he a card?' or 'What an extravagant fellow' – and that she might previously have mistaken for compliments now took on an entirely different complexion. As Charles had noted, Yuri was Emil's equal in loudness or joviality but she didn't hear anybody speaking about him as if he were some kind of jester or worse, a performing animal, whose champagne they would drink and whose food eat, even as they had their fun with him.

An image – her formerly smiling self moving amongst her guests – returned to her mind's eye. How proud she had been of her own appearance, which now, seeing herself through the lens of their disapproval, thoroughly embarrassed her. Her guests were all respectably dressed but they were also all quite drab. Marjorie's faded, dated frock fitted this company better than her own peacock display of sparkling jewels and expensive dress.

What an idiot she had been. Like a child flaunting her good fortune. And now it was as if she had been stripped naked and left to stand amongst strangers.

How naïve to assume that, in marrying Emil, all her problems were at an end. They had just become more complicated. Her mother must have had an inkling of this. She had tried to tell Evelyn that you don't marry a man in isolation: that you also marry everything that comes along with him. Which, in Emil's case, means the way he flaunted his riches. The same extravagant behaviour that had first attracted her to him, his very 'Emilness,' now included her. She was his trophy just as he had been hers. They were joined together to show each other off and, knowing this, all she could feel was shame and a longing for a general exodus that would leave her free to go upstairs to bed.

By the time she got up to her bedroom Evelyn had undergone another mercurial change of mood. By this time she had also stood at the front door, the object of many extravagant parting compliments. 'A marvellously interesting mix of people,' they'd said as they sauntered out, or 'You really must come over to us next time,' or 'I must say, you lot certainly know how to throw a party.'

Charles was wrong. The party had been a complete success. She had read too much into everything. She was out of sorts – that's all – from moving countries. It was only to be expected.

It was late and it was dark. She pressed her face against the hard cold of the window pane.

Despite her new optimism, she couldn't help thinking that, if this had been Ceylon, the garden would have been bathed in moonlight and lit by stars. A smudge of diffuse yellow light rose up from the garden's furthest end telling her that Emil must be in the greenhouse he kept heated, night and day, so as to keep safe the orchids that came, in the list of his many enthusiasms, second only to her.

He was such a wonderful husband, and such a generous man. She was ashamed of her doubts.

Going to the dressing table, she thought about some of the many ways Emil displayed his devotion. Take this table with its matching circular stool. It would not have occurred to most men that their wives might need a dressing table. The fact that it was here when she first arrived was a mark of Emil's unusual thoughtfulness. He had even found the perfect spot to catch the morning light, adding lamps for the night or for when (a more frequent occurrence than she could bear to acknowledge) the day was dark. And as well there had been tissues, cold cream, and a brand new bristle hairbrush (all of them the 'best', or so he said) in case she had forgotten, or used up, hers.

Holding back her blonde hair with a wide cotton band she slathered on cold cream, working it methodically into her skin. She could hear the faint clattering of clearing up. By the morning all evidence of the party would have been expunged. She hoped the noise would not disturb Milton who was safely tucked up in bed and she also hoped that, at least for Emil's sake, Milton would not get up.

She looked to her reflection. Covered in a slick white layer of cream she looked old. Like her mother, albeit a bigger-boned, blonder version of her mother. She wiped away the cream and as she did, her youth returned. One more tissue and she had removed the last vestiges of her bright red lipstick.

'Tired, darling?'

She nodded gratefully. 'A little.' Thinking that Emil had, as ever, hit the nail on the head. She was just tired.

He came up behind her. She could see him in the mirror leaning down. She felt his lips graze her neck. She could smell his familiar sweetness and underneath, the faint aroma of the loam in which his orchids grew, a smell that got stronger as his fingers fluttered at the base of her neck. He undid the catch of the string of sapphires and laid it on the table. 'Quite a triumph, I think,' and yes, she thought, it had been a triumph.

'But now.' He yawned. 'I'm also very tired.'

He was about to turn away. 'Emil?'

'Yes, darling?'

'Who was that man? One of your partners? Charles, I think he said his name was.'

'Ah, so you met Charles. Lord Charles, to us commoners. Or at least lord-in-waiting if such a category exists. Did you take to him?'

'We only exchanged a few words.'

'That's odd. Charles is usually the most loquacious of men. That's one of the reasons I took him into the business. He has that perfectly polite way of saying nothing that is the mark of the true ruler of the empire.'

'He didn't strike me as a rubber expert.'

'Well that's because,' Emil laughed, 'he's anything but. I hired him for his connections. His family might be over-extended, practically on its uppers, but the name still opens doors. And that matters here.'

'I see.'

In the mirror, Emil's eyes met hers. 'You didn't take to him, did you?' he said which, she thought, wasn't strictly true.

Mistaking her silence for assent, Emil said, 'Can't say I blame you. Charles can be a cold fish. The mouth may move but not the eyes. Don't worry, darling, I had to invite him – he

127

insisted on meeting you – but there's no need to have him round again.'

She said, carefully and with as much studied indifference as she could summon, 'That might be for the best,' as he began to ready himself for bed.

The door inched open, light from the landing shafting in soon to frame that small tousled figure of their son. His curly black hair was all fluffed out from the pressure of his head against his pillow and his long black eyelashes were still weighed down by sleep. He didn't say anything and neither did he venture any further into the room. He stood thumb in mouth and precious blanket trailing down.

Her heart went out to him. That he was having trouble adjusting was only natural. He had lost everything that was familiar – his warm garden and his cosy bedroom, the chattering of the monkeys that he loved to look at, and the young son of their cook with whom he used to play, his ayah who always slept at the foot of his bed, and Minrada who had been like a grandmother to him. And as well, in the time Emil had been away, Milton had been able to claim all of her attention; he might also be feeling he had somehow lost his mother. She pulled back the covers.

Emil stopped her. 'Let me,' and even though she didn't want to, she let him.

Milton did not move. He didn't even blink as his father pulled on a dressing gown to cover his night-time sarong.

And she as well, she forced herself to lie motionless, hoping against hope that Emil would not show too much of his frustration to his son since the more impatience he displayed, the more fear Milton expressed, so setting off a circle of misunderstanding that usually was ended by Emil's throwing up his hands as he loudly forsook all claim to the management of his son.

Now perhaps things might go differently. For as Emil came abreast of Milton, he did not raise his voice. He leaned down, scooping up the child, saying, 'Let's get you to back to bed, my boy.' His voice was soft, tender almost, so that, although the rigidity of Milton's splayed-out limbs made visible the extent of his guardedness against his father, he made no verbal protest.

She lay quite still after they had gone. Ears straining, she tried to hear how they were getting on. Emil must have closed Milton's door. She couldn't hear a thing. Not for an age and then beyond. She knew she should not give in to impulse and go and check on them but it was an effort not to do so. Images she couldn't for the life of her understand – Emil smothering Milton with a pillow, or Milton scratching and biting his father – kept coming to her. She told herself that this, as that mocking crowd had also been, was just the product of her imagination, but despite this was on the point of getting up to make sure (she'd tell Emil that she had come to rescue him) when Emil came back. He was smiling.

'I think the little fellow is at last beginning to trust me.'

She matched his smile with one of hers. As he took off his dressing gown, she lifted the bedclothes, inviting him inside.

He was cold. She pulled him closer so that he might warm himself on her. She could feel the smooth, soft silk of the chest she had always loved and she could feel his interest quicken.

He tucked one arm around her. Eagerly she responded. In that moment that terrible sense of isolation, of her foreignness, that seemed to have enveloped her since she'd first stepped foot on land, dissolved, its absence filling her with a longing that she had thought had gone and which, in going, had brought its own stern necessity – her version of Milton's stiffened limbs – to keep her distance. Now she no longer felt this way. He was her husband and, just as she had never doubted his love for her, now she felt how much she also loved him.

Had Evelyn's mother been alive, would she have recognised her younger daughter in this well-dressed, calm, staid woman who was waiting so patiently in a queue? Perhaps. Of all the people who had known the young Evelyn, only Edie calmly used to insist that, just you wait and see, her rebellious daughter would one day settle down. And yet even Edie might have been surprised to see how very neat and how very constrained Evelyn had become. She was as beautiful as ever but it was as if, just as the quality of daylight had dimmed when her ship had steamed across the oceans and into the north, some of her inner light had also leached away.

There she quietly stood. She had thought of telling Emil she wasn't feeling very well in response to which, she knew, he would immediately have summoned up water and a chair, then to have her sit and wait until he had brought the car round to the front entrance. And after that, he would have practically carried her out, in the car to cover her with the softest of rugs (if he didn't already have one he would buy it) and take her home and put her to bed and cosset her until he was sure that she was properly well. But the thought of all that upheaval was just too exhausting. She would, she decided, say nothing when Emil and Milton came back. Until that moment she would keep their place in the pedescope queue.

It was Emil who had insisted that Milton should be fitted. Only the best for his son, and for his wife, was his watchword which meant, in this case, only the most scientific method. So Milton must put his feet in the pedescope box and then all three of them must look at how his bones were shaping; for the second time in as many weeks, as Evelyn had already brought to her husband's attention. But, once he had made up his mind, there could be no gainsaying Emil. 'Look how rapidly the boy expands,' he'd said. 'You must know, darling, how absolutely vital it is at his age never to pinch the toes,' this sentence delivered with one of his most engaging smiles, which, as ever, had melted her resistance.

He was one floor up in the department store where she knew he could be found lifting Milton up to the counter so the boy could point his chubby finger at whatever caught his fancy, secure in the knowledge that whatever it was would be added to Emil's account and soon afterwards, delivered to the house. Father and son shared a love of shopping. On their return, they'd be equally wide eyed as they described the absolutely latest dinky toys, or the wind-up cars, or the jigsaw sets or anything else that had happened to catch the eye, all of which Milton already possessed and in abundance for Emil was as generous to his son as he was to her.

Until they did come back, however, she must keep their place in the queue.

The nausea she thought she had swallowed down rolled through her once again.

Her swaying attracted the attention of the woman behind her. 'Are you unwell?' The woman reached out a steadying hand.

'No, not really.' Evelyn patted her damp forehead. 'But thank you.'

'Ghastly isn't it? That they keep it so hot, I mean.'

'Yes,' Evelyn agreed. 'It is intolerable,' her smile a response to the realisation that she, who had never ever thought to describe the muggy Ceylonese heat as intolerable, must finally be on her way to being fully anglicised.

'We could ask them for a chair.' The woman absent-mindedly smoothed her hand over her small daughter's ponytail.

A chair might help. But then Emil would want to know what she was doing in one. 'Thank you,' Evelyn said. 'I'll manage,' adding, 'I'm not actually ill. I'm pregnant,' which surprised her.

She hadn't meant to blurt out the news – not until she'd told Emil as she was planning imminently to do – but when the woman smiled and said, 'Congratulations. Is it your first?' and when she looked at Evelyn with renewed respect after Evelyn answered, 'My second. My husband is upstairs with our son,' she was glad she had said something.

'A husband willing to set foot in a department store. Lucky you,' and Evelyn thought, yes, she was lucky, and soon would be more so because Emil would be overjoyed by news of the pregnancy.

Shooting an irritated glance at her wristwatch, the woman now said, 'Really, this is taking for ever,' indicating with her head the general area around the pedescope where a mother was putting her five youngsters through their paces (all of them oohing and aahing at the projection of their skeletal feet on the fluorescent screen). 'You'd think we were in a museum for the advancement of the uneducated.'

'Well, I'm not sure . . .'

'Why anyone would choose to have so many children, especially in such rapid succession, is beyond me.'

Another snob, Evelyn thought, this country was littered with them. But the woman had been kind to her and so she held her tongue. Her attention was anyway distracted by the sight of Emil and Milton who, hand in hand, were making their way towards her. She gave them a quick wave and mouthed, 'we're next'. Which is all the encouragement Milton needed. He let go of his father's hand and, new red wooden fire engine outstretched, started barrelling over. She knew she shouldn't be encouraging his riotous behaviour (and Emil's) but the sight of those hard-pumping, chubby little legs, Emil not far behind calling, 'Milton!' both of them laughing uproariously at the chase, melted her heart. She opened her arms wide, welcoming Milton and he ran straight – boomf – into them as a puffing and laughing Emil screeched to an exaggerated halt. Such a happy little unit the two had been since the night of the party when Milton had let his father put him back to bed. And soon we'll be a foursome, she thought, thinking she would tell Emil as soon as they got home.

'Next, please,' she heard the saleslady saying. Still smiling, she turned to present herself.

But the woman who had been behind her now stepped up smartly to the front. 'It's our turn.' She pushed her daughter at the sales assistant. 'We're next.'

135

'No.' Putting Milton down, Evelyn also stepped forward. 'I was next,' and then to the woman, 'You know I was in front of you.'

The woman flicked her hard eyes. Down to Milton. Across to Emil. Back on Evelyn, before turning to the sales assistant to say, 'It's my turn.'

'But I was next.'

The shop assistant's moment to move her head. First to look at Evelyn. Then to look at Evelyn's adversary. And then, head turning, she glanced past Emil to the now crying Milton who was standing by his father's side. Having completed her circuit and looked her fill, she said, 'This way madam, if you please,' to the other woman.

Like a slap. All Evelyn's resolutions since the party – that she must contain herself – must keep her dignity – must learn to act as other Englishwomen did – deserted her. In their place came fury which she would . . . she knew she would have expressed if not for the fact that she felt Emil's breath hot in her ear, and heard his whispered, 'Don't.'

She was too angry; she made to step forward.

His hand restraining her. 'You won't win.'

'Please, Emil.'

'She's an ignorant person,' Emil was speaking loudly, as if this was a theoretical point. As if the woman wasn't there or couldn't hear. 'Don't give her the satisfaction of an argument.'

'Please . . .'

His voice dropping. 'It's not like you to make a fuss.'

She looked at him, wondering furiously why he was saying this. He was after all the man who, when he wanted to, would make as much a fuss as he felt like making. Just this once, however, when her old self (the one he had loved and married) reasserted itself, he wouldn't even stand up for her. Bile rising in her throat, and riding behind it, nausea. 'Please, Emil.'

'We can come back another day,' he was saying. 'Or we can take our custom elsewhere. The boy's cupboard is anyway bursting with shoes.'

'Please Emil, could you find me somewhere to sit. I don't feel very well.'

Emil was all solicitude and action. He found a chair, curbed Milton's crying by telling him roughly to 'buck up, boy', before swooping down, picking up his son and carrying him away to fetch the car.

'Sit,' he'd told her, and she had sat holding on to the smeared glass of tepid water that he had commandeered for her.

She could see her white hand holding the glass and she could see the skirt of her frock and her shoes and the pattern on the carpet and apart from that – nothing else. She wished she could likewise cut out her thoughts. But no matter how hard she tried, all those other, previously swallowed slights kept rising to the surface. The downcast looks, for example, whenever she and Emil walked together into an unfamiliar room. The insinuating little coughs that accompanied this avoidance of gaze. The manner in which people would smile when she was alone, and frown when she was with Milton. That man the other day who, instead of holding open the door as he had just done for another woman, swung it shut.

Even at her own party. The things she had told herself their guests could not have been saying – well, now she was more habituated to the place, she knew better than to doubt what she had heard. And these from Emil's partners and his supposed friends. No wonder strangers went one further.

And what did Emil do when faced with this? He kept on smiling, that's what he did, and he carried on. He told her 'Don't', as, adamantly resisting change, he continued to act his same nonconforming self. He was so consistent in his inconsistency, she sometimes felt like ramming the beatific self-control that sat so uneasily with his flamboyant behaviour, down his throat.

'Feeling better, love?' A woman leaning in.

So caught up had she been in her thoughts, Evelyn had almost forgotten where she was. She said, quickly, 'Yes, thank you. I am much better,' seeing the woman's honest look of concern. 'And thank you very much for this.'

How strange the uneven movement of time. She had thought she had been sitting for an age but the sight of Emil and Milton's still retreating backs told her that it hadn't been very long. Now as she watched them go, her husband and her beloved son, she became aware that she wasn't the only one watching. They were like two moving points of magnetism, first repelling – the space in front of them, despite the fact of the shop being crowded, mysteriously cleared – and then attracting, heads turning after they had gone. And she, as well she knew, she was a magnet in her own right, the end point of this choreography of turning heads and also of words. Whispered murmurings to accompany those darting movements.

138

She couldn't hear what they were saying but she knew the import of their words. They were asking what she thought she was doing with those two and how she dared to show her face in public. And even worse, they were talking about the things she and Emil did in the privacy of their bedroom.

It was this knowledge that drove her from her seat.

She began to walk and as she walked she could almost touch the contempt of the other customers who kept pace with her. Faces in and out of focus. Fleshy lips snarling. Yellow teeth bared. High foreheads, distorting faces. And that chattering of voices so that what she wanted to do was to close her ears and shout to drown them out. Instead, all the energy she had must be used to drive herself onwards. To protect herself and her unborn child from this monstrous invasion, trying not to say the thing that kept going round her head.

She must not think it. Must not say it. Certainly must never say it out loud, *Please God*. And no, she must not even say it to herself. *Please God for the child's sake* . . . (Not for her sake. Never . . . She would never love anyone as much as she loved Milton) . . . but still, the same refrain: *Please God (for the child's sake) let this one not turn out too black.*

'On your own, are you?' the doctor asked as he ushered Evelyn out of the consulting room.

'That's right. My husband is tied up at work.'

'Well, do send him my regards.' The doctor shook Evelyn's hand. 'Good as ever to see you, Mrs Reymundo.'

As she went to make her next appointment, Evelyn couldn't help wondering whether this doctor, the most expensive Emil could find to oversee her pregnancy, had asked after her husband as a politeness or as a way of pointing up his modish views on the man's involvement in maternity care or just to emphasise his general liberality. Might he, she wondered, have heard about that awful moment on her first appointment when her entrance with Emil had heralded the abrupt cutting off of the genteel hum of waiting-room conversation?

Not that Emil had noticed. In his view it was all in her imagination.

She didn't know whether he was right or just blindly intent on ignoring the malign stares that usually greeted their togetherness. But as the receptionist now said, 'Same time in two weeks?' she was smiling as warmly at Evelyn as she smiled at all the other women.

Except, Evelyn went to get her coat, if she was imagining things, why had Emil conceded to her request that she keep the appointments on her own? She took the coat down from the rack, nodding at another woman who, having just arrived, was hanging hers.

'It's jolly brisk out there,' the woman said.

Evelyn nodded again, and turned away and as she did, it occurred to her that Emil, who didn't seem to be able to distinguish a casually passing pleasantry from a planned introduction, would have tried to engage the woman in further conversation. It was so much simpler, she thought, wrapping herself in the fur folds of the coat, when he wasn't around.

She was in her eighth month of pregnancy and the coat no longer did up. Emil had wanted to buy her another, just for these last few months, but, his unstinting generosity feeling sometimes burdensome, she had dissuaded him. Chilly or not, she had told him, it is still autumn.

She opened the door. As she stepped out, her baby gave such a sudden, and such a sharp, kick that she couldn't stop herself from gasping. Another reason to be thankful for Emil's absence. He would have made a fuss and tried to hurry her back to see the doctor. Standing, and waiting for the spasm to abate, she rubbed her distended belly.

This pregnancy had been different from her first. Then, cocooned by Mimrada's care and Emil's love, she had floated through the first stages, until, at her mother's sudden death, grief took the place of contentment so that she hardly remembered anything of her last few months' confinement. But still, that pregnancy had stuck in her memory as a golden time. Not like this one.

The doctor had told her it was normal; after all, she already had a child for whom she had to care. But she didn't think Milton was the problem. How could he be? She loved him so, her adorable little cherub, who only had to look at her to make her smile.

She took the lift down to the ground floor. Despite the clarity of a light, bright blue sky and a sun that was, for once, visibly present, a chill wind cut right through her. She considered hailing a taxicab – Emil had only consented not to wait because she had promised him that she would get a cab – but then she remembered that the doctor had said that a little exercise might lift her spirits. She began to walk down the pavement. Hampered by her own great bulk, she moved, at first, quite slowly until, realising that the doctor was right, and her mood was lifting, she picked up her pace. Despite the chill it was a glorious September's day, the air, for once, bright and clear, the leaves, already turning brown, shining in the sun.

'Evelyn?'

She thought to keep on walking.

'Evelyn Williams?'

Whoever was calling was someone from her past. She stopped to find a man and a woman who, having just emerged from a shop, were looking in her direction.

'Tommy?' Something, and it wasn't the baby, seemed to give a little skip. 'Is that you?' Not a question she needed to ask because, although his skin was whiter and his face much older and more tired, it could only be Tommy, a certainty that was doubly confirmed by his, 'I'm sorry, I forgot. I should have called you Evelyn Reymundo,' as, with familiar, eager boyishness, he made his way over.

Despite having visibly matured, Tommy still seemed driven by similar impulses as he reached out for her hands and joyfully clasped them. 'How wonderful to see you.' There was not even a hint of the awkwardness that had attended their parting. But then Tommy never had been one to bear a grudge. And besides, 'Barbara,' he said, summoning his companion over, 'come and meet Evelyn Reymundo. Evelyn, this is Barbara Cornish. My fiancée.'

'You're engaged! Congratulations.'

'And to you as well . . .' He took a step back, his admiring gaze acknowledging the advanced stage of her pregnancy. 'It's your second, is it not?'

Just like Tommy, she thought, to have kept abreast of her news.

'How wonderful,' but as he said this, his smile faded. 'I was sorry when I heard about your mother's untimely demise.'

She looked down.

'She was such a lovely lady.'

'Yes.' Her voice cracked. 'She was.'

Silence. They had been so pleased to see each other, each assuming that the familiarity of their shared past could be carried through into the present. Now, however, there arose between them that discomfort that people who once thought they knew each other can feel when it dawns on them that they have always been strangers.

'Well . . .' Tommy said in accompaniment to his fiancée's, 'It's cold. We should let you get on,' and yes, Evelyn agreed, it was bitterly cold and she really should be going.

*

Before she had time even to think of getting out her key Emil, who must have been listening out for her, pulled the front door open.

'You've been a long time. Is everything as it should be?'

She put her bags down on the table. 'I did a little shopping while I was in town.'

'I could have organised a delivery.'

'Oh I didn't mind. And yes, the doctor says that everything is perfect.'

He beamed and leaned closer, meaning to kiss her, but when she said, 'Do you mind, darling, if I first take off my coat?' he quickly helped her out of it.

'I've had a fire laid in the lounge.'

'How lovely. I'll fetch Milton from his room and then we'll join you there.'

He was standing under the lit chandelier, light glinting against his dark, black hair, and still holding on to her coat. When he said, 'Yes, good idea,' she thought she saw his face darken. But no. She must have been mistaken. He was smiling as he moved to put her coat away.

Lying in the darkened bedroom, Evelyn shut her eyes. She heard her husband softly walking over. The bed shifted as he sat down on it. She kept her eyes tight shut even though he knew, as he always did, that she was still awake. A fluttering in the air before he began to stroke her forehead. 'Tired, darling?'

'A little.' Why – she didn't understand it – why was she having to resist an impulse to move out of his grasp?

'Anything I can get you?'

She shook her head. 'No. Thank you,' thinking that his touch was actually quite comforting. He always had been able to intuit her physical needs. As he began to circle his fingertips, massaging her forehead more heavily, but not too heavily, she felt the headache of which she'd only been half aware begin to lift. And she felt herself relax.

He felt it too. Another shifting of the mattress. He was moving closer. She smelt his familiar, slightly sweet scent, and she felt his lips grazing her forehead. She seemed to feel again the crisp of cotton sheets beneath her skin, and she seemed to hear something close by rustling in a warm breeze, and see his skin glistening in the half-light and to remember the passion he had coaxed from her. The touch of his lips against hers and . . .

And then she couldn't help herself. Without even being conscious that she was going to, she moved away.

Which is all that was needed to make him instantly remove himself to the other side of the bed. She could sense how his hurt radiated out.

'I'm sorry.'

'I know. It's this pregnancy. I'll let you get some rest.' He left the room.

Long after he was gone, she continued to lie there. She was dry eyed – crying was not a luxury she would permit herself – and yet she was also awash with sadness. For the loss of the ease that she and Emil used to share and, even worse, for their passion.

Perhaps Emil was right, perhaps the culprit was her pregnancy. But the guardedness she felt when she was with him wasn't purely physical. It was also an absence of enthusiasm for his conversation, and a lack of sympathy for his concerns. Gone was the sense she'd once had, that he could do no wrong, or that if he did, he would be instantly forgiven.

Once she had thrilled to the merest glimpse of Emil. No longer. Instead she had been shocked by the way her heart had lurched at the sight of Tommy. Not, she told herself, that she had even the faintest regret at having refused Tommy. She never would have made him happy. Nor he her. And yet, having seen the way that Tommy and his fiancée had stood, gazing into each other's eyes, as she had been driven off in a taxi, she had been filled not only with regret but also with anger. At Emil and his insistence on being so different from everybody else.

If Tommy could get over the humiliation of her rejection, she had thought, which clearly he had done, then it was possible for any man to change. For any Englishman like Tommy, she thought. But not, apparently, for Emil.

1957

When her father said, 'Why not climb over, my darling girl?' the seven-year-old Vanessa instantly complied. She clambered over the back of seats that smelt of leather and of lavender until she was in the place her mother had just vacated.

Her father straightened her white hat, making sure to curl the feathers forward as well as to tuck away a wisp of straight black hair, before his smile told her she was perfect, a judgement that was confirmed by his 'Now, together, we can take on the entirety of good old Blighty,' as he opened up his door.

In parallel with all those other parents and all those other, younger siblings, they stepped out, this general mobilisation punctuated by the sequential closing clunk of the doors of Rovers, Daimlers, Humbers and Armstrong Sidleys, symbols of their common, moneyed comfort. And, after that, men's polished black shoes and women's elegant, heeled pumps crunched over gravel and on to grass, there to pick out and move with their sons to the receiving line as, all the time, cars kept sweeping in, the full complement to celebrate sports day.

In contrast to convention, Vanessa's father did not immediately walk on. At the grass verge he stopped and there continued to stand with Vanessa by his side. If she was surprised that her normally decisive and determined father should hesitate, she didn't really mind. She was a dreamy child, at home with silence and delay.

Above the patched and stuccoed, wooded windows and gabled roofs of the mock Tudor school building hung a light, midsummer sky of sunlight and feathery cloud. The school was so big, she thought, if it was hers, she would always have felt lost. She was grateful she didn't go there, a silly thought (as her thoughts usually were, or so Milton would have said) since it was a school only for boys.

Her gaze wandered past the buildings and across to the smooth mown laws where families had gathered by hyacinth and hydrangea beds and the bountiful oak. There she saw her mother and her brother. They were standing apart from all the rest beneath a tree whose darkened leaves spread shadows across their faces. Something about the sight sent a shiver down her spine. But at her father's 'Into the breach', she began to walk.

With her buttoned-up, tight-waisted, fast-flared, petticoated white dress accessorised by a white band hat, white socks, white pump shoes and – that killer stroke – short, white gloves, Vanessa was a perfect little parody of rectitude. All early fifties perfection, in fact, although this was 1957 and she was hardly on her way to church.

And what of that man, her father whose short legs propelled him forward at a pace that almost set her to running? Well he had (in this as in almost everything) chosen a different route to respectability. He had on one of his bespoke double-breasted suits that Vanessa knew her mother considered altogether too city (and not grey flannelled enough) for sports day.

Vanessa was conscious of her parents' different social stratagems and of the tension these differences could cause. That morning she had heard her mother asking her father whether he would not 'at least try and blend in'. She hadn't needed to hear his reply to know what it would be. He would not change. Not even for her mother. He was proud of his wardrobe and of himself. He was proud of being noticed, although, as he would always quickly say, everything in moderation. And so he had chosen this thin, dark stripe especially because, although it wasn't grey, it wasn't quite black either. 'Just a hint of black,' he would say as his tailor smoothed the jacket across his shoulders, 'made dark, but not dark enough to put them off their stride.'

She glanced across at him. How handsome he looked. She saw that he was smiling. Which made her also smile. She loved having the day off school and she loved being with her father. She felt safe with him. And so with him beside her, she skipped, skippetty skipped over to her brother.

She had been hoping for at least a twinkle of recognition from Milton, the minimum she would have got at home. But Milton had on his earnest face. He held out a hand – 'hello there' – which she knew she must touch and let go so that he could then proffer it to his father, an action he accompanied with a clipped, 'How are you, sir?'

She saw how her father's deep-set dark eyes narrowed. She knew that he, like her, would have preferred to hug his son as he would have done at home. But Milton was ten and this was his terrain and even her father had learned, at Milton's school, to keep his preferences to himself. So all he did was reach out and slap her brother on the back, saying heartily, 'How goes it, my boy?' a progression that made Milton flinch not, she thought, because either the phrase or the back-slapping were improper or out of place but because they were executed with too much verve and in a voice that was far too loud.

Her mother said, 'Emil.'

In her father's answering smile Vanessa could read those tiny inconsistencies she knew so well, embarrassment at being caught, defiance at what he had done, and both of these undercut by the way he always looked at her mother, so full of love and pride.

Vanessa shifted her gaze downwards to the ground and the spiky blades of grass, her attention caught by the sight of a lone ant that was trying to negotiate a twig. Such an unequal struggle. Its antennae flittering, its leg barrelling, it tried and failed, once, twice and three times, to overcome the obstacle. She considered bending down to help it over, and was about to, when, too late, her mother's tan high heels moved to cover up both ant and stick.

In hope of the foot's removal and the reappearance of the ant, Vanessa continued to look down. But when her mother did not move her foot, Vanessa let her gaze inch up. She took in the sight of her mother's seamed stockings (perfectly in line) and then the crisp, stiff flare of her mother's striped navy and cream dress, and up again, beyond her mother's cinched waist, past three buttons and to a rounded collar, a slow tilt that was perhaps an attempt to read her mother's expression but as her eyes drew level with her mother's face the sun came out. All she could now see was the outline of her mother's head and her blonde hair framed by a startling brightness that bleached out all her features.

Her father bent down. He untied and then retied one shoelace. He was down so long Vanessa thought he might even be looking for her ant until he raised his head suddenly and, having winked at her, straightened up. For a while there they stood, her parents, locked in their mutual and un-peaceful isolation.

In the silence that descended, Vanessa imagined herself up in the high branches of the tree under which she stood. As if in training to be a cartographer. Or a bird. From this great imagined height, she seemed to have access to a shifting point of view. She could look all the way down to her earthly body, a tiny white encased pinprick in layers of green, seeing those other, jovial family groups, busy with their eager beaver greetings and their hearty handshake blurs as they met and parted, a fluid and cheery composition of politeness and normality. She could almost trace the pattern of their engagements – over there a small child darting off only to be lassoed back in, or two women conversing in low tones, their heads so close their hats merged, or a knot of boys lazily kicking at a clod of earth. Greetings, *'My, my, haven't you grown!'* and *'I know, who would have thought it?'* and *'Yes, of course, we really should'* kept drifting over. She let them pass. She wasn't interested in them. Where her imagination took her was to look directly down to where the four, frozen members of her family – the family Reymundo – stood, solitary in an ocean of affability.

They were different from the rest and visibly so.

Because he was Sinhalese, her father's skin was a light honeyed brown, and this, together with his slim build, wiry frame, black hair and jet dark eyes and, more than this, the way he held himself (like a peacock, she had heard people say) proclaimed his foreignness. And there next to him stood her taller, blonder, larger, whiter, English mother.

The mixing of their blood had worked its way through their children in unpredictable ways. Vanessa was white like her mother but with her father's slim, small build and his sleek, straight black hair and on top of that a butter-wouldn't-melt-in-her-Eurasian-perfectly-neat-and-unadorned bow mouth.

In Milton's case the coming together of their parents' genes had forged a different composite. He was much darker even than their father, but with their mother's big-boned build and her looks, his face a large circle to his sister's petite oval, his cheeks broader and much wider while his hair was a black, fuller, wilder, curlier version of his mother's permanent wave.

That's why, Vanessa knew, her family always stood on their own on school occasions. Because they were a patch-work four in a part of England that was otherwise almost entirely white.

The receiving line having done its work, all the other visitors had been siphoned off to the playing fields, leaving only the headmasterly couple to bid the laggards welcome. When her father said 'Shall we?' Vanessa rustled down her imagination from the tree and back to earth as her mother set off like all

154

those other ordinary and dutiful wives, at her husband's side, her two children trotting obediently behind.

Vanessa would have liked to talk to Milton. She would have liked to ask him whether he got the special chocolate parcel she had sent. Or tell him about the secret place she had built in the orchid house. Or she could even have found out from him (boring question) how his term had been. But Milton had closed off his expression; it was his way of ordering her to hold her tongue. So she walked, silently, beside him and behind their parents until they reached the spot where the headmaster and his wife were waiting.

Vanessa's part was now to stand quietly by her mother's side as her mother smoothed down Vanessa's hair and the headmaster shook her father's hand, this gesture accompanied by a hearty, 'Mr and Mrs Reymundo. It is, as ever, wonderful to see you here,' and afterwards beamed and nodded as punctuation to his wife's repetition of the word, 'Wonderful.'

'Always a delight to visit the playing fields of Eden,' her father said.

The downward pressure of her mother's hand on Vanessa's head grew heavy, and heavier still as her father turned to the stout figure of the headmaster's wife to give an exaggerated, flourishing bow before lifting her hand up to his lips.

Vanessa loved it when her father did things like that – he was so funny – but she saw how the gesture brought out Milton's scowl. But Milton must be mistaken because the headmaster's wife laughed – as did her husband – both of them quite loudly. So loudly in fact and for such a long time that Vanessa began to think that something odd might be going on although in her position, almost bent double in an effort to release her knees and thus escape her mother's crushing inattention, everything would seem odd.

'Well . . .' the headmaster said as his wife dropped her hand to its habitual place by her brown spotted dress.

'Well,' the headmaster said again.

'Well.' This from her father.

The headmaster's wife's hands seemed to be copying her mother's, smoothing down her skirt while the headmaster pointed to the playing fields. 'Ad astra.'

'Ad absurdum,' her father replied, softly enough so that (hopefully, hopefully) only his family heard.

Vanessa didn't know what either of these phrases meant but the tightening of her mother's lips told her that it would be wise to keep any questions to herself.

There were straight backed chairs for the adults and tartan blankets for the young. Vanessa sat, cross legged, on a blanket on the grass, leaning against her father's legs. They were three again, Milton having gone to join the other non-competitors of his year, all of them bunched together in their tallying and re-tallying of the scores.

The competition so far had been vigorous and it had been wild. Boys had blasted themselves over hurdles. They had strained neck muscles to hurl javelins. They had launched themselves feet first into the long jump, or sideways over seemingly impossible heights – and all of this for the glory of house points.

A few races in, Milton's house was in the lead. It then was overtaken by another but soon afterwards had inched itself back into contention, the two streaking ahead of all the rest without managing to shake off their rival, so that by the time the last race, the four times 100 yards relay was announced, they were neck and neck. 'The decider,' the headmaster said, as if it needed saying.

Vanessa looked to where Milton stood out so strongly in that sea of white faces. She, who knew him so well, could read his eager excitement and his anxiety. She could see how much the race mattered to him. She felt herself tensing.

On the track, boys in long grey shorts and white sports shirts, one from each house, strained forward. They were like graceful animals, quivering as they waited out the starting signal. And there it came. 'On your marks, get set . . .'. The crack of the pistol followed by a collectively shouted, 'go' and the boys leapt forward. Necks straining, legs working piston strikes, they pounded out the first 100 yards where batons were passed from hand to surging hand, and on to the next 100. Her brother's fervour having transmitted itself to her, Vanessa moved with the rest of the craning crowd. A normally reserved child, she was caught up in the moment, her excitement rising in her throat. A hundred more yards and the two competing houses were neck and literal neck, her father's enthusiasm having catapulted him to his feet and she to hers as well because everywhere she looked other spectators were rising. The crowd was now so keyed up that it felt as if what was unfolding was less a school race and more like something much bigger, the Melbourne Olympics perhaps, she thought, but even better, for in place of those grainy black and white television pictures there were full frame, fully realised, flesh and blood, determined runners, running as if life itself was at stake as, to egg them on, their house comrades drummed their sand-shoes against the grass, their voices rising and their parents joining in, the whole crowd on its feet, even her mother, the runners and their houses urged on to greater effort by her father's sudden, 'Come on you buggers!' that rent the air as the last baton was passed on, two boys neck and neck and one from Milton's house, Milton's voice now dominant shouting, 'Come on Castleton . . .' and where Milton led so did others follow, his cry taken up by the crowd. 'Come on Castleton,' and even Vanessa, usually so quiet, caught up in the excitement, her reedy, 'Come on Castleton' joining with the others.

Which, it seemed, is what Castleton had been awaiting. He kicked so hard against the ground and against his opponents' efforts that it was as if a draught blew his opponents way off course. The crowd strained to watch the beauty of the forward thrust of those long legs, this sight of a boy completely free, running so fast that when finally he crossed the finishing line and collapsed, all the other runners seemed very far behind.

Victory! Peaked flannel caps flying high as boys rushed at their sprawled and panting hero. A score of eager hands, Milton's amongst them, lifting and bearing Castleton back along the course, parents congratulating or consoling each other, as Vanessa stood and watched her brother, foremost amongst the bearers, her heart swelling with this visible proof that, in this place at least, he really did belong.

Behind her she could hear her father's softening, 'Come on Castleton,' a refrain that seemed to die out long after all the others.

Tea and lemonade and scones and iced biscuits were served, family groups merging. Only Vanessa's family sat in each other's company. The chink of cups against saucers and the murmuring of pleasantries drifted over as her father smiled and sipped his tea and her mother looked brightly around before turning to Vanessa's father to say in a very soft voice, 'You're not going to, are you?' to which her father answered absently, 'Going to what?' – this answer telling them that, yes, he was going to. In response to which, Milton got up with Vanessa following suit.

Vanessa had thought they might even go out, down the drive and through the tall gates (and where would they go then?) but Milton led her in the direction of the school. He pushed open the heavy oak doors, announcing, 'This is the entrance hall,' as if she might otherwise not have guessed.

Given the scale of their Bishop's Avenue house, Vanessa was not easily impressed by size. But the age of this school building and the decay evident in the grand, if crumbling, entrance hall with its high beamed rafters and fading Victorian portraits lining the dingy beige walls, made her jaw drop. Which was what Milton had been hoping for. There was a new swagger to his walk as he led her inside. Only to stop in front of a wooden plaque on which a list of names was painted.

She knew him well enough to know by the way he was looking in her direction that it was now her task to read out the names and so, 'Ploughman, Roger,' she dutifully began, 'Stableworth, Hugo, White, Sebastian, Johnston, John,' repeating this with a giggle, 'Johnston, John,' Milton's disapproving glowering leaving her in no doubt that this was a serious business and not to be taken lightly, she hastily pulled herself together to continue, 'Castleton . . .' She couldn't help herself. 'Castleton?' she said. 'The one from the race?'

'No, of course not, silly. This one here is Castleton Major, not Minor.'

She nodded gravely as if she understood.

'There are three of them. Each as talented as the one before. Perhaps even more talented. Rumour is that Castleton the Third will be an even better all-rounder than Minor. They will all naturally expect to make head boy. Three Castletons on the plaque,' Milton said in a musing, and vaguely amused, kind of voice, before he looked at her, his nod indicating that it was her turn to contribute to the conversation.

Scrabbling through memory, she pulled out one of the phrases she'd heard strangers use on hearing of her mother's childhood in Ceylon. 'How fascinating,' she said, and seeing this met by a nod, she risked a supplementary, 'How enchanting.'

'Yes, isn't it?' Milton walked on.

But soon they must both stop again, this time in front of a thick, smooth oil painting of a smiling and uniformed man.

'That's Fergus, the headmaster's only son.' Milton dipped his head respectfully and, only after he was satisfied by her hasty replication of his gesture, continued, 'Fergus was a war hero, don't you know. Shot down in '40 during the Battle of Britain.' She tried to imitate his grave expression that must befit a tribute to a hero. 'That's why they converted the house into a school,' he said. 'No one to carry on the line,' and, although this seemed to her insufficient explanation as to why anybody would turn their home into an institution, she nodded so as to mirror his nod and, as he set off, trailed after him.

As he led deeper into the bowels of the school she registered how what had previously been straight backed and deliberate was now a semi-slumped and aimless drifting along an endless and dingy sludge-green corridor, feet rubbing parquet, past painted and closed doors all of which Milton ignored, save to mutter the occasional 'out of bounds', until they came adjacent to a room whose bounds, apparently, were not so tight.

'The rec room.' With a dramatic flourish, Milton flung open the door.

She took one big, bold step in, before some sixth sense brought her to a halt.

What she could see: a large, scruffy space, in which were three battered, greasy and threadbare benches, a ping-pong table by the window and, in pride of place, dominating the room, a huge, green baize table. But what prevented her from proceeding further was the sight of two boys much taller than Milton by the billiard table. She didn't like the way they were looking at her or the lazy drawl one looped through his voice to say, 'Ah, the king himself.'

She shot Milton an uneasy glance.

'And the princess sprog, I assume.'

Milton kept his eyes fixed on the billiard table.

Following the direction of his gaze she was in time to see the boy who had spoken leaning over the table and stretching back his cue arm. 'Shut the door, on your way out, there's a good man.' He thrust his arm forward, cue tapping a ball that bounded and ricocheted against three sides of the table before coming to a full stop.

His partner grinned. 'Bad luck,' he said and began to stalk the table.

Milton pulled her into the corridor and quickly shut the door.

*

Her brother's mood had darkened. She knew she should hold her tongue, but she couldn't help asking. 'What's a sprog?'

'A baby. A greenhorn. An idiot, you idiot.'

'And why did he call you the king?'

'The name.' His scowl deepened.

'The name? You mean Milton?'

'No, you stupid girl. *Our* name. Reymundo.'

She had no idea what he was talking about but knew she must not press him. He was anyway already on the move, down the corridor, shoulders set in an anger which her childish stupidity must have provoked. For a moment she wished herself outside and away from the complications of a relationship that seemed to have grown more sticky as the years of their separation increased. But then they had both come in because neither of them wanted to be out. And so she trailed after her brother wondering how far this set of corridors could conceivably stretch and how long they could possibly keep on doing this. She was on the point of asking, despite the trouble this might cause, when Milton flung open another door. This time he didn't hesitate but boldly led her into a cavernous dormitory.

Slim iron bedsteads, about twenty of them, lined the walls while, running in a line down the middle of the room, a series of dark and stout chests of drawers was planted back to back. Metallic lockers stood like soldiers beside each cot.

'Cosy, don't you think?' Milton's softened voice suggested that if she played her cards right, she might be forgiven. And so she did enthusiastically agree that it was cosy even though

163

she thought it looked more like the painting of a war hospital her teacher had recently showed her, than a bedroom.

'And look.' Milton drew back one of the dark green curtains that ran along a jointed and rectangular set of metal railings. 'Isn't that ingenious? Once they're closed, you hardly notice the bod next door.'

'Yes.' Although in truth if it had been she forced to sleep so close to someone else, she certainly would have noticed. 'It's so grown up,' she added, a winning line, for Milton relaxed sufficiently to point out his bed. 'But don't you dare sit,' he warned. 'It takes for ever to get it this neat,' the perfect flatness of the rough brown blanket, the symmetrical folding of the eiderdown by the foot and the creased overlapping of a greyish white sheet bearing testimony to this.

'Can I see inside your locker?'

Another success. Even though Milton sighed in exasperation at her childishness, the alacrity with which he produced the key told her that her request had been spot on. Shifting a coat hanger ('for my blazer,' he explained) he undid the padlock before stepping back to reveal the interior.

She saw two metal shelves. Almost empty. She knew her role was to admire but privately she couldn't help comparing what was here with home which contained all the latest in consumer goods – refrigerators, vacuum cleaners, Kenwood mixers and washing machines – the best that money could buy. As for Milton's Dinky toys, well, despite his insistence that he was too old for them, the scale of his collection was beyond compare. In contrast, in Milton's locker were so few items. Two biscuit tins. He opened them to show her that one contained chocolates (so he had got them) while in the other was the last slice of the fruitcake their mother baked and weekly posted. Apart from these comestibles there was a furry and almost shapeless tennis ball, a much-thumbed copy of the 1955 *Dandy* annual and there, right at the bottom and poking out, some silky material, apricot coloured, which, she thought, might be one of her mother's chiffon scarves but Milton closed up before she had a chance to check.

She looked around. There must be something else to see.

'We had better,' Milton said.

She struggled to put what she knew they must both be thinking into words, but, 'Isn't there . . . ?' was all she could come up with.

Milton knew what she was trying to say. 'No can do,' he responded, adding an explicatory, 'Everything else is out of bounds.'

Out into the sunlit afternoon they went, those two children of the 1950s, steeled, like other children, by respect, by ritual and by rationing, schooled in conformity, obedience and the unquestioning reverence for authority. Exotic in a time when exoticism was not a quality to be admired.

Slowly they walked and reluctantly. No need for words. They each knew that the other would also inwardly be praying that the moment they both feared had passed.

No such luck. Rejoining the gathering, they could see that even though the sun was lower and the conversation more muted, everything was much as it had been, groups scattered beside the playing fields as plates were gathered in. They hadn't missed a thing – or at least, they hadn't missed the thing that they had ached so to miss. And yes, it was clear that the moment they dreaded and their father professed absolutely to adore – absolutely being his favourite word, always delivered with relish in his perfectly enunciated foreign tones – was upon them. The parents' sack race was announced.

Their mother was already on her feet. Their father was seated and looking up at her. He smiled and for one grateful instant Vanessa misread the smile to mean that he would not rock the boat. But his smile turned out to be a sop to throw them all off scent. And it worked. Her mother looked away. Which is when her father leapt up and was off.

By the time her father joined the other volunteers the women had already begun to take off their shoes while the men displayed their eager readiness by rolling up their sleeves. Innocent normality, enforced harmony, born out of war and its relief. Adults acting like big children, ungainly and ill at ease in their forceful enjoyment as the clamour of their children's shrill expectation rose, the assembled company joined together in that moment of imminent hysteria, all of them save Vanessa, the red-faced Milton and their tight-lipped mother.

Their gazes were concentrated on a single point. On that lone man, Emil Reymundo, whose position, slightly distant from the others, belied his determination to be a central part of what came next.

A pile of hessian sacks was lying on the grass. Vanessa counted off the participants in twos. It wasn't easy. The excitement of the volunteers sparked movement, their movements making them merge and separate in constantly changing combinations. She knew she must be careful not to accidentally double count and when she got to fourteen – an even number – she, a stickler for accuracy, distrusted the count and set herself to making double sure. This time she tried simultaneously with her count to tick off each of the contestants as they were added to the whole. When she did that, the tally was fifteen. Fourteen, perfect. Fifteen, impossible to pair. But which of her two counts had been correct?

Tradition dictated that the pairs – one father, one mother, two per sack, no couples permitted – be decided by the headmaster. In anticipation of this, the grown-ups now divided themselves by gender. All of them including her father who was, as ever, slightly apart from the group but smiling, just like all the others, as the headmaster began to pair them up.

The headmaster's finger pointed before moving on. 'Mr Edwards' – in response to which a man detached himself from the group. Then the finger singled out a woman, 'Mrs Bridges,' the two laughing heartily, something that, in the crowd, was echoed by husband Bridges and wife Edwards before their spouses came together to shake hands. And then the chivalrous Mr Edwards fetched up their sack and held it open for Mrs Bridges as all eyes swivelled back to focus on the headmaster and his moving finger. 'Mr Harrison,' and this time a mustachioed father Harrison unpicked himself from the knot of other men, his pressed grey-flannelled legs stepping smartly out in time to greet his partner Mrs Brown, her dress the colour of her name and her laughter bashful, before they also took part in the ritual of greeting and sack selection as behind them a Mr Parsonson was chosen to partner a Mrs Wheeler and on, one by one, these disparate pairs united and, having been united, going, two by two, to fetch their sack.

'Mr Crawley,' the headmaster said and Vanessa saw, as did all the watching crowd, the relief with which Mr Crawley hurried over to greet his chosen 'Mrs Jackson' and to fetch her sack.

Only three remaining. Vanessa's father, one other man and one woman.

'And here we have,' the headmaster said, puffing it up to make it right, 'our final heroic pair.'

No laughter now as the finger made its final allocations, Mr Last-but-one-man-to-be-picked partnered with the Last-remaining-woman, relief causing them both to almost fall into each other's arms before they backed diffidently away. Stranding Vanessa's father.

It was so quiet. Everybody keeping watch.

So quiet that Vanessa thought she could hear her mother's thoughts, her mother's prayers that her father would do the decent thing and step aside, pretending that he hadn't ever intended taking part but was merely there to congratulate and egg on the others.

A moment's soft murmur, the collective make-believe that nothing of significance was taking place, against a silence that was otherwise so total, so even a skylark could be heard.

The innocence of nature mocking the complications of man.

Vanessa looked straight ahead. She could not bear to see the expression on her mother's face or on her brother's. She stood watching her father's defiant stand and here time did slow, so slow it didn't move at all, their family for once united with the others in trying to work out how this catastrophe might be resolved.

From the rest of the company came misplaced coughs and the clearing of a score of throats, handkerchiefs dabbed on faces, the temperature spontaneously increasing, and feet shuffling as if, throughout the crowd, scores of differently shaped shoes had simultaneously begun to pinch. And all the while Vanessa's father held his ground, his expression set to unperturbed although even those who didn't know him must surely have been able to sense that what lay behind this apparent detachment was a fearless determination. What previously he had told her mother was coming true – he would not be overlooked.

'Lydia.' The headmaster's bark so sharp it hinted at his bite. 'Lydia', and the headmaster's wife, his Lydia to command, squeezed her stout body from the centre of the throng. 'We need to make up numbers,' he said, either because he thought she was too stupid to understand what was required of her, or else to reinforce her resolve, this latter confirmed when Vanessa saw her wobbling double chin firm up as she barrelled herself forward, going up to Vanessa's father to say in a bracingly loud voice, 'Oh, Mr Reymundo, it looks as if it is to be you and me. What fun.'

And wasn't she so right? What better thing to do, on a summer's day in 1957, than watch the adults at play?

What fun.

What fun to watch as each couple settled clumsily into their sack. What fun to see them manoeuvre, awkwardly jumping, edging forward with disjointed steps, to the starting line. What fun to pick out her father and the headmaster's wife, her body a huge Hessian outline and his thin fibres pushing forward, his striding and her struggling, her face red and his set grim. What fun to hear the firing of the starter's pistol, and see her father and Lydia jerkily set out and almost immediately trip each other up, sprawling down on the running track. What fun to see arms flailing as they struggled, while the other couples were in motion down the track to the sound of those jovial cries *Harold. I'm warning you,*

170

unhand my wife,' or *'That's right, Charlotte, you show him who's in charge.'*

What tremendously daring, terrifically brave, spiffing, utterly combustible, heart-wrenching fun.

Night had long since closed in, bathing the car in darkness, the monotony of the journey home broken only by the occasional, passing beam that flared garishly against the leather interior before rolling across the roof and out. Stretched out on the back seat, and lulled by the dark, Vanessa was on the brink of sleep when her mother's, 'Why did you do it?' cut through her reverie.

Vanessa was instantly awake, although careful to give no sign of this, as she heard her father's, 'Why did I do what?'

'You know what, Emil. Why did you join in?'

Vanessa watched as her father turned, briefly, to glance at her mother. 'It was a game for all the parents.'

'But you knew – we discussed it – what was going to happen if you took part.'

'You think I'm the one at fault, do you?' Vanessa could see that the sinews in her father's neck were stretched tight and then she saw the shaking of her mother's head,

'No. Of course not.'

'There's no "of course" about it.' Her father sounded very angry.

Holding her breath Vanessa watched as her mother stretched out a hand, lightly, to touch her father on the shoulder.

Not seeming even to register the touch, he said, and more loudly, 'My money's the same as theirs.'

'Yes, Emil.' Her mother sighed. 'So it is.'

'Then why should I not join in?'

Because of Milton, Vanessa almost said, and perhaps she did say this out loud because her mother's head whipped round. Eyes tightly shut, Vanessa folded herself deeper into the seat.

'Not now, Emil . . . Vanessa,' came her mother's voice, sharp and full of warning, and after that – silence.

Evelyn shouldn't have said anything. Not until she was sure that the already sensitive Vanessa was safely asleep. In silence she faced forwards, looking straight ahead, out into the night.

Emil was a good driver, she could barely feel the motion of the car. She watched the yellow headlights illuminating short sections of the road before sweeping relentlessly on, white lines and hedges and twigs blaring in and out of view.

Emil was angry with her. Well, let him be. She was equally angry with him, and it wasn't new. For what seemed like an age it was the way things had stood between them, the matters of which they no longer could speak having built into a wall so high that neither was capable of breaching it. Yet she could not afford to give in to despair. Her children, and especially Milton, needed her.

Her attention was caught by a rabbit frozen in the head-lights, its panicked immobility reminding her of her son similarly frozen in the glare of his father's obstinacy. As soon as the race was over he had run off, afterwards refusing point blank to come back and say goodbye. She had tried to coax him out but he wouldn't come. Not understanding that there was nothing she could have done to change what happened, or to stop it happening again, he had been equally angry with her.

Emil steered around the rabbit, then smoothly picked up speed. As the car swept past, she turned back. In the fading red of the back lights, she could see the rabbit slipping into the undergrowth. She wished for a moment that she could follow it and likewise vanish.

'It hurts me that you take their part.'

The relaxation in Vanessa's limbs telling her that the child was now genuinely asleep, Evelyn said, 'I don't take their part. I take Milton's. Didn't you notice how upset he was?'

'Of course I noticed.'

'But you don't care?'

'That's beneath you, Evelyn.' His dark eyes flashed. 'What Milton endures is not of my doing. I can't do anything to change their behaviour, can I?' He was gripping the steering wheel so tight that the flesh around his knuckles was shiny and pale.

He hated arguments, this she knew. And she also knew that he did care about their son. 'I don't know why you can't just ignore them,' she said. 'Keep out of their way. Like you did last year.'

'Yes, so I did, but only because you were so adamant that I should. I've had a year since to think about it. What I've realised is how cowardly it was of me to play their other game – pretending that I don't exist.'

'It's just a game, Emil.'

'Yes. It is just a game – for *all* the parents – but that's not the point. It's the principle of the thing. Or do you think that principle is unimportant? Is that the lesson you want our son to learn?'

'No.' Her voice rang out so loudly it startled them both. For a moment afterwards they were quiet, looking straight ahead, the nub of their disagreement – he the idealist, and she the pragmatist, he stubbornly determined to take his own path, and she trying to smooth Milton's way – seeming to stretch out into the dark night until finally he said, very softly, 'What do you want from me, Evelyn?'

I want, she almost said, I want you to make it like it used to be. I want us to be happy. I want us to be in love again, joined together in our shared understanding. Yet how could she say that? And so instead, 'I want you to understand that by sticking to your principles you are hurting Milton. I want you to put away your pride, and think, just for a moment, Emil, about our son.'

'And if I did? If I played by their rules, do you think that would help him?'

'Well it might at least give them time to get used to us.'

'How much time do you think they need, Evelyn? How much time to deceive themselves into believing that Milton is white? How much time for him to learn to pretend that he's not black?'

'Oh Emil.' She gave an angry little laugh. 'It's not about that.'

'Isn't it?'

She held her tongue.

In the rising of silence she couldn't help looking at him. He didn't seem to feel her gaze and so she looked her fill. She saw how he was concentrated on the road and frowning slightly. She thought how handsome – no, she didn't mean handsome, she really meant beautiful – he was. How dare those snobs not see him for the generous, lively, unmalicious, loving man he was? Her man, and yet they were slipping away from each other.

'We never should have sent him to that school,' he said.

There, at last, lay the disagreement that had dug its wound into their marriage. For it was she who, after Milton's prep school headmaster had cast doubt on his ability to pass the eleven-plus, had insisted that Milton be sent to boarding-school. In this she had been uncharacteristically unyielding. She was determined that her beloved son (her wonderful Coloured son), should grow up with a proper sense of his belonging. If sending him away would aid him in this, then she'd had no compunction about forcing her husband to bend to her will.

'He shouldn't have gone there.'

'So you keep saying.' She let her sigh stretch. 'But he's there now.'

Silence, broken only by the faint pattering of Emil's fingers against the steering wheel.

She looked down to where her own hands lay folded in her lap. She couldn't make out anything other than their outline.

If the light had been better she knew she would have been able to see those first faint brown spots that were the symbol of her ageing. Hers and Emil's as well.

Her heart went out to him. He was a good man. He did, in his own way, love his son.

'I was sorry to see the boy upset.' He stretched out an arm, beckoning her closer.

As he waited for her to snuggle in one could be forgiven for thinking that, having reached the crossroads of their disagreement, it might have been better if they had tried to talk it out. Perhaps if he had told her how much he disliked her new-found conformity. Perhaps if she had countered with her exasperation at his always having to flout convention. Perhaps if they had found a way of talking about the different ways they felt, then perhaps it would have turned out differently. But they were a feeling couple. Talking or truth-telling never had been the basis of their relationship.

Evelyn moved across and nestled in the crook of Emil's outstretched arm. There she breathed in that scent of the food he loved, that spicy blend of curry powder and chilli in which onions, cinnamon, cardamom, ginger and garlic had all been fried, that always somehow seemed to cling to him. It was the smell also of their country, Ceylon.

Her proximity always soothed him. She felt him relax. And so sat for a long time and only when the time felt right, said, 'I'm worried about Milton. It might be an idea if I were to pay him some special term-time visits,' not adding the 'without you' that was running through her mind.

'As you like.'

She sighed again, heavily, and settled deeper into his embrace, sinking into a silence which she was now determined to keep.

The snub end of a piece of chalk was well aimed and it hit Milton centre forehead, jolting him awake.

'Still with us, Reymundo?'

Milton framed his heavy head into the semblance of a nod.

'Well then?'

He let his sleepy eyes play over the blackboard.

'I haven't got all day.'

There was nothing on the blackboard that needed answering and neither were there any eagerly waving hands. Which meant, most of the boys in his class not usually being willing to forgo any opportunity to show him up, that it could not have been a question.

The boy in the adjacent desk, one of the kinder ones, was jerking his head, excessively, to the right. No clue in that direction either, if you didn't count the section drawings on the wall that had been up since 1066.

'Well?'

Something at the door? But no. The door was shut.

'Well, boy?'

Milton gave a hopeless (sometimes hopelessness placated them) shrug.

'What Jones and his idiotically convulsive twitching is trying to signal,' the master said, 'is that your mother awaits.' The master glanced down at the note that some small boy must have brought in while Milton had been daydreaming. 'An appointment with the oculist, apparently. Such a dubious succession of appointments you have. Especially for a boy who never actually acquires a pair of spectacles.'

'Thank you, sir.'

'Hurry, boy. Don't keep her waiting.'

He wanted to break into a run, but since running indoors was forbidden he walked forward as smartly as he could.

She was downstairs in the entrance hall with a master to keep her company. Milton could see how close the master was to her and how cocksure, almost preening, like all the masters always seemed to be in her presence. He knew, because he'd heard them saying so, that they thought she was a 'beauty' and a 'veritable English rose'. And to think she was his mother!

No need to run. He should savour this. He started slowly to descend. When he was halfway down the door opened to admit a group of seniors. They came in casually enough but at sight of his mother straightened up and, as if they were still on the parade ground, forward they marched, their footsteps as synchronised as any cadet group's. When they passed him on the stairs, he heard an unmistakable 'Lucky bugger', which he knew was aimed at him. But even this approval was a trifling pleasure when all he needed was to say, softly, 'Mummy,' and, fawning master discarded, he got her whole attention.

'Darling.' She bent – although not as far as last time; he was growing – to kiss him on the cheek, a gesture she accompanied by a comforting little squeeze. He was elated by her touch and almost delirious that she had visited him again without warning and on the flimsiest of excuses, as she had done sporadically since last term's sports day.

'We'd better hurry.' Her smile joined them in the conspiracy of their series of bogus medical appointments and he would have left if not for the master's, 'Your coat, Reymundo?'

What a fool. During the winter term none of the lower school were permitted out of doors without full uniform.

'Don't worry.' His mother was always so understanding. 'I'll wait for you,' and even the master was smiling (happy to be alone with her again), which, as Milton knew, in any other circumstance he would certainly not have done.

He was grateful for the coat and even more grateful that she, never the most confident of drivers, had come all this way in such dreadful fog.

She took his hand. Unlike his father who tried to break the bounds of convention by hugging him in public, she always was correct and so taking her son's hand would be something every other mother would have done and also something that everybody, especially in the lower school, would permit, and, besides, the fog was too thick for anyone to see. He gave her hand a special squeeze. 'I'm so glad you came, Mummy.'

She was a slow driver. With the yellow beam of fog lights washing over the eerie space beyond, she handled the Rolls as if it were a decrepit thing. He saw the high gates looming through the drifting haze. No need for him to jump out and open them; a gardener having already been dispatched, she didn't even have to stop.

There: Milton released from captivity. Sitting in companionable silence as slowly she drove to town. He rested back, happily, in the front seat, his feet up on the dashboard. He could see shapes that parted open the drifting fog. There a barely visible portion of a long, low hedge that suddenly seemed to fall away, or here the bare talons of a spreading tree reaching out but not so far that it might get him. He felt so very snug. So safe.

'Hatches?' she said and he nodded enthusiastically, Hatches being his all time favourite place for lunch.

Hatches was half full, mostly with women although Milton could also see a smattering of other boys. Boys his age, but not like him. Ordinary boys, white boys, wearing ordinary clothes, pressed slacks and open-necked shirts that seemed to mock his short, grey flannel trousers, his maroon blazer with its house badge on the breast pocket and his matching striped, maroon tie and cap (which hastily he whipped off). He sniffed the air, like a dog sniffing home, luxuriating in the rich meaty smell. Such a contrast to the pong of stewed cabbage that clung to the refectory walls.

'And you, sir?' A waiter, having helped his mother out of her coat, was waiting to take his.

His mother nodded, encouraging him to give it up and he would have, he truly would have, if he had thought that this is what she wanted, of course he would, he'd do anything for her, but if it wasn't absolutely essential then he'd rather not expose his school uniform, thus making himself, in this town ambience, seem even more exotic.

'Sir?'

'Still cold, darling?'

His nodding was all that was required for the waiter to leave them free to follow another to their table where Milton could slip off his coat and because of the huge fuss they made of helping his mother into her seat, squeeze unnoticed into his.

The white tablecloths were thick with starch and the cutlery shone in the soft light. He felt so very happy opposite the most beautiful (as his father always called her) woman in the restaurant. He picked up the luncheon menu, letting his eyes pass down the list even though he knew what he was going to have. She did as well. 'Prawn cocktail?' and without waiting for his nod, she told the waiter, 'and to follow, the gammon and roast potatoes,' which is what he also always had. For herself, she ordered the baked mushroom caps and a buttered Dover sole and then their drinks – dandelion and burdock for him and a dry sherry for her – that they sipped, companionably, as they munched cheese straws and crackers on which they had spread a smattering of Peck's fish paste.

'How's Vanessa?' he asked, afterwards listening in a lordly manner to her telling him how Vanessa was well and doing well at school, and that she was also busy with her maps, this last delivered with a quick smile that he returned in their fond complicity for the oddness of his sister's quirky insistence on mapping everywhere she ever went.

'Your father is very proud of her.' His mother speared a

mushroom with her fork, an action he caught because, surprised by the edge to her voice, he had quickly looked up. But she was smiling as she popped the morsel in, her manner so unperturbed he must have been imagining things.

He reapplied himself to the catching up of the last drops of the thick, pink prawn sauce before the bowl was whipped away, its place taken by a fat slab of honeyed gammon with a glossy pineapple ring and crispy-edged potatoes over which dark gravy had been slathered, the extra large amount she always ordered, and for a while all he did was attack his food, tucking in so happily that he caught himself humming with the joy of it, a habit that would have drawn a disapproving grimace from his father but only made his mother laugh out loud. 'Do I gather that the food at school has not improved?'

'No,' he said cheerfully, 'it's utterly filthy,' putting a forkful of meat and fruit and gravy-sogged potato in his mouth.

'And other than that, how is school?'

'It's fine, thank you,' he said, just in time swallowing down the 'sir' that automatically had risen at his sentence end.

'Is it really?'

Something in her voice made him glance up to find her watching him with grave attention. She had barely touched her fish.

He felt uneasy. As if he were about to sit an exam for which he had forgotten to prepare.

He said, 'Well . . .'

But this, he realised, was no exam. She was his mother. With her he could say anything he felt like saying. And so he said, 'Well, it's not exactly fine,' which understatement was enough to release, from deep inside him, that cry he usually held back. I hate it. I hate it so much, Mummy, his voice loud enough to halt waiters in their tracks, Please – and stop forks from reaching mouths, Please take me away, mouths unhinging and dropping open, as he shouted, I promise, I'll work harder in the future, I'll do anything as long as you let me come home . . .

A juddering of time and Milton was returned to his own skin. Back to the restaurant where his mother was looking at him, brightly and encouragingly, waiting for a response that she had already foretold. She thought that he was happy. She expected him, no, more than expected, she *wanted* him to be happy. She would be terribly hurt if he told her exactly how miserable he really was. He couldn't tell her. He could not.

'Your father thinks the school might not be suitable,' she said.

Ah, so that's why she was asking. The school had been her choice. A difficult choice, he knew, because she hadn't wanted to send her special boy away. And yet she had suffered the loss of him for his own good. How could he tell her how much he hated it?

'And after sports day . . . he heard her saying. She left the sentence hanging, for which small mercy he was grateful. Best not to dwell on that. Ever.

'Is your father right?'

He couldn't. He just couldn't. 'I like poetry,' is what he said, 'and I can always remember it,' and seeing how pleased she looked he tried to please her further by adding, 'and I also particularly like Latin.'

His instincts rewarded. Her smile widened. She wanted so much for him to like school. She needed him to. And so he detailed just how very interested he was in Latin and how good his marks were, across the board (taking poetic licence since geography hardly counts) and when she nodded and smiled her approval seemed to swell inside him so he was almost trembling with excitement, especially when he confided what previously he had not even owned up to himself, that his secret ambition was one day to become a Latin teacher. Having blurted this out, he heard an echo of his own voice, high and wavering in its boyishness and also over-eager, so childish that it almost made him blush except that his mother's, 'That's an idea,' was delivered with such gusto, and she showed such interest in what he next had to say that he felt himself to be interesting. When she asked just the right question about his friends and how they spent their recreation time, he had no hesitation in keeping the conversation going, right through the slice of Black Forest gâteau that he gratefully wolfed down along with a double scoop of vanilla ice-cream.

Many years later, looking back, he would summon up the sight of them basking, not so much in the abundance of good food or the luxury of being warm and comfortable on such an inhospitable day, as in their mutual admiration. His of his splendid mother and she of her chatting, sparky son. Both of them sitting companionably never dreaming that all of this soon would be lost. But by then, of course, it would all be far too late.

How tempting, when you're boarding, to forget those moments of transition between two worlds. Easy, perhaps, because to remember is constantly to stir up the pain. But as his mother paid the bill, and as reluctantly he rose, his awful dread returned. He spent the car journey talking brightly to hide from her (and from himself) how dismal he felt.

Only when they had rounded the last corner and were close to the gates almost entirely shrouded by fog did he let himself remember how it had felt to walk into the restaurant. He remembered how grateful he had been because his coat hid his scratchy school clothes, himself so tiny and so unschooled in the ways of the outside world. Lunch and his mother's attention had made him grow, until he'd walked out of the restaurant a normal, full-size boy.

Now the opposite effect. As if somebody had scattered magic beans to enlarge the school. Either that, or his journey into town and his eating had diminished him.

There stood the school whose forbidding exterior no fog, no matter how thick, could completely mask. It was its own empire, its separate kingdom. His throat constricted, almost choking him.

No gardeners this time. He must get out of the car and, with great effort, push open the high wrought iron gate. Back again into the warmth, head down, as she drove on until soon, too soon, she drew up. She applied the hand-brake. 'Well, darling . . .'

She hated these partings as much as he did. He blinked and saw her also blinking and he saw how moist were her eyes. Suddenly afraid, he blurted out, 'Are you quite well, Mummy?'

She sniffed. 'Yes, darling. A slight cold. Nothing serious,' although there was something in her voice, he knew it was there, that made him doubt what she was saying and made him hope that she would ask him again whether he liked the school, thus allowing him another opportunity to tell the truth.

She stretched across and kissed him. 'You better go.'

This was part of their unspoken agreement: she would come into the school to fetch him but not on their return.

'See you soon,' she said.

'Yes.' He had to be brave. 'Soon. Goodbye.'

Out he went, quickly.

'Goodbye, darling.'

His goodbye had already been said. Only once. That's the rule. He must not repeat it.

And neither would he look back. He walked up the stairs, hearing the car tyres trundling into motion, not looking back – he wouldn't and neither, she had promised, would she – his hand on the door knob, and pushing through and then the heavy door swung shut behind him.

The light was fading as Evelyn stepped out of Gunter's. Her companions, a neighbour and two of her friends, were already on the pavement. Standing in the doorway, seeing them gaily chatting, she found herself thinking, as she often did, about Milton.

'Coming, Evelyn?' This from the neighbour whose car was parked near hers.

'No, not just yet.' She went to join the group. 'I've got some errands to run,' which wasn't strictly true but, it being one of the days when Emil and Vanessa were due to spend time in the orchid house planting his latest acquisitions, she wasn't inclined to hurry home. 'Do go on without me.'

'Well if you're sure,' one of the women said. 'It's been a pleasure to make your acquaintance. We'll see you again, soon, I hope,' which sentence set off the sequential nodding of other heads before gloved hands were pressed briefly into Evelyn's.

Evelyn unfastened the clasp of her handbag and took out a small notebook. With ballpoint pen poised as if intending to add something to her list, she watched them walking away. They were all old friends, comfortable with each other and they were walking slowly. From their serious exchange of nods, she guessed that they were talking about their husbands and how hard they worked. If she had been with them she, too, could have joined in, although she had noticed that when she did talk about Emil's work they always seemed a little puzzled. Their husbands were top civil servants, or doctors or something respectable in the City. They didn't do strange things with oil and rubber like Emil and Yuri.

It was kind of them, she thought, to have included her in their outing. It had been pleasant to sit in that spacious, well lit tea-shop and let their conversation wash over. Even so, she had found herself assailed by a familiar thought – that no matter how long she lived in this country she would always be an interloper. A thought now given strength by the moving together of those four heads and the quietening of their voices. By which she knew she had become the focus of their conversation. She and her exotic husband. Quickly, in case they happened to glance back, she lowered her gaze.

'Spying on someone?'

Startled, she looked up.

'Mrs Reymundo. Evelyn, if I may make so bold.'

She frowned.

'Don't worry. You're not being accosted by a stranger. We have met before even if it was a good seven years ago. In your house. Remember? At your party.'

'Of course.' She remembered how he had also sneaked up on her then. She held out her hand. 'How nice to see you, Charles.'

'I'm flattered that you remember me,' he said. 'Especially since that was our only meeting and so long ago. I'd begun to think your husband was jealously keeping you at home.'

What arrogance. She didn't quite stamp her foot although she felt like doing so. 'Do you really think that I let my husband dictate what I may or may not do?'

'*Touché.*' His whole face seemed to move with the grin that now consumed it. 'I spend so much time in society dreaming up preposterous things to say, I've forgotten how to stop. I hope you will forgive me.'

He sounded so genuinely apologetic she felt awkwardly wrong-footed. All she managed, by way of reply, was a 'Well . . .'

'So, were you?'

'Was I what?'

'Spying.'

'No. Certainly not.' She shook her head. 'I was looking at my list.'

'I see.' He leaned over and cheekily plucked the notebook from her hand. 'Let me see.' He held it up high. 'You need to buy . . . hmmm . . . air . . . blank space . . . air . . . and a few ruled lines. What an extremely long and demanding set of requirements.' With a flourish, he shut the book. 'Perhaps I could be allowed to help you work your way through it?'

He was teasing her as if they were old friends. An impertinence. And yet she was enjoying herself.

'Look, and do forgive me if I'm speaking out of turn,' Charles said, 'but if I'd just had tea with a bevy of such . . . mmmm . . . delightful ladies I might also have invented a pressing shopping list.'

How rude he was and also how right. Strange. Not even Emil had guessed at her discomfort.

'When I saw you with the quartet,' she heard him saying, 'I wondered how much you all had in common.'

She shivered. Not so much from shock as from recognition. She dressed like her companions. She talked like them. She even looked like them. But when she was with them she found herself trying so hard to match herself to them that her every sentence, her every gesture, even her laughter, felt fraudulent.

'You look as if you could do with a spot of cheering up. Would you care for a drink?'

'A drink? When?'

'Well . . . how about now?'

No, she thought, knowing that she should say it, no.

'Before you refuse,' his grin was engagingly boyish, 'let me play on your heart-strings by telling you what a complete bugger of a day I've had. No, on second thoughts, I'll spare you that boredom and instead repeat, and I hope you don't think me presumptuous, that you don't look ecstatic yourself. Please. A disgracefully abject, clumsily begging please.' He laughed. 'You will, won't you?'

No, she thought, I will not. And said, not only out loud but also very loudly, 'One drink. It can't do any harm,' her volume, she knew, to convince herself that to give in to innocent impulse as she once used to do was exactly what she needed.

She had expected him to walk her out in the general direction of Park Lane. He steered away from it. It occurred to her to ask where they were going but she couldn't think how to do this without sounding overly suspicious. Which wasn't necessary, he was a partner of her husband's. There could be nothing wrong in spending half an hour – that was all the time she would spare – with him in a public place. And so, on she walked and as she did she imagined herself arriving home and saying to Emil, 'Can you guess, who I bumped into?' and when Emil drew a blank, she'd tell him 'Charles', after which she had no trouble imagining his amusement as he said, 'Good God, Charles, was it?' And then he would fill her ears with scurrilous tales of Charles's derring-do.

So caught up was she in her imagining (it's what happened to married people, she thought, not only do they finish each other's sentences, they can construct entire conversations) that she didn't notice that Charles had stopped.

'After you.' He had even pulled out a key. Now he nodded to indicate a few steps up which she was meant to go.

She looked to left and right. They were standing in front of an anonymous door in a quiet, residential street. 'Is this your house?'

A beat before: 'There is the club,' he said, 'but those old boys would rather fall on their swords than let in a lady. So I thought . . . But if you'd rather not?' He said this casually as if to say that if she'd rather not, he would naturally understand. That if she said no, he, the perfect gentleman, would escort her to her car and wave her off.

She didn't actually feel like saying no. The old Evelyn – the impulsive one – said, 'Half an hour, and then I really must head back.'

'Of course.' He nodded. 'After you.'

Up the stairs she went and in to be struck, once more, by incongruity. Instead of finding herself as she'd expected in an entrance hall that would then lead on into the rest of the house, there was a numbered door and a set of steep and uncarpeted stairs.

'Straight up,' he said.

Even the old Evelyn hesitated.

'Not as grand as Bishop's Avenue, I'm afraid.' He pulled such a charmingly apologetic face she was ashamed of the manner in which she had so quickly leapt to judgement. I've been here too long, she thought, as she started up the stairs, I'm also turning into a snob. And indeed, now she remembered Emil telling her how he'd recruited Charles into the business, not for money ('Charles hasn't got any') or for expertise ('that, he'll never attain'), but for his connections. 'It's that benighted English practice,' she seemed to hear Emil saying, 'of fathers who use the promise of a future filled with plenty to control their sons. Poor Charles must make ends meet until at his father's demise he, being the elder, will inherit what remains of the family dosh.'

'All the way to the top,' Charles said.

She kept on going. To the top. But when he had unlocked that door and stood aside to usher her in, doubt returned. With its tiny entrance hall and its dingy corridor, the flat had nothing of a home about it. Certainly not the kind of home that would have belonged to somebody of Charles's class.

'Last door on the left,' he said.

She must leave, now, before it was too late.

'The flat belongs to an old school chum,' he said.

At the end of the corridor she turned left.

She found herself in a shabby lounge with Charles coming up behind her saying, 'Tim's the complete country bumpkin. Does everything he can to avoid coming up to town. He's been kind enough to let me have a key.'

Oh, of course, Charles must also live in the country. Emil would confirm this when she got back.

'Now. Let me see.' From a long, low teak sideboard Charles took out two glasses and a jug. 'What else?' He was talking to himself. 'Ah yes, ice. If this place runs to it.' Taking the jug to the door, he paused long enough to say, 'Please, make yourself comfortable,' before leaving.

The room he left her in never was going to provide much comfort. It had a neglected, unloved feel about it, a low, armless sofa and two wire chairs being, along with the oversized sideboard, the only pieces of furniture. There were no pictures on the wall. No photographs on the sideboard. And, apart from some greyed and hanging lace, no curtains.

Charles's muffled, 'Damn thing's frozen up,' was followed by the sound of banging.

There was another door she had noticed off the hallway. She retraced her steps and, quietly pushing it open, went in.

She found herself in a bedroom even more neglected than the lounge. A rickety double bed was inadequately shrouded by a crumpled lemon-yellow candlewick bedspread. And that was all. No side tables. No mirrors. No bedside lights. Not even a wardrobe. Only thick, sludge-green curtains that clashed with the wallpaper's wild pink swirling roses.

'Evelyn?'

It wouldn't do for him to catch her here. She hurried back to the lounge.

'I'll be with you in a jiffy,' she heard him calling.

At the window she pushed aside the lace, there to stand apparently looking out, although if someone subsequently had asked her, she would not have been able to describe a single feature of the view. She was too caught up in thoughts that seemed to stab at her in the way that, by the look of the bucket on the sideboard, Charles must have succeeded in stabbing out some ice. This was not a home, she thought. It was a no man's land. The kind of land to which men might bring their mistresses. The kind of land, therefore, into which a respectable married woman should not venture.

Yet here she was feeling strangely altered and simultaneously recognisable. More herself than she had been for ages. Not so much because of the deprivation of this flat – though they had been poor their home, unlike this place, had always been comfortable and well tended. Rather what being here did was summon back the person she once had been.

It was as if she had spent a long dark winter, a winter of many years' duration, huddled in the shell of a new woman. That respectable wife who balanced her husband's forthrightness with her own dignified silence. That mother who always put her children first. And now again that girl she had been, the girl who never had been afraid to break the bounds of dull convention, was back.

But, came the reluctant thought, I should go. I really should.

Her heart was racing with the realisation that Charles was by her side. She didn't turn to look at him. She didn't dare.

She could feel the heat of him and she could hear his rhythmic breathing for what seemed like ages before he said, cheerfully, 'Another filthy fog.' She let drop the edge of the lace curtain.

'Here you are.' Somehow he had found time to fill two glasses with ice and alcohol, one of which he held out to her. 'It's whisky.'

He seemed so sure that she would want it, she almost felt as if it was something she often drank. Dutch courage, she thought, taking it.

'All there is, I'm afraid. Bloody Tim letting the stocks run down.'

Feeling the glass cold against her skin, she wondered whether he helped pay for the 'stocks' and, if so, on what basis. By the serving? she wondered. The bottle? Or – and she couldn't help thinking this or noticing how the thought seemed to make her heart race faster – by the woman?

He had lifted up his glass. 'Cheers,' although, instead of drinking, he just stood there with it raised.

Feeling his scrutiny like a burn, she blushed and looked away. Silence as she stood, eyes downcast, wondering if he were still looking. And then she heard 'So what do you think about Sputnik?'

'Sputnik?' She was so surprised she couldn't stop her gaze from meeting his.

'The Russian earth satellite,' he said. 'Yuri calls it Sputnik, which I presume must be its authentic name. Did you know that it can circle the world in less than ninety-five minutes?'

'No.' She smiled. 'I didn't.'

'Imagine that – say it's above Panama at one o clock, well then at two it might be in . . . in . . .'

'Reykjavik.'

'Precisely so. Reykjavik for coffee and then, where else? Detroit? Yes, why not? Detroit for a *digestif* and after that . . . hmmm, it's a Russian innovation, so we must not neglect Russia. So perhaps it will be tea in Moscow and aperitifs in Vladivostok.'

'Sounds like it's going to be well fed and extremely drunk.' Who was this woman standing with this stranger's whisky and talking his same nonsense? Who was she?

He seemed also to be wondering this. His eyes on her for what almost felt like for ever until, eventually, he said, 'Christ.'

It sounded like despair. She couldn't help herself. 'What is it?'

'You're so beautiful. You take my breath away.' He grinned sheepishly. 'I'm sorry, I'm making an awful fool of myself.'

If he hadn't said that, and if he hadn't also looked so mortified – like a naughty schoolboy – he might have scared her. But there was something so unthreatening about the way he now was regarding her and, she had to admit this, if only to herself, also something wonderfully flattering.

Emil loved her – or so he said – but he did not look at her with love. While here was a near stranger whose admiration was clear. She couldn't help savouring the moment and wishing it would last.

'Come.' His voice was soft. 'Let's drink to our chance encounter.'

He put his hand around hers so as to help nudge up her glass. It was a light touch he had. Gentle and without pushing. The feel of his skin against hers made her gulp so that she didn't so much sip her drink as physically inhale it. The whisky, which she was anyway unused to, went down her windpipe. She began to splutter and then to choke.

He took her glass then hit her lightly on the back until she had stopped coughing.

'Better?'

She nodded.

Another long, slow look before: 'You're a fraud, Evelyn Reymundo.'

What? Her startled gaze caught his wide stretch of grin.

'There I was, thinking you were a woman of the world but you turn out to be such an utter greenhorn you choke on the tiniest sip of whisky.' His grin was so infectious that she also started smiling and, for a while, that's all they did – two foolish adults standing and smiling at each other. She couldn't remember when it was she had last felt so carefree.

'But there's something sad about you.'

She blinked, surprised to find herself on the brink of tears. What a stupid fool she was. And how ashamed. If he had come even an inch closer, she would have run.

He stood his ground and, when he said, gently, 'What is it?' it sounded as if he really wanted to know.

She shook her head. She couldn't tell him.

'Was it those women?'

'I shouldn't,' she said. 'They are so kind.'

'And yet?'

'And yet . . .' She had tried, truly she had, but now she could no longer stop what she had to say from spilling out. 'And yet when I am with them, I feel so out of sorts. As if I don't belong.'

'Do you think you're the only one?'

'Yes, I do.'

'Why? Do you think any of the rest of us ever really feel as if we belong?'

'Don't you?'

'No, I don't think we do. Or perhaps it's just us English. All of us in our separate little boxes worrying that we're the only ones not to fit in.'

'But not someone like you – surely not.'

'Me? I'm the worst of the lot.' He gave a brittle little laugh. 'I'm a laughing-stock. A member of the aristocracy without a penny to my name. To have my ancestors and my income – it's absurd. So yes, I have the silver salver and all the right calling cards and all the right invitations, but when I walk into a room, do you know what people are thinking?'

She tried, 'They're thinking what a handsome—' but he, refusing her consolation, interrupted her. 'They think if, that is, they bother to notice me at all, what a stupid arse I am. And they're right. At home, there's always my father breathing down my neck. This is the only privacy I have. But look at it. It's sordid. And to think I brought a woman like you here.'

Her heart went out to him. Without thinking about consequences, she moved to him.

She felt how he tensed up before relaxing into her

embrace. He smelt of cologne, and tobacco and whisky. A very manly smell, she thought, so different from Emil's.

She shouldn't be here. Shouldn't be doing this. She felt his hand gently stroke her cheek.

'Please,' he whispered. 'Stay here with me.'

Wraiths of grey-white fog swept up and over and beyond the windscreen, again and again. Although the black blades of the windscreen wipers also kept arcing to and fro, they did nothing to improve Evelyn's vision. She could barely see the road. She was going much too fast. She braked, and stamped down on the clutch, but her leg was juddering so violently that, as her hand changed down a gear, her foot jumped off.

The car jerked and bumped, throwing her forward so that her head banged on the steering wheel. She could hear the horn blasting out into the thick, dark night, a plaintive cry like the one to which she wanted, but had not been able, to give voice.

Her hand went up to her forehead. It came back dry. Straightening herself and sitting back, she waited for her breath to calm. It was a mercy there had been no car behind hers. She had been lucky, she thought, at the same time as she couldn't stop herself from admitting the thought that a crash – and particularly a bad one – would have acted both as punishment and as solution.

The wipers swept from side to side. To no avail. Moisture almost immediately seeped back into the places they had vacated. It must be raining, she thought, although, the fog having dulled all sound, she could hear no rain.

Through the dark veil of the road ahead something was heading towards her. First the blur of its yellow headlights and then two low, looming beams of light lit up two long, low streaks of fog before a dark, unwieldy beast – a bus – reared into view. Now it was close enough for her to see a high lighted interior framed by the dense black night. There was a conductor standing on the platform and he was holding up a fog lamp. As he drew parallel to her he used the lamp madly to gesticulate, swinging it from left to right so that it inscribed streaked arcs of light that seemed to linger in the dark.

He was signalling to her and he was right. Not only was she endangering herself, she was also risking the safety of other drivers. The fog was just too thick. She never should have ventured out. She should have found a phone box and phoned Emil knowing that, if she had, he would have come to fetch her, a thought so ludicrous, given what she had just done, it made her laugh out loud.

Her laughter was as unfunny as the very idea that she would be laughing. Abruptly she cut it off.

She turned the key. The engine kicked and strained and died. Her turning must have been too forceful. She made herself sit, taking in a breath and then slowly breathing it out and only afterwards turning the key again. This time, and to her great relief, the engine sparked into life. She steered the car to the side of the road, the bump of tyres telling her that she was alongside it. Leaving on the headlights for protection, she switched off the engine. And sat.

Charles had tricked her. That is what happened, she thought. But even as she was sealing the thought with a confirmatory nod, she knew it for what it was: a lie. She had been so very willing.

The musk of the candlewick bedspread and that stronger, earthier, acrid scent of him. The rasp of his chin against her cheek and his insistent touch, such a contrast to Emil's gentleness – although she hadn't thought this at the time. She hadn't thought anything. Her body had taken over, arching up, involuntarily, her breath joining and flowing with his. No thoughts, then, to hold her back. Just feeling.

Only afterwards and after he had cried out and after his weight had slackened, then she had begun to admit a doubt.

Not his fault. He had been the perfect gentleman. Shifting off his weight, he had begun to trace the curve of her body with a gentle hand, whispering, 'You are so lovely, Evelyn,' as if he had known that what she needed then, more than anything, was reassurance. And yet, she had not felt reassured. What she hadn't been able to do was stop herself from contrasting his reaction with hers.

He was so slow, satisfied and happy. Her nerve ends seemed to be afire. His self-assurance troubled her. Everything he did, the manner in which he had got out of bed, for example, and had quickly covered himself, or the way he had left the room so that she might dress without the embarrassment of being observed, had reinforced her doubts. And when eventually she had emerged, he did not make her walk the corridor alone. He had been waiting with a glass of water and a kiss that was neither cloying nor demanding. He had been so considerate, so attuned to her every need that she had understood that his behaviour was so perfect because it was so practised.

So what? He was a single man. Why shouldn't he have done this before? And yet, although she stood by this thought, at the same time repeating to herself that she was no innocent, no deflowered virgin, still she couldn't help feeling that, to him, this was just a game.

She hadn't stayed long. He had understood. He had offered to accompany her and again had understood when she'd said it would be better if she made the return trip, even to her car, alone. He had shown just the right amount of concern about her driving in the fog. The only false note had come on the doorstep when he said, 'Perhaps best to keep this between ourselves?'

Again, the right thing to say and she hadn't trusted it.

'Be careful in the fog.' His voice had been distant as if, by stepping out of the house, she had made him fade away. A soft click, muffled by the fog as she stood in the dank, dark air, trying to get her bearings.

And now half an hour later she was encased by fog, conscious of the foul taste in her mouth and of how thirsty she was and how tired.

Slowly, slowly she pulled out, and slowly she drove home.

The house was, as always, lit up. Emil's doing. Unlike real Londoners who, trained by wartime rationing and blackouts, would go from room to room turning out lights, Emil would make special forays into places he had no intention of occupying specifically in order to turn them on. Which meant that, as she quietly pushed open the front door, she had no idea where he might be.

No need for her to know. As soon as she stepped in, she heard 'Evelyn?' coming from the lounge. He was so alert. He'll know, she thought.

'I didn't think you'd manage to get through this fog.'

'Yes, it is thick.' Her voice, like her body, was trembling.

'You should have phoned me to come and fetch you.'

She thought about going straight upstairs but if she did he would be bound to follow her. She walked through the hallway under the hanging chandelier. How proud it had once made her feel; now its shattering shards of light only seemed to mock.

The door to the lounge was ajar. She stood to one side, peering in.

She could see Emil on the sofa with Vanessa on his lap. 'You see,' he was saying to Vanessa, 'I told you she would be back, and so she is,' in reply to which Vanessa nodded, her straight black hair swinging from side to side, almost purple as it caught the light. And then Emil (he was so attuned to her) glanced up. 'Is that you?'

She could not hide from him. Never had been able to. She must reveal herself before he got to her.

'Good God.' He put Vanessa down. 'What on earth?'

'What do you mean?'

'Your forehead.'

She put her hand up and he was right. Her forehead hurt.

He hurried over. 'Was there an accident?'

She shook her head and, without meaning to, found herself backing away. 'No,' she said and quickly afterwards, 'I mean yes. The fog. I had to brake suddenly. Must have hit my head. I did. I remember. I couldn't see . . . I . . .' she was babbling as she kept backing up so that they both ended up in the hall.

'Evelyn.' He stretched out an arm. 'Calm down.' He held his hand up, palm open, as if she were a frightened animal he was trying to calm. 'You're safe now.' Moving closer. 'Come, you should sit.'

She cried out, 'But I don't want to,' thinking how much she didn't want him near her in case he sniffed her out.

He stopped abruptly. Looked at her.

Had he read in her expression what she had done? Did he already know?

'Where are you going?'

'To call the doctor.'

'But I don't need a doctor.'

'You may have concussion.'

She said 'Emil,' so loudly she stopped him in his tracks. 'Please.' Smiling at him as he turned, or at least trying to. 'Don't. Honestly, I'm fine, I'm just a little shocked.'

'Are you sure?'

'Yes, I'm sure. It wasn't so bad. Go and look at the car, there's not a scratch on it.'

He said, 'I'm not worried about the car,' but at least, by walking back to her, he showed he wasn't going to call the doctor.

She must not move away from him. Must not.

She let him put his arms around her.

He hugged her, carefully, so as not to bruise her further. Feeling the warmth of him, and his gentleness, she also felt the depth of her betrayal.

'Are you sure you don't need a doctor?'

She pulled away from him. 'Yes,' she said. 'I am sure. What I need is a bath.'

She locked the bathroom door and immediately after that tried it again to make sure it was properly locked. She turned on both taps before peeling off each item of her clothing. She dropped them on the floor from where, she thought, she would later pick up and permanently dispose of them.

Steam rising and almost filling the room. She swiped her hand across the mirror. In the moment before it misted over she looked at her reflection. Her eyes were wide, her hair browned and tousled by the rain and there, on her forehead, the reddening bruise that Emil had noticed.

The water was hot enough to burn. Her just deserts. She stood until she had grown more accustomed to the heat and then, gingerly, lowered herself down. And there she lay in the scalding water.

As quiet as she was, and half holding her breath, she still could make out the murmur of Emil's reading to Vanessa. He did so every night, and every night Vanessa (who was surely too old now to be read to) would drink in the folklore of her father's childhood that she already knew by heart, this ritual being one of the many things they shared.

Evelyn slid down deeper into the bath until her head was also covered. Breath held, willpower making her endure the steaming heat. What a relief to cut out all noise. She wondered, as she kept herself down, what it would be like to listen to her stentorian breaths as they came slower and slower until they altogether died away and, with them – what a merciful relief – consciousness.

She burst up, gasping, through the surface of the water.

'Are you all right?' she heard Emil calling.

Why would he not let her alone? 'Yes, I'm fine.' She lay back in the water. As she lay it came to her that irritation with him and her own self-hatred were not the only things she felt. For, into her consciousness, now crept a once familiar sensation. A feeling of liveliness. Of breaking out. As the memory of the excitement she had experienced surged through her again, it dawned on her that it had been an age since she last had felt this alive.

Noises. In the house and out. They all heard them even if they heard them differently and never related what they had heard.

Emil waking up to a noise that seemed to have faded in the moment before he properly awoke. Looking over at the sleeping Evelyn and thinking that she must have called out something in her sleep. Stretching out a hand, thinking to touch her. His sleeping beauty. But his hand withdrawing.

Down the landing, Vanessa also wide awake. Unable to lull herself to sleep. No sounds that she can hear and yet, should she close her eyes, the noises will return. Of this she is frighteningly aware.

While Evelyn sleepwalks through life. Her noises the everyday sounds of her husband and her daughter going about their everyday lives. Speaking in voices she knows so well. Saying things to which she nods although she cannot hear.

Her ears are attuned to another sound. To Charles's siren song. Her thoughts caught up in resisting the awful knowledge that soon, today, tomorrow and the next week, she will be with him again.

Vanessa couldn't sleep.

It had been like this for weeks. No matter how tired she was, no sooner did she close her eyes than she was instantly on the alert. Just lying there waiting for sleep to come didn't work and so she was up and trying to occupy herself until fatigue got the better of whatever it was that was keeping her awake.

She had been up for hours. Had worked on her maps (she was putting the final touches to the route from home to Milton's school). Had put up her hair in rags, rolling through long strips of torn-up sheets, trying (even though it had never worked before) to fluff out her straight, black locks. Now she needed something else to do.

Her room was ordered, everything in place. She let her gaze run along the line-up of paper dolls and outfits she had cut from *Bunty*, toying with and then rejecting the idea of undressing and re-dressing them, before her gaze moved on past the pile of jigsaws and the coronation mug to settle on the much-thumbed set of miniature, tan-coloured, hard-covered, one shilling books that made up her complete 'I-Spy' collection.

First was *I-Spy Spotter* book Number One (spotting famous cars series A). An old favourite, her first and her most successful. She flicked to the end pages on which she had inscribed the place and date of her sightings. Of the 10.97 horsepower MG Midget, the 1.5 litre Jowett-Javelin with its flush-fitting door handles, the 4 cylinder, Austin A40, and on, through the hubcap-badged Rover and the Jaguar Saloon. All the cars required by series A, bar one, the 6 cylinder Rolls-Royce Silver Wraith.

The Silver Wraith was, in theory, the easiest car for her to spot – all she need do was go to the garage where her father's was parked. But just as her maps were drawn freehand from observation and without any reference to a printed map, the inclusion of a car that belonged to her father had seemed like cheating. She had therefore set herself the task, thus far unsuccessful, of spotting an earlier model – the one with the radiator lady still on her feet.

Now, for completion's sake, she told herself that there was nothing in the rules to say that a car had to belong to a stranger. She was going to claim her father's Rolls. She deserved to. 'A lady's privilege,' she muttered to herself in imitation of something her father liked to say.

Her pencil having been sharpened (a good, sharp point was required), she applied herself to filling in the empty lines. She wrote the date *24 October 1957*, the place *our garage*, the car, *Rolls-Royce Silver Wraith, new model*, open brackets *'ours'* close brackets and there it was – her spotter's log complete.

The completion of this task didn't make her any sleepier. She went over to the window.

While the front of their house was all fat pillars, regularly spaced windows, clipped hedges, high gates and a sweep-in driveway here, at its back, Ceylon had come to London. The garden's deep borders had been planted with as many of her parents' native country's species as would take root so that, in summer, an abundance of roses, climbing, standing and tea (that her father also adored), sat amongst hibiscus and rhododendron and under the spiky purples, pinks and deepened crimson of flamboyant flowering trees.

The garden was Vanessa's favourite place, especially at night and especially in winter when it was the shape of things and not their colour that stood out. The fearless child she occasionally felt herself to be loved the stark skeletons of trees. She loved the manner in which the contours of the few remaining leaves were fattened by their shadows, and how the offshoots of vines had turned to gossamer threads. In the winter garden, she could imagine herself in that other country, an explorer mapping the connections between two worlds, the embodiment of the house's front façade travelling to its back. Mostly, though, she loved the garden because it was her father's favourite place, and the site of his beloved orchid house. He was often out there, especially at night. Even now, this late, she could see there was a light on. Having spent many happy hours with him there, she knew he'd be humming to himself as he misted his latest acquisition, the dark reddish-brown *Miltonioides leucomelas*, the so-called black orchid whose name, and nickname, had so tickled his fancy he'd gone to great trouble to get one sent from Guatemala.

I could go see him, she thought. In fact – this idea making her giggle – I could sneak up on him.

The more she thought about it, the more right it felt. She could picture herself moving softly to the bottom of the garden then opening the orchid house door, experiencing that comforting blast of heat and light as she announced her presence with a dramatic star jump, legs wide, arms up and stretched out in a V and an accompanying clarion 'tarah!'. In response to which her father, once he'd got over his shock, would play along, even pretending to be more surprised than he actually had been until, as her reward for his play-acting, she would laugh and laugh. And after that, he would let her help him with the misting and finally would take her back to bed where he would read or, even better, tell her a story, something he did and that she loved him to do despite, or perhaps because of, what her mother said about her being far too old. And after the story was finished, well then she'd be able to fall asleep.

No one on the landing. She tiptoed down the carpeted stairs.

Standing under the chandelier she looked into the dining room where the polished mahogany table reflected back the light. She turned her head to look into a lounge that was all brown velveteen sofas and russet thick pile. It was equally well lit and equally empty. Her mother must be out, she thought, or else upstairs in bed, this realisation giving her the courage to pass quickly through the hall and into the kitchen, past the washing room and through the back door.

The night was dark and moistened with reminders of a fog that still, vaguely, smeared the air. As she moved across the lawn, she could feel damp seeping through her slippers. Her father didn't like her getting her feet wet, especially at night and in the winter, and he wouldn't have liked the way the hem of her long flannel nightie was trailing. But she wouldn't let that stop her. Dipping down, since he was a master spotter himself, she flitted jerkily over the lawn. She was a firefly in her whiteness, crisscrossing the pulped remains of dead plants. Mud oozed over her slippers' edge and between her toes. She swallowed down the slick edge of the repulsiveness that rose up in her throat and pressed on.

The last few feet were the most exposed, especially when the orchid house was lit. She scooped herself down, bending almost double as she scurried over to the red-brick base that supported a wall of glass.

She was halfway there when she heard voices.

Voices in the orchid house were wrong. Her father didn't go there, not with anybody. Not unless that anybody was her. Gingerly, she raised her head.

The glasshouse was well lit. A bright, light box in the darkness out of which she was peering. She could see her father and her mother over by the far glass wall. They were standing close together, her father with his back to her.

She'd not previously thought of the garden as a hostile place. It was her playground, its night-time scariness there to thrill and not to frighten her. But now the flutter of excitement that had sustained her in the darkness dropped to her stomach like a stone. The disquiet that seemed recently to have taken hold of her, intensified. She turned away from the orchid house.

There was light behind her and light splaying out in front. Between the two lay that long stretch of dark garden filled with shadows that seemed to beckon her. She was wet. Shivering from cold. And fear. The thing that she had been feeling for weeks, the conviction that something terrible was about to happen, possessed her.

If she couldn't go back across the dark – and there was no way that she could – then she must reveal herself. She would go in and tell them that old truth – that she couldn't sleep – and the new one – that she was scared – and when they saw her, wet and with her teeth a-chatter, they'd believe her and yes, why would they not believe her? she thought as, still on all fours, her hands padding dirt, she make her way towards the door.

Slow progress as the faint hum of their conversation, her father's emphatic clip and her mother's murmuring response fluttered out. Until, that is, when she was inches away from making her presence known. Then her father raised his voice. 'Did you think I wouldn't find out, Evelyn?'

The crouching Vanessa was transfixed by this vision of her furious father, and more so when she saw him raise up his hand, to shout, 'Could you really be that stupid!' this careful, kind father of hers who never raised his hand to anyone but who now swung it so wildly that a pot he hit went crashing to the floor. When he shifted slightly to his right Vanessa could see how his hand had gripped her mother's throat.

Vanessa was gone. Running through the garden as if her

216

life depended on it, through the back door and up the stairs and to her bedroom and when she got there, she threw herself into bed, pulling on the eiderdown until she was completely covered.

Evelyn was fighting. Not to get away from Emil but to stop herself from fighting back. She was conscious of the sweet scent of his cologne and of the heavy musk of the loam in which his orchids were planted. He pressed harder and she welcomed the pressure even as it choked her. If I don't resist, she thought, I might lose consciousness. Better still: I might die.

Turned out she was too feeble even for that. She couldn't stop her gasp from sounding out and when it did, he immediately let go. Emil, no matter how angry, was no killer.

Letting his hands drop, he gave a disgusted 'pah' and moved away from her. As far away as he could get and still be in the orchid house. 'You're such a coward, Evelyn.'

She was such a coward, she couldn't even look at him.

'First you betray me and then you expect me to forgive you.' His voice was muffled as he turned and caught hold of one of his beloved orchids. With one deft movement he pulled it straight out of its pot and, closing his fists over its dark brown flower heads, ground and crushed them. An orchid ending, she thought, to match the beginning in a clearing in a jungle in Ceylon.

'Is it really possible that you didn't know I knew?'

'Who told you?'

'Why would anybody need to tell me?' The malice of his smile cut her more keenly than his throttling fingers had. 'From the very first, that day when you came home with your fantastic tale of car crashes to explain the marks your lover had left on you, I knew.'

Was it true? Had he really known, and from the beginning? And every time after that as well? Had he seen through each of her smiles of false cheer? Her little faux-fond gestures of denial? The manner in which she had kept out of his way until she had washed herself? The nights she had lain beside him in bed hoping that he wouldn't think to touch her? Never dreaming that she might be the one who revolted him. She felt such outrage at *his* deception she couldn't help herself. 'Why didn't you say?'

'What was I supposed to say?' He began to tap the ledge on which was sited a long row of orchids. 'That I knew you went with Charles to that godforsaken place he and his chummery keep for their nefarious purposes?' Tap, tap. 'That I knew you were continuing to go there?' His fingers drumming against the wood. 'That I knew I was being cuckolded by such a man?'

He's itching to get hold of me, she thought.

'Was I supposed to tell you that?'

And yes, she thought, if only he had – it might have kept her from the worst of the madness.

His voice rose up. 'How could you have made such a mockery of me, Evelyn?' It seemed to be seeking concealment in the dark but instead rebounded against the glass of the orchid house so that it was almost as if she could hear her name repeated . . . Evelyn . . . Evelyn . . . Evelyn . . . again and again and again. Such a melancholic lament the like of which she had never imagined Emil giving voice to.

She felt so sorry. So very sorry. She wanted to reach out and hold him close and tell him so. But the man she wanted to hold was the Emil she had once known and not this familiar, unfeeling and untouchable Emil who was saying, and coldly, 'I will not play the part of sacrificial lamb' as he began to walk towards her. 'I will not open my veins so your lover Charles can suck me dry.'

Such fury in his regard and nothing she could say to mute it.

He let the silence stretch. On and on. She waited for a blow – verbal or physical, she didn't mind which – to fall. She waited in the silence trying to meet his gaze. Waited thinking that she had broken her own heart. And his as well.

'I never thought you hated me that much.' This cry was so pitiful that once again she was gripped by an impulse to reach out. But all she could equally plaintively say was, 'It wasn't to do with you.'

As if a cold wind had entered the orchid house. She saw it, icy hard, in his expression.

'Is that what you tell yourself?' His smile, that was no smile, stretched wider. 'It is, isn't it? You tell yourself that Charles was interested in *you*, didn't you?' Cruel laughter spilling out. 'You do know, don't you, that the whole purpose of his seduction was to hurt me?'

If this was what Emil wanted to think, and if letting it pass was the price that she must pay, well she owed him that at least.

220

'I see you don't believe me.' So cruel he looked. So hard. 'Well, it happens to be true. Your generally acknowledged loveliness –' his tone was soft and conversational. He might easily have been referring to some expensive, if meaningless, acquisition he had made – 'naturally would have served as an added bonus for a conqueror like Charles. But believe me, Charles tracked you down . . .'

. . . it came to her, then, how Charles had unexpectedly appeared that afternoon . . .

'. . . because, by possessing you, he would be getting something that belonged to me. There are scores of women who'd jump at the soon-to-be-vacant position of Lady Charles.' Emil's voice drumming as insistently as his fingers had previously drummed on that shelf. 'Charles may not be the wealthiest peer in the realm, but he still will be a peer. Class counts. He can have any woman he wants. He's not interested in you.'

Not true, she thought. Not true.

'What really stirred his blood, what kept him after you, was that you are the pure white wife to whom I, a jumped-up Colonial Coloured and, by the way, also his superior, had no right.'

She thought of the way Charles's face used to light up at the first sight of her and of his languid satisfaction as they planned their next tryst. It wasn't true, Emil was only saying this to hurt. 'It isn't so.'

'Isn't it? Ask yourself this, Evelyn. Hasn't Charles wanted me to know what you were up to? Hasn't he been egging you on to spill the beans? Isn't that why you came to me with your touching confession?'

221

No . . . And yet . . . from the time of their second meeting, hot in her ear . . .

'*Does Emil know?*'

'*Do you think he might suspect?*'

'The most astonishing aspect of this whole affair,' she heard Emil saying,

. . . the fantasies Charles had liked to weave

'is how skilfully he played you . . .'

. . . all of them involving her husband finding out about their affair. '*What do you think* . . .' He was always asking this. '*What do you think he'd do?*'

'Only to be expected. The kind of school the likes of Charles are sent to . . .'

Why wouldn't Emil stop?

'. . . the kind to which you insisted on sending our son, excel in teaching pupils to play the game.'

Why wouldn't he?

'In this case, Charles's little game was first to seduce you and then to push you hard enough until you had to tell somebody about it because he knew. . .'

'*What do you think, Evelyn darling? What do you think?*'

'. . . that you'd end up telling the only person who cared.' Emil bit down on the 'd' before repeating and completing the phrase, 'who ever really *cared* for you', his expression so hard it might have been carved from stone.

In all the ten years of their marriage, he had never looked at her like this.

'You have never stopped casting yourself in the role of sacrificial heroine,' he said. 'And all because you married a darkie. The things I sacrificed for you never even entered your mind. My family, for a start. From whom I have been estranged. My country. *My* country in which, with you, I could not live. Because of you and your ridiculous ambitions we came here to this place where I have done my best to hold up my head in the face of unrelenting humiliation and abuse.'

He was standing on the threshold, his eyes averted. Light from the orchid house was spilling out. Beyond it, darkness. Such a short distance that separated them.

If only either of them had been able to take that first closing step. She tried. 'Emil?'

He tried. Just by saying, 'yes?'

She had done too much and simultaneously had never done enough. What was there left for her to say? She swallowed.

'Cat got your tongue?' A pause and then, lightly, 'Well, no matter. I do have something to say and it is this: I want you to go. And to be clear, I don't mean from the orchid house.' He grabbed her by the elbow, propelled her to the door.

'You can't . . .'

Out she was pushed, so hard that, to steady herself, she had to thrust out both hands as her, 'But where am I to go?' rent the air.

He closed the door but not his mouth.

His voice sounding through the glass. 'I will not change my mind.' His rigid back encased in lit-up glass was all that she could see. 'You should go. Now. Before I have you forcibly removed.'

She turned away. Dropped her head. Buried it in her hands. That way she did not see him turn to look at her.

She stood in the ring of light outside the orchid house. She had to go. Could not resist him. Could not argue with him. Never had been able to.

'Leave,' she heard him saying.

In the bathroom of her boarding-house was one, small, tarnished mirror. It was hung so unnaturally high that Evelyn must stand on tiptoe so as to look into the face of a woman who had become a stranger. Surely Evelyn's face had never been this gaunt, or her skin this pale? As for her hair – no matter how much she brushed it, she could not tone it down. It was wild. Unruly. Impolite. Like (no, she told herself, she would not think of him) like Milton's.

The last of Charles's pay-off had been sufficient to tide her over for only a short time. She had no rouge and no money to buy any. Not that she would need rouge where she was going. She pinched both cheeks, pinching hard. Because pinching was all that she deserved.

Leaving the bathroom she went to the cold, damp, ugly cell that had served as her temporary stopping place. There the tears she had wept had seemed only to add moisture to the veins of dirty yellow that bulged and broke the wallpaper. Her suitcase was open on the ex-hospital bed with its bent metal frame. Where she was going, she would have no need of it. Not taking it, however, might raise suspicions.

Only one thing left for her to pack – the sapphire necklace that Emil had insisted that she keep. She tucked it in a glove that she wedged into a corner. The necklace would, she hoped, find its way back to Emil, who would pass it on to Vanessa. She closed the case and locked it. She dropped the key into her purse.

She smoothed down her pencil skirt and clipped on the pearl earrings and the single strand of pearls that had been her mother's. She pulled on her three-quarter-length coat, shrugging herself into the soft black wool, feeling how the mink collar nestled against her skin. Then she left the room.

She was all paid up but her landlady anyway came out to witness her departure. She saw the other woman's surprise at her outfit, pearls and all, and could read in her response the landlady's unspoken, *who do you think you are?* That was the question that was these days often beamed at her. Especially on those rare occasions when she opened her mouth to speak. *Who do you think you are with that stuck-up accent and yet so poor? Who do you think you are?* Having got the landlady's agreement to hold her suitcase for a few hours, she said goodbye and left.

It was grey and foggy as she pushed open a neat little gate to walk slowly down a neat little path. Nothing was familiar – a fact she knew better than to blame on the fog. Although there had been some sporadic polite sippings of tea in town, over the years, along with the occasional duty call by Marjorie to Evelyn's children, this was only Evelyn's third visit to Marjorie's home. And the first one unannounced.

The hand that she raised up to the bell hesitated. She even half turned away. But then, telling herself that the things she had done had removed her right to want anything, she jabbed the bell. Once and sharply. Hearing its dissipating ring, she thought again: this is a mistake. Yet when there was no answer, her relief at being spared humiliation was shot through with anxiety. Where was she to go? What was she to do? Without Emil, she had nothing. She was nothing.

'Evelyn?' Marjorie was suddenly in the doorway. 'I was in the back yard,' and pushing away a long strand of dark, dank hair. 'What brings you here?'

Had her sister exhibited even the slightest pleasure at the sight of her, Evelyn might have spilled out her story. As it was, Marjorie's distracted display of annoyance meant that Evelyn said, and as lightly as she could manage, 'I just happened to be passing.'

'Oh.' Marjorie seemed to crane round Evelyn. She must be looking for the car. Which she wouldn't find but, Evelyn hoped, Marjorie would tell herself that this was because the overwhelming grey had obscured it. And sure enough, 'What a nice . . .' pause . . . 'surprise. You better come in '

Following her sister down the narrow hallway, Evelyn could see a slight hunch to Marjorie's back at the point where her thick pinafore straps crossed over. Was this new, she wondered, or had she just never noticed it before?

'In here.' Marjorie, having opened the door to her front room, was greeted by a billowing wave of hot, wet air. Quickly, she moved to close the door but not quickly enough to stop Evelyn from seeing the lit gas fire and, arranged around it in a semicircle, a sheet-draped settee and two chairs covered with steaming clothes.

'You're busy with your wash.'

'Yes . . . well . . . it is Monday. Let's go to the kitchen.'

Had Evelyn been in Marjorie's kitchen before? As her sister bustled about, freeing up a chair and moving the clothes-horse away from the range and putting on the kettle, she realised that she hadn't. Or if she had, she certainly didn't remember the dirty brown linoleum, or the deep shelf by the open window on which some eggs and a bottle of milk sat, or the fat sink full of unwrung washing.

A dreadful memory rose up in her – her boastful showing off of her own kitchen. How could she have been so insensitive? No wonder Marjorie had kept her distance.

Having warmed the pot, Marjorie threw out the water before carefully measuring in tea leaves over which she poured more boiling water. She put a cosy round the pot and, leaving the tea to brew, arranged a ring of plain biscuits around the edges of a floral patterned plate that she had fetched down from the top shelf of the dresser. This was something she must have done a hundred, a thousand, a hundred thousand times, taking out cups and saucers and teaspoons and a jug into which she poured some milk and seeing how automatically, and how efficiently, everything was accomplished Evelyn couldn't help conjuring up a picture of the kitchen free of Monday's washing and of a table already laid for tea, around which Marjorie's friends and neighbours, whom Evelyn knew Marjorie must have and in abundance, would be arranged.

'Milk or lemon?'

'Milk, please.'

Marjorie poured tea over a careful measure of milk. As she handed the cup across Evelyn seemed to see in Marjorie's expression not this middle-aged Marjorie but the younger one, and seeing this she also seemed to hear Marjorie's furious, *Why do you always have to be different?* in reply to which the young Evelyn had asked, *Why would I want to be ordinary like you?* Now, taking the cup, Evelyn knew that Marjorie and her mother had both foreseen the costs of her refusal to conform.

Once she had contrasted her own courage with Marjorie's faint-hearted conformity. No longer. Now she saw that her sister was, and always had been, sensible while she was just indulgent. And also blind. She had refused to understand that rebellion for its own sake was far worse than Marjorie's more prosaic search for stability.

And now: the dream that had started on a roadside in Ceylon was over. She must throw herself on the mercy of the sister she had shamed.

Marjorie put down her cup. 'What brings you here, Evelyn?'

It was too late. She was already lost.

So thick was the fog it had turned day into night. Evelyn was grateful for the protection of her coat. She stood an age until – at last – she stuck out an arm. The bus was moving slowly, so slowly that even if the driver hadn't seen her until he was almost abreast he still had time to stop. She climbed in, the conductor waiting until she had seated herself before ringing the bell to signal the driver to slowly pull out.

She was going. For ever and for her children's sake.

For Vanessa who was young enough to forget her, and for Milton for whom it would be much harder. Although, she sternly told herself, it was for Milton's sake that she had made up her mind. If she stayed in the state she was, and in her situation, she would only hold him back.

Tendrils of fog kept drifting in and clinging to the other passengers who were sitting closer together than normally they would have done. Only Evelyn, the pariah, up front, was separated from the rest. She leaned forward, pressing her face against the front window. This was her last journey. All she could see was the blear of yellow light drifting through the void of grey outside.

Milton, she told herself, would be safe at the school he

loved. Yes, he would mourn her, but he would recover. And then he would learn, as she had never properly learned, how truly to fit in. 'If I can't belong,' she sent out her thoughts to him, so far away, and never to be seen again, 'then you will, my darling Milton. You will.'

'Cannon Street station.' She got off the bus.

The booking hall was crowded. She stood under the clock in a crush of other passengers, all of them gazing hopelessly at an announcement board that foretold nothing but delays. The air was thick with the resignation while the dank, dark smells of fog lingered on the press of dampened coats. She was impatient to get on. What rose up as she stood amongst it was hatred of this crowd. This place. This country.

The sudden incursion of a marching beat. An overladen man skirting the edge of the crowd. On his back a huge drum against which a series of roped levers ensured that his moving feet beat a stick at the same time as the wide sweep of his hands clashed a set of cymbals together. He's beating out the time, she thought, or the end of me.

She saw two helmeted bobbies approaching the man, each taking hold of one elbow and so moving him off. No one would miss him, she thought, just like no one would miss her. She looked up at the board. There were only two trains due to depart. Randomly she picked out one before, separating herself from the crowd, she made her way to the platform.

On the day their father drove them to their mother's grave Milton chose the back seat, sitting silently as a London he didn't know passed by. He watched a long series of grim red-brick terraces giving way to bigger and more detached houses, their place eventually taken by hedgerows and rolling meadows. He did not speak, not even to ask his father when they would get there. He liked the silence. He wished it would go on for ever. Which thought seemed enough to provoke Vanessa into saying, 'I learned a new one today,' before singing out,

> *Down by the river, down by the sea*
> *Johnny broke a bottle and blamed it on . . .*

Raising his hands up, Milton turned them this way and that, inspecting them for the stains that were habitually there.

> *I told ma, ma told pa,*
> *Johnny got a spanking so ha ha ha.*

Sure enough there were ink blotches on his palm as well as a long splodge of ink running the full length of his index finger. He also knew, without needing to look, that there was an ugly gravy splodge on his shirt. He'd seen it earlier. He had even considered washing his hands and changing the shirt for another. But not wanting to gratify his father, he had decided against.

> *I had a little puppy,*
> *His name was Tiny Tim*

Now he realised that he'd made the wrong decision. It wasn't for his father that he should have changed. It was for his mother. She had always liked him spick and span.

> *I put him in the bathtub, to see if he could swim.*

He spat into a hand that he then rubbed across the stain. That didn't help. Worse. The more he rubbed, the more it spread until, instead of just a drip of gravy, his shirt was filthy. Tears of frustration spilling out, he happened to look up at the rear view mirror. He saw his father's eyes on him. Scowling, Milton sank down deeper in his seat.

> *He drank all the water, he ate a bar of soap*
> *The next thing you know he had a bubble in his throat.*

'Shut up.' He said it once and then couldn't help repeating it – 'shut up, shut up, shut up.'

'Milton!'

'Well what does she think she's doing' – he couldn't bear to look at her – 'reciting all those stupid skipping rhymes?'

A pause and then, 'We are all trying to deal with things as best we can,' his father said before stretching out an arm to pull Vanessa close. 'Don't cry,' he said, and as she sobbed harder, 'Milton didn't mean it.'

And Milton sat thinking that his father for once was right. He hadn't meant to make her cry.

'Let's keep quiet for a moment,' his father said.

The silence Milton had thought he craved grew almost unbearable. To distract himself, he inserted various wishes. He wished he hadn't been so mean to Vanessa. Certainly he did wish that. But more than that he also wished for those most fervently held, and contradictory, desires. The first that he could have his mother back. The second that he had told her, that time, how much he hated school. If he had, she would have brought him home. And if he'd been at home he could, maybe, maybe have stopped her from getting on that train.

Stupid. He scrunched down, deliberately dulling thoughts and that way forcing himself into a frettingly deep sleep.

'Milton.'

He opened his eyes to find his father and Vanessa standing in front of a long low wall beyond which was a gate and a path that led to a spired church. A picture book sight, green and quiet apart from the chirping of birds.

'We're here.'

His father sounded so uncharacteristically gentle that Milton bit back a sarcastic, *yes, I can see we're here.*

Vanessa's sweet, shy smile was aimed at him. She's so small, he thought, and so pretty with those dark wide pools of eyes. He was sorry for the way he had snapped at her. He said, 'I'm sorry . . .' to which his father said, 'No need, my boy. No need,' stepping back then to let Milton out and afterwards ruffling his hair. And then, 'It's time.'

Milton did not want to think about what lay ahead, nor have it happen either. He looked up. The day was so bright. It was the kind of day his mother had always loved, the blue of the sky ruffled by only the occasional white of a feathery cloud. He set his top teeth to chewing his bottom lip.

He wished that they could leave. That they had never come. No matter that he was the one who had nagged and nagged until his father had agreed to bring them to her grave. He didn't want to see it. He had changed his mind.

'Here, my boy.' His father was holding up a clean white shirt. 'I thought you could do with this.'

Afraid that if he opened his mouth he might not be able to stop his tears, he did not thank his father. He took the shirt and put it on.

'Perfect.' His father straightened his tie before reaching into the boot, this time to bring out two roses. 'Here.' He made as if to pass one to Milton but he must have seen something in Milton's expression that made him withdraw. 'I'll keep hold of it until . . .' With a nod in the direction of the gate, 'After you, my boy.'

Head lowered, eyes downcast, Milton walked through the gateway.

He could feel Vanessa close to heel with their father drawing up the rear. Having gone into the yard Milton stopped and turned to see his father's head darting from left to right, as if he were expecting somebody but, since the place was deserted, he took the lead, his children following, round the church and to the graveyard.

First glimpse of the sea of graves made Milton remember those first nights that had stretched out into months. Those long nights of feigning sleep in his dormitory bed. Tears soaking his hard pillow so that during inspection, the yellow beam of torchlight flickering over the rows, he must turn himself face down so as to cover up the wet. And all those other long nights when, to staunch his tears, he had steeled himself against the knowledge. Had fooled himself into believing that she wasn't dead. How could she be dead? She was so alive to him. So alive in him.

'Come, my boy.'

They walked in single file, picking their way through gravestones that were big and old and crumbled with moss and hard carved words until they had passed through into the newer section where everything was scaled down. There were plastic flowers, now, in dirty stone vases with wilting half-dead real ones. And finally, and most frightening of all, there were the newly planted graves with makeshift crosses over uneven humps of earth. If his mother was under one of those suffocating mounds, he would not be able to bear it.

Stopping, he averted his gaze.

'It's all right, Milton,' he heard his father say. 'I have done her proud.'

Her grave was separated from all the rest. It was in its own section in front of a long, low hedge. His father had told the truth – he had gone to town like only his father could. There was a high, fat stone, so white that if Milton hadn't known better he would have thought it was plaster of Paris, not stone. But he did know better.

Vanessa was hanging back – so was his father – both of them expecting Milton to make the first move. When he took one small forward step, he could feel their gaze hot on his back. Trying to blot out this awareness which made him too self-conscious, he read the carved words, *Here lies Evelyn,* he read. *Beloved wife of Emil, devoted mother of Milton and Vanessa. Killed by a runaway train.* And underneath, her dates, *1928–1957.*

He read the epitaph again. 'Killed by a runaway train.' His face contorting with the pain of it. 'By a runaway train.' He said it out loud, screwing his expression tight. And then something that he hadn't meant to happen, and didn't want, happened. A strange sensation rising, like a bubble, up his throat. Unstoppable, although he did try to stop it by swallowing. Without effect. Up it burst – an inexcusable giggle – out into the air. 'Killed by a runaway train.' His own shock at this appalling flouting of respect made him . . . it made him laugh out loud, this eruption seeming to feed itself so that the more he laughed, and the more ashamed he was of laughing, the louder he laughed.

He looked to his father. His father would stop him.

He saw how his father's brown skin had turned a furious red, and he saw how his father's full lips had tightened into one thin, hard line, his neck sinews bulging, all of these such obvious signs of his father's rage that, instead of bringing an end to Milton's unacceptable behaviour, they provoked him to laugh more. It wasn't funny but still he laughed, hating this awful, boyish, fat self that was standing in front of his mother's grave and laughing. He looked at Vanessa.

She smiled, her smile widening and then – despite his unspoken *please no, please don't, not you as well* – she, too, began to laugh. She was laughing because he was. Because it meant she was forgiven. Because she followed him in everything.

He saw his father swallowing. Saw his father's eyes filling. Don't cry, the laughing Milton thought: hit me and stop me laughing.

His father threw back his head and then he, too, began to laugh.

Now with each of them fuelling the other's hilarity, there was no stopping them. How awful, and yet at the same time it was as if they had been restored miraculously to a time (before Milton had been sent away and before his mother's death) when they would be joined together in a conspiracy of improper behaviour of which his mother would have always disapproved. Foreigners, all, too green to know that no Englishman would think of carving anything as inappropriate as 'Killed by a runaway train' on a gravestone, never mind on one that was so much more extravagant, in size and opulence, than its fellows. And so they laughed. At themselves and who they were and who other people thought they were but laughing also just for the sake of laughing and for the togetherness it brought them. Laughing so long and so loud that Milton must hold his stomach, laughter seizing hold of him so hard that he kept on long after his father and his sister had stopped, tears rolling down his cheeks as if they would never stop. His body hiccuping with something that wasn't funny, until at long last it abated, a series of sobs issuing out.

Now he felt his father's arm on his shoulder and heard his father's gentle, 'Come on, my boy.'

That's all it took. His laughter staunched, he felt himself deflate. He stood, so small. So full of loss.

He took the handkerchief his father held out and used it to wipe a face that was as wet as if he had been crying. He didn't know where to put himself. Or where to look.

His father seemed to know. 'Here.' He held out a rose. 'They were her favourite. Red roses in particular.'

With the rose gently cosseted, Milton went up to the gravestone. He stood for a moment in front of her but looking up. He saw that the sky was now an unmarked clear light blue – as if his laughter had chased away the clouds. He lowered his head. Silently he spoke to her.

He told her how much he missed her and how badly he wanted her back. And after that he thought-told her how dreadful everything had been since she had gone. Sniffing and crying and thinking his thoughts to her until at last there was nothing left to say.

Now the realisation came that she, who could no longer see, must not see him with his face so full of snot. He wiped his arm across, clearing it away.

What next?

He went closer and laid down the rose, thought-saying one word, 'goodbye', although he didn't really mean good-bye. For always, for all eternity, he would keep her with him. He stepped back. And stood, calm as he had not been calm since hearing of her death.

He was vaguely conscious of his father nudging Vanessa and, in response, of Vanessa moving, head bowed, to the grave. She didn't look entirely serious. She was probably counting to herself, as she often did. Standing in imitation of what he had seemed to do, without knowing that he had spoken to his mother. Had spoken out the truth. So that when his father put a hand on Milton's head and said, quietly, 'Well done', he thought it also to himself: Yes, he thought, it was done well.

1963

Six years later

To the sixteen-year-old Milton had fallen the responsibility of a number of different jobs. He was doorkeeper designate, finance director and early warning, each of them essential to the success of the enterprise. He was also a major investor (he had financed the half-term trip to Soho to buy the *Playboys*) and self-designated observer of hilarious behaviour.

Standing guard outside the bicycle shed and holding the tin whose float had now been augmented by, on his last reckoning, more than three pounds and fifteen shillings, he watched boys making their way over. They came, as per strict instructions, one by one. Some sidled as if, by turning sideways, they would not be seen. Ditto for those who crouched down as they scurried across the lawn. They were all so funny in their furtiveness. He chortled to himself even though he was careful to hide away this amusement before they got to him.

The most entertaining of all were the ones who walked across the lawn in a haughty 'I-am-not-going-to-a-masturbatorium' kind of way but rather 'I'm-taking-a-lordly-stroll-through-the-grounds'. As if, Milton thought, anybody ever bothered strolling to the bicycle sheds.

These Arrogants were the ones Milton liked infuriating. They were such easy targets. All he had to do was take ages to write up their slips and give out their change. No matter their insults – these were the sign of just how much they were salivating at what awaited them in the shed. He took an extra sixpence off them as well, making them pay for the condescending manner in which they said things like 'Just old copies of *Titbits*, I assume?' And if they were extra specially patronising – well, these he gulled into taking up his special 'two for half a crown' offer which, rather than have him think they couldn't come twice, they always paid.

Having got their money, he would open the door for them. In so doing, he would also check, in a proprietorial manner, that everything was in order. That each new entrant had been found a place by one of the bicycle racks and that they'd got hold of their magazine of choice. Each time he did this, he was met by the same mesmerising sight. Boys standing trousers unbuttoned (and on occasions, down), tongues panting, hands pumping, pictures of big-breasted women fluttering in agitation as officers patrolled the ranks to make sure that the magazines did not get dirty. Having looked and seen, yes, everything was in order, Milton would then close the door in preparation for the next new arrival. And so it had gone for the last half-hour.

Now at last the trickle of newcomers had died away. If his masturbatorium comrades kept their promise, one of them should soon be relieving him of his post. They should, in fact, have come out some ten minutes ago. He wondered what was keeping them.

Since, as an extra security precaution, he was only meant

to open the door in the case of a new customer, he put an ear to it. He heard a sound. Loud it was, louder than could issue from out of the mouth of any boy. Pressing his ear harder into wood, he thought it sounded like a steam train starting up. He came away from the door and, in case a build-up of wax had him hearing things, briskly rubbed the inside of his ears. As he did, he happened to catch sight of one of the masters who, emerging behind a far bush, began to amble across the lawn. The master had the look of someone out for a casual stroll but if the noise in the shed got any louder he would be bound to hear and, having heard, to investigate. This being a potential emergency of which he must dispose, Milton opened the door.

All he had intended doing was to order a general piping down. What he saw, however, was so astonishing it both silenced and immobilised him. When last he had looked in, the boys had been busy in their separate racks. No longer. Milton's first thought was that some unwieldy beast had gate-crashed the bicycle shed and spread its tentacles, absorbing all, but soon it dawned on him that the beast actually was boys joined up in one snaking line and masturbating in tandem. Magazines discarded as, mouths slack, masturbatorium officers and customers combined, big boys and little ones, all caught up in a single pooled rhythm of pumping arms, the grunted sound swelling, air taken in and air expelled and something deeper, the beast moving to its climax, and Milton too startled to even call out a warning although later he thought he must have said something, he must have, to try and warn them. But if he did, it was too late.

'What on earth?' That outraged adult master's voice was enough to break the beast. Pandemonium as it fractured into pieces that turned into individually panicked boys scrabbling one on top of the other, limbs flailing, arms punching, bicycles crashing, planks bashed through, backsides disappearing into makeshift holes, such an incredible imbroglio, such a rumpus, a dance of panic choreographed to the master's blasting on a whistle, so that Milton, standing open mouthed, couldn't help it: he laughed.

His laughter is what dropped him in it. That, and his failure to rid himself of the money. As a mass of half-dressed participants pushed frantically through the door, both Milton and master were swept aside. Milton, who had never even joined the beast, didn't feel so urgent. In keeping his grip on the tin, he didn't see the master reaching out and so by the time the master had caught hold of him with one hand – and with the other, the unfortunate Adams who'd been sidelined in the crush – all the rest of the boys had fled.

The forced marching in of Milton and Adams. Not a single face at the window. Not a boy in sight when they got in. Milton nevertheless knew that they would all be there, crouched down, eyes peeking over sills, and he also knew they would be present on the landings pressed against the walls, watching and waiting and vanishing as he and Adams were hauled through what had taken on the appearance of an abandoned building.

'Wait.' The master tapped on the Head's door, and hearing an impatient 'Come,' took the tin from Milton before going in.

Silence. The whole school holding its breath and Milton at the centre of the storm.

Although there were chairs outside the study, neither he nor Adams dared to sit. They stood there, dwarfed by the oak panelling and enfolded in that awful silence so uncharacteristic of the daytime school when chatting, talking, fidgeting, farting boys usually filled every crevice. Standing, Milton could feel, and also hear, the hard beating of his heart. But gradually, as time passed and the master did not reappear, he began to feel calmer.

So many boys had been involved in the venture, they couldn't punish them all. There was therefore no need to be troubled by his possible fate. In fact, remembering that vision of a mass of masturbating manhood, he couldn't stop himself from smiling. He looked to Adams, meaning to share the joke.

Adams's eyes were firmly downward fixed. To break the tension, Milton said, 'Like waiting for the firing squad.'

Adams gave no sign that he had heard. He was white faced, his fists clenched and his jaw juddering. The grapevine had it that his father was a martinet which, Milton thought, explained this terror. 'Chin up,' Milton said. 'They can't blame it all on us,' and then he couldn't help jumping, along with Adams, as the bell for prep sounded out.

A roar of noise to break the silence, drumming feet against wooden floors, and prefects shouting for the boys to slow down and then the sequential slamming of doors.

Silence again and Adams even whiter.

'They're trying to wear us down,' Milton said. 'But you know the drill. Name, rank and serial number.'

Adams's whispered 'Yes' in reply was so soft Milton might have imagined it.

No time to check. The door had opened. The end of waiting. Fear rising but, it being easier to get a beating over than to wait in contemplation of one, and to help stir Adams into courage, Milton stepped up.

The master placed an outstretched hand, flat, against his forehead. 'Where do you think you're going, Reymundo?'

'I was . . . I was . . .'

'Are you deaf, boy? Did you not hear the bell for prep?'

'Yes sir, I did.'

'Well then what are you waiting for? Get along now. We'll deal with you later.'

As they were marched, side by side, into the prep room Milton whispered to Adams, 'So they're going to make us sweat.'

'Don't you think you've done enough damage for one day?' the master said, which question earned Milton one of Adams's furious looks as Adams stalked over to his desk.

Milton knew why Adams was cross and he knew that Adams was right, his own smart-alec tongue always did have a tendency to run away with itself. He would, he decided, keep it on tight hold when they were with the Head. He opened his book. Like Adams he was scared – this he was man enough to admit – but, unlike Adams, he was proud of being so much the centre of attention, something that, since he wasn't much good at sport, didn't often happen. Later, he thought, after lights out, he and Adams would show off their wounds to widespread admiration for their heroic silence.

'Not got any prep to do, Reymundo?'

He picked up his pen. To start, he chose his Latin prep. He liked Latin. It was neat, logical and ordered and, unlike his untidy and inaccurate stabs at spelling English words, he always got the Latin ones right.

The piece they had been given was fittingly military. He parsed each sentence, separating participles from ablative absolutes and conjugating verbs to check he'd got it right, and as he worked his way down the piece, gradually he grew calmer. So involved did he become in his work, in fact, that the first he knew that they'd called for Adams was when he heard the reluctant scrape of Adams's chair.

Poor Adams, the stoop of him and his haltingly slow walk to the door showed how terrified he was. And it was especially scary, Milton thought, if they were going to be picked off one by one, a thought he must soon discard because, having shot a silent question to the boy in the next door desk, he got an exaggeratedly mouthed, 'his father' in return. Which was followed by, in case Milton hadn't understood, the boy holding his fist up to his ear to show that Adams had gone to speak to his father on the telephone.

Adams was gone an age. Must mean they were taking the whole affair awfully seriously. Expecting imminently to be summoned to the phone to speak to his own father, Milton got into an awful mess with his Latin and with an army that now seemed to be marching backwards, which he wasn't sure was the same thing as retreating. He was so busy looking at the door, anyway, that he kept losing his place on the page.

At last the door opened to readmit an Adams who had the

look of somebody straight from a most terrific scolding. His head hung down but not far enough to hide how red his eyes were and how smeared his skin. Milton couldn't imagine that, when his turn came, his father would be anywhere near that ferocious. The opposite, in fact. From Emil there was more danger of mockery than reproof.

Not that his father did phone. Perhaps he had just laughed them off, or perhaps they hadn't yet got hold of him. Whichever it was, although Adams remained downcast and isolated from company, Milton soon began to enjoy his newfound notoriety. As he tucked into supper with his usual gusto, he was conscious of how he had become the centre of attention, the focal point of whispered conversations and nodding heads, of respectful silences and strained half-smiles. And yes, he was also conscious of the imminent dressing-down and the inevitable caning, but if he didn't think too much about it, he would get by.

They didn't call them after supper. Must have decided to make them sweat. It bothered Milton, but not overly. After lights out, he even lay happily in bed, proud of being the target of darkened whisperings and flittings about. Not that anybody came near him although, in circling him, they muttered loud enough for him to hear, 'don't tell, don't tell', until he went to sleep dimly thinking they must know that they were safe, he would take his punishment like a man and never tell. Name, he vaguely thought, rank and serial number.

He drifted into dreaming about ranks of boys, and smiling women, lips parted, teeth teasing tongues and a voice saying, 'Name, Rank and Serial Number,' the dream gradually turning to confusion that stretched on, a strange beast transformed into a machine that began to chase him and he, even knowing he was dreaming, was unable to get away and so he ran the whole night through until at last, mercifully, he was wrenched from sleep by a hand that roughly shook him as a voice said, gratingly, in his ear, 'Get up and go and wash and dress. You're wanted by the Head.'

As his son was preparing to face his headmaster Emil, with half an ear open to Vanessa's chatter, sorted through the post that the housekeeper had just brought to the breakfast table. He separated the envelopes into two piles – those to be taken to the office and those to be left for consideration at home.

The batch was almost perfectly predictable: in all cases, bar one, he could guess who they were from. He picked up the exception. It was a folded blue airmail letter and it was postmarked Ceylon. The ungainly block capitals of his name and address seemed familiar. He turned the envelope over – no return address – and as it came full circle, it dawned on him why he recognised the handwriting.

It was Evelyn's writing. This letter was from her.

The shock he felt was physical. First a kick of adrenalin, and in its wake a high fluttering of exhilaration at finally having heard from her, both replaced by a heavy jolt that seemed to knock the air from him.

She was alive.

It was six years since she had disappeared. Six years since, in desperation, he had fed his children that awful lie that she was dead. Six long years in which he had never stopped thinking about her, or wondering where she was. Six years when, although the pain of her defection had not faded, at least he had begun to think he had got away with the charade he had enacted for his children's sake.

This letter was the sign that he had not.

It was as if a bomb had blasted him back to the moment when, incarcerated in the orchid house, he had stopped himself from calling out to her. His ears were ringing. So many different thoughts tangling so wildly they created a clotted panic that blocked out any thought.

'Daddy?'

Vanessa was looking at him oddly. He must have made some kind of noise. He pocketed the letter. 'Get moving,' saying this brusquely, adding, 'we're going to be late,' the sight of her, so clearly wounded by his tone, provoking him to a further, 'Why do I always have to chivvy you?' in a voice that was also uncharacteristically harsh.

Vanessa scurried off. Thirteen years old and still such a sensitive child. He'd most likely made her cry. He ought to go after her. But what could he say that might explain his inexplicable behaviour?

As they were about to leave, he reached for her hat. His aim was to put it on cock-eyed, as he always did. But she snatched it away from him, ramming it down firmly before, a furious little hurricane, she stormed out of the house.

She didn't say a word on the way to school. Neither did he. He couldn't think of anything to say. When they got to school she had the door open almost before he'd even stopped the car. Hurtling out, she began to walk away.

He rolled down the window. 'Vanessa.'

She turned, angry, but with hope.

What could he say?

He couldn't tell her, baldly, that her mother was alive. Not now, like this, after all this time, and not in such a public place. But if he couldn't tell her the truth, he was equally disinclined to pile on another lie. So all he said was, 'Have an enjoyable day,' wincing at his own false cheer in response to which she nodded, angrily, before pushing through the gates.

Why had Evelyn written? Why? Now, after all this time?

Six years ago he had waited to hear from her. Then each ring of the telephone had brought a surge of hope, as each knocking on the door had also done. The rage that had infected him in the orchid house had worn away: if she had got in touch with him then he would have taken her back. And if she hadn't wanted to come back, if she had asked him for a settlement or access to the children, he would have – he was almost positive – he would have agreed to both.

She hadn't bothered ringing. Or visiting. Or writing.

Now, a full six years later, the sequence of his remembered emotions came back. First off, his fury at what she had done. No, not so much at that. What most had angered him was her singular refusal to understand what it was she had done. After a few weeks, however, when still there had been no word, that image of her desolated retreat from the orchid house started reverberating and he had begun to worry that something terrible had happened to her. He had grown increasingly anxious, so much so that he had swallowed his pride and asked Charles where she was, but Charles had either lied or genuinely had not known anything, and neither had her sister. The only clue Emil managed to glean from these humiliating interviews was Charles's offhand mention of a boarding-house somewhere in the vicinity of Cannon Street station.

Then it was that he had heard about the Lewisham crash. He had leapt to the conclusion – it was the only possible explanation – that she must have been on that fated train from Cannon Street. The knock on the door he then expected was the police come to inform him that his wife was dead. Except there was no knock. Gradually, and as the names of the dead were made public, he grew increasingly convinced that she could not have been on that train. That she was not dead, only disappeared. And by her own volition.

Still, he had waited.

To hold off the children, he told them that their mother, a victim of the flu sweeping Britain, had gone to recuperate, and would soon be back. But when they kept asking for her and when still he received no word, it dawned on him that she might never get in touch. His anger had come again then, and worse. That she could walk out on her children! And that she could also walk out on their ten years of marriage without so much as a backward glance, well that told him that she didn't love them, or him, as they and he (still) loved her. She never had loved him. Had married him for his money and her passage from Ceylon. And to think it was for this mercenary woman that he had quarrelled with his family and burned his boats to travel to a hostile land.

And now. The letter fluttered in his trembling hand, the only visible sign that the hole he had dug and filled with lies was waiting to receive him. He wanted to tear it up while simultaneously wanting to know what she had written. He used his paperknife to slit it open.

Dear Emil, he read.

Dear Emil! He flicked the letter away. Stared at the far corner of his desk where it landed, imagining the satisfaction to be gained from tearing it up unread.

He stretched across and smoothed it out again.

Dear Emil ~~It's~~ has been a long time

After the high point of the greeting, the letter was a mess. A muddled clutter of sentences crossed out and spelling mistakes out of which a series of self-pitying excuses struggled. The story he gleaned – what irony – of an Evelyn on the brink of suicide, saved by her last-minute decision not to take the train that ended up in the Lewisham crash. This, she wrote (underscored, crossed out and rewritten) she had taken as a sign that she should not kill herself. So she had sold some jewellery and used the money to fund her passage to Ceylon where her old ayah Minrada had helped her put the pieces of who she was (she actually wrote *who I am* as if all those previous years she had never been who she really was) back together. That was it, except. Oh yes, she missed the children and that now she was ~~(able to in a state)~~ back together she wanted to be put back in touch with them.

That was all. The bare bones of an explanation and nothing more. No regret at what she'd done, nor protestation of (former) love. Just bathos at her own predicament.

The relief Emil had felt at finding her alive was replaced by one – *What?* – hammering question – *what am I going to do?*

Of all the terrible deceptions of which man is capable, the worst, he thought, is self-deception. He had told himself a lie and the lie was this: that he had killed Evelyn off for his children's sake. Much easier, he had thought, that they think of her as dead rather than find out how he had sent her away and, more importantly, how easily she had gone. But now to tell them this truth was simultaneously to let them know that he had lied and was implicated in her disappearance.

He couldn't do it. Look at how angry Vanessa had got that morning, and only because he had lost attention during breakfast. As for Milton, his response to the news of his mother's death was burned in Emil's memory. That awful and unending refrain *I don't believe you, I don't believe you* filling the space, *I don't believe you* resounding as Emil had walked out of that cursed school and down the steps and into the car *I don't believe you* and all the way home and after as well, *I don't believe you, I don't believe you,* through Emil's waking, and his sleeping hours, for months. *I don't believe you* – and Emil knowing that Milton was right and that he was not to be believed.

Such an easy lie, born out of anger and desperation. With the Lewisham train crash in mind, he'd told them that, weak from flu, she had accidentally fallen on to a railway line. He could get away with it – he was estranged from Charles and from Margaret while Yuri, who must have seen the lie for what it was, was friend enough to keep his opinions to himself. But then, having let loose this lie, Emil was led on to another. The distraught Milton having insisted on seeing a grave, Emil had to have a fake one built. The worst lie told for the best of reasons, to calm Milton down. To settle him. And it had worked.

How could Emil now admit to what he had done? And if he did, well, how would that help them?

To discover they'd been betrayed by both their parents would be devastating. He would risk losing them as surely as he had lost his wife.

He could not tell them. Not when Milton had just climbed out of the long period of isolation into which the loss of his mother had sunk him and was about to sit his O levels. Not now, at this moment. Later, maybe. When they were older, stronger, better able to understand.

In the meantime he must stop them from inadvertently finding out.

Now at last, Emil's confidence reasserted itself. He phoned through to reception to cancel his appointments and put his calls on hold. He locked his door, tore her letter into tiny pieces, put the pieces into an ashtray and set fire to them, watching as they disintegrated.

As soon as that was done, there came a further thought – what would happen if she wrote again? And if she wrote directly to the children? What then?

He phoned a carpenter and issued instructions, after which he placed a call to his housekeeper to tell her of the imminent arrival of the carpenter who would be building a lockable box to hold his post. Then he picked up the receiver, intending to ring the school and tell them that a disturbed relative (of which he knew they thought he must possess many) was causing disruption, and so as to protect Milton, who was anyway, as they already knew, delicate, any post should be sent in the first instance to his father.

'Get me Milton's school,' he said.

'Ooh that's funny' – funny? – 'Mr Reymundo,' he heard his secretary saying, 'the school has just rung for you.'

In only a few months Milton would have left the dormitory. That glorious privilege – your own room, your own corridor, your own autonomy – that every boy in his form was eagerly awaiting. All the indignities of the lower school reversed. Their chance to sneer at and scorn the younger boys, or else, with magnanimity, to condescend to them. Long trousers in the place of shorts, high boys' voices settling to the serious gruff tones of men who would leave, two years later, with qualifications and cups and velvet school caps and photographs, all of which they would be sure to keep for the rest of their days, these props to remind them of this time, their best, when they had all been their younger, better selves.

For Milton, however, this will not now come to pass. Matron's presence in the doorway, and her grim expression, confirmed it. With a reproachful shake of her head, she indicated his empty trunk. 'Haven't you even started?'

'I was going to.' He despised the unreliable wavering of his voice.

'Do you need help?' Although her voice was harsh, she was trying to be kind.

The hardship he could take, the kindness he could not bear. So when he said 'I can do it,' he said it coldly to put her off.

Her pupils contracted, her pale green eyes hardening. 'Get a move on. You won't want to keep your father waiting.'

As the echo of Matron's stout clicking pumps grew gradually more distant, Milton's hope drained away. He never should let hope in. That lesson he learned when, after his mother's accident, he finally had been forced to acknowledge that there could be no reprieve from his loss. As now. There would be no reprieve from this expulsion.

He piled up his spare uniform, his shirts, trousers and ties, to which he added his cap, sports gear, outdoor shoes and his underwear, trying to garner up the lot. But things kept slipping out and so in the end he grabbed a chaotic armful and dumped it on the bed before going back for more.

Tears kept rolling down his cheeks. He swiped them furiously away. Thank heavens there was nobody around, it wouldn't do for them to catch him snivelling. They'd think it was because he couldn't take his punishment and in this they would be wrong. The tears were a result of an image of his mother that had come, unbidden, into his mind and of his younger self watching as she had folded and tucked and smoothed his things into this trunk. He remembered how carefully she had put in each layer so that, in her charge, the trunk had seemed almost bottomless, and fragrant as well, with the rose petals she always scattered through.

Banishing this memory, he leaned into the trunk. To make

room, he swept an arm across the row of books he had already packed – so roughly that his hand snagged a page and tore it. Bloody hell, things were bad enough already. He pulled out the book. It was *Tom Brown's Schooldays* and it wasn't that badly damaged. Easy enough to put it aside for subsequent repair.

But it was as if his hands had a life of their own. They tore wildly at the book (like those boys' hands), the Flashman inside him ripping out the pages. He was going to disembowel the bastard thing, along with this shitty, stubborn, spine. The notion fuelled his fury. He leaned into the task, tearing at the book. But no matter how hard he tore, the spine stayed as it was.

What a failure. Even at this simple task. As he threw the lot into the bin he knew that not only was he the weakling that they said he was, but also all the other things they called him. Like

Useless.

Stupid.

Weak.

Corrupt.

(And, although they never said this out loud, Black.)

From the start, they had disliked him. Now they had found a way to chuck him out.

No point in being fastidious. He grabbed up armfuls of clothes – he would not, could not, fold anything – and haphazardly shoved them in. It being better not to add vandalism of a book to his list of known offences, he emptied the contents of the bin into the trunk, layering in the torn pages (his rose petals) so that if Matron chose to do one of her inspections, she wouldn't spot them. He pushed down, forcing in the bulk.

They had been crystal clear in their instructions: all traces of him to be removed. Undoing the padlock, he opened the locker.

In it were his most personal possessions. He hauled everything out. His only photograph of his mother, her final letter to him, a scarf of hers that had accidentally infiltrated itself into his first trunk-load and that he'd never remembered to return, along with the other detritus – sweet wrappers and half-eaten boxes of Kipling cakes that Vanessa sent – of his life at school, that he then stuffed, chaotically, in the trunk.

He was left holding the padlock, which provoked another brief and unassailable snatch of memory. Him with his parents in Harrods. His mother, having ticked most items off her list, looking up to say, 'and a padlock please,' an incident that had stuck in his memory because of his father's, 'We pay them a king's ransom and they can't even supply a padlock?' that had made his mother blush, his father being too brash, too loud and altogether too insensitive to know better than to talk this way in front of a member of the Harrods staff.

Shoving the padlock into his pocket, he went to close the trunk. It was crammed tight. He had to sit on it to force down the lid. Just in time for Matron's return.

'Finished?'

He nodded.

'It will be waiting for you at the end of the drive.' Which is how he learned they wouldn't let him linger here until the other fellows had come back from games.

He'd already imagined the scene – them slick from showers, towels flicking out in play, loud voices, tired old insults exchanged and some of them, he was sure, some of them would want to come over and deliver their farewells.

'Come along, Milton. The Head is waiting.'

He had no option. He came along. Having walked slowly to the door, however, he found Matron standing in such a way as to block his exit. 'What's that in your pocket?'

He pulled out the lock.

She reached for it. 'I'll take that.' She wasn't expecting opposition. When he kept hold of one end she didn't at first realise that he had. Only when he pulled back, did she bother looking down. First at both their hands, fastened to the lock, and then up again at him. 'Hand it over.'

He shook his head. 'No.'

'Don't be silly, Milton.' Her face was red. 'The Head has already told you, all school property must remain at school.'

'But this is mine.'

'No it is not. The locks are all ours. We issue them at the start of year.'

'Now you do, but not when I first came.'

She didn't remember and she didn't believe him. She gave another tug. 'Do you want to be known as a thief?'

As well as a blackguard, he thought, which is how he would be described after he had gone.

'Do you?'

Of course he didn't want to be known as a thief but how the school knew him was no longer in his gift. And the fact remained, the lock was his. He said, loudly (he being, after all, his father's son), 'It's mine. I brought it with me.'

Like every other member of staff, Matron dearly loved to win. And she could have done. She was strong. She could have wrenched the lock from him. But she could also tell when a boy had reached the point of nothing left to lose and she knew the tussle could end in her loss of dignity. 'Not worth the trouble,' she muttered to herself and then, to him, 'Well if it's so important.' She wheeled away.

Her visible, defeated fury was his one, small victory.

Walking behind her, he watched the swaying of her broad bum, the origin of her nickname 'Horse-bottom'. These boys' designations, one for every member of staff, were handed down from year to year, a custom that always brought Milton joy, reinforcing, as it did, his sense of belonging. But now he had to remind himself he didn't belong at school.

'In you go.' Walking had brought her back to her control. Holding open the door, she even saluted his passing with one of her small, tight smiles.

That smile almost did for him. It made him vulnerable to a resurgence of hope. The headmaster, this hope assured him, is going to back down. It was almost as if he could hear their great, generous headmaster saying that he had decided expulsion was too drastic a punishment, before he ordered Milton over the chair to give him ten of the best.

First sight of the headmaster was enough to kill off hope. For the headmaster did not look dutifully pained, as was normal prior to the administration of corporal punishment. Rather he had on his severe I-have-made-up-my-mind expression which was accompanied by a low-voiced, 'Ah, Milton. A pity it has come to this.' A pause during which the headmaster looked at Milton as if it was Milton's turn to speak.

Other boys might boast of their time at school, speaking of accusations and confessions, retributions and repentances, but Milton was not like other boys. He held his tongue. The right decision; the headmaster's silence had been mere dramatic pause. Now he wheeled round and went over to the window, there to stand looking out.

'Unfortunate timing, I grant you.' His back was to Milton. 'A day school might be persuaded to take you on for A levels, but, since you will have failed to obtain a single O level, this is unlikely.' He said this musingly, as if it had been Milton's preference to enmesh them both in that prolonged agony of expectation, Milton lying awake for nights on end waiting for the hammer to fall until eventually the headmaster had decided to expel Milton late, but not late enough for him to sit his O levels. 'I am of the opinion,' the headmaster now continued, 'and I have shared this view with your father, that further schooling is unnecessary. I understand you anyway will be going into the family business. A tradition amongst you people, is it not?' With this last giving Milton a quick backward glance.

Milton held himself very still.

'Well, your father should be . . .' The headmaster was looking out. 'Ah yes. I think. Yes, is that his car?'

Knowing how scrupulously on time his father always was, Milton knew it must be his father's car. Which meant this was Milton's last chance. 'Sir?' he said.

No answer.

Again and louder. 'Sir.'

'Yes, boy.' The headmaster wheeled round. 'What is it?'

'What's going to happen to Adams?'

'To Adams?'

'Yes, sir. What's going to happen to him?'

'Is that any of your business, do you think?'

'No, sir. But I would like to know.'

The headmaster looked vaguely at Milton. As if he were a tiny thing and very far away. He's not going to tell me, Milton thought; this followed by another thought: if he doesn't, well then, I just won't go.

Perhaps this was all that was required – Milton's determination – to break the headmaster. Who anyway must know that an expellee, even one as friendless as Milton, would be bound to find out. 'Adams has been gated.'

Gated! 'For how long?'

'For a week.'

A week!

'It's a blot on his copy-book.'

'A week?'

'Yes. A week.'

'But sir . . .'

'We have passed the point of ifs and buts, Reymundo. Adams was led astray. It is, of course, reprehensible that he showed such little self-control – there is undoubtedly effort to be put in there – but this is effort that I am confident will be rewarded.'

'But sir . . .'

'Yes, Reymundo.' There was threat, now, in the headmaster's voice.

'It's not fair.'

'Fair?' Coming one, menacing step forward the headmaster also seemed to rise up, the better to tower over Milton.

'But it isn't, sir. Adams was equally involved. And so was—'

'Snitching on your fellows, are you?' Another threatening step. 'Only to be expected. From the outset there were different customs, different standards.'

Different customs . . . different standards. Those words striking Milton as he heard the headmaster's, 'I have bent over backwards to try and integrate you into our little community. Unwisely, as it now appears. One bad apple. That's all it takes. But I am ready to acknowledge my misjudgement, and to remedy it . . .'

By expelling me, Milton thought. And said, 'You've made me a scapegoat.'

The headmaster clapped his hands together. Twice and very loudly. 'Enough.' Three hard claps this time, palm slapping beefy palm, as if he meant that way to crush Milton. Except his clapping had only been his way of summoning Matron. 'Show out the boy,' he said.

What a dolt Milton was, and how slow. He should have known. From the start when Adams had been called out of prep. That was when the other boys would have guessed. Only Milton had failed to nurse even the vaguest of suspicions as to how very hot his goose was being cooked. To think he'd actually felt sorry for Adams being on the receiving end of such a scolding! And that night. Those hurried dartings from bed to bed and those almost imperceptible '. . . chin up . . . that's right, Reymundo. Don't tell, don't tell . . .' Well, even then he hadn't understood.

Five days, *don't tell, don't tell,* is what it took for him to realise that his father was right and fair play was only for the fair haired. They had banded up against him. Adams had bought his freedom by squealing on him and by getting all the rest to back him up, thus dropping Milton into the worst trouble a schoolboy could be dropped into – insurrection and on his own account. His fate was sealed. The axe had fallen. And he hadn't even realised.

There was usually somebody around even during lessons. A boy scurrying to the sanatorium, or a cleaner singing under her breath as she wiped down the picture frames, or a parental pair with their small child nervously in train. But today . . . Not a soul.

Had they emptied the place especially? They must have done. The driveway was similarly clear with only his father's Rolls at its very end. The gate was already open. They didn't want to waste a second in getting shot of him.

He could see his father supervising the hefting of the trunk into the boot and, after that, dispensing largesse. The crunch of gravel as Milton and Matron's paths crossed with the two gardeners who stepped off the path, one of them tipping his hat. 'Ma'am.' The boot of the car closed with a sharp click. Horse-bottom speeding up while, behind him, Milton knew, many eyes would be following his eviction.

He knew those boys. He'd lived amongst them long enough. Now that they'd got shot of him, they'd be pitying him. His fists clenched. Blood rose to his face. That they should dare! Those who had betrayed him. He would not give them the satisfaction of looking back. Them and their bastard compassionate looks that he had always strived valiantly to ignore. Their pity not enunciated but nevertheless clear, that he was not and never would be like them, this motherless brown boy who had so much to learn he never would catch up, though take his money, why don't we, because we pity him . . . rage rising to the surface as Matron said, 'Ah. Mr Reymundo. Here, in safe custody, is your boy.'

His father, who the boy in question knew would understand what he was feeling, for this is why his father always had loathed the school. Well now Milton would band together with this same father and wreak his own revenge. He'd tell his father what had happened, from the beginning until the end, and then his father would tell him what they would do about it. He would, he thought, looking up.

Risen fury draining as he saw that there was somebody in the car. He could hardly believe it. 'You brought Vanessa?'

'Yes. I thought you could do with the company.'

How could his father have thought that? How could he have brought Vanessa to witness Milton's humiliation? Vanessa who so admired him? How was he going to say, in front of her, how terrible he felt? He'd already lost his school. He couldn't also risk losing her admiration.

How heartless, Milton thought, hearing his father's tentative, 'Did I . . . did I do wrong, my boy?'

Two things wrong with that question. The first, that his father could be so clueless. And the second, that uncertainty in his father's voice. That unsure vulnerability. He needed his father strong, not looking away as he was doing now, as if to look Milton in the face was too much.

'I'm sorry, Milton.'

He didn't need his father sorry. He didn't want him so. 'It's fine, sir,' he said in response to which he stood witness to the hardening of his father's expression until, 'You can drop the sir,' his father said.

His father was right. Milton's school-days were over. He could drop the sir.

He pulled his door closed so roughly that even the great, big, solid monster of a car seemed to give a little shake.

'Good riddance to . . .' Emil began, his phrase cut short by Milton's tight-lipped, 'Don't.'

The boy was right, Emil thought, best not to make light of the expulsion. He nevertheless completed the phrase – *good riddance to bad rubbish* – to himself as he concentrated on leaving that blasted place.

The more distance he put between himself and it, the more weight seemed to lift off his shoulders. In fact, he thought, as he accelerated, the school had stood between him and Evelyn. No – it was worse than that. The school had stood as a symbol of their different approaches to life and as a sign that matters had got out of hand long before Evelyn had ever entangled herself with Charles.

One glance in the mirror showed him how far down Milton had slumped. If only he'd say something, Emil thought, give voice to his rage. Adjusting his mirror, Emil looked to the back where Vanessa also seemed to have folded in on herself. Such a sensitive girl, she knew that, in this circumstance, it was better for her to hold her tongue. Perhaps she had even seen, as Emil had, how Milton's face had crumpled at the sight of her. It often went like this, with Milton jealous of his sister and of the ease of her abilities.

A rare and glorious summer's day, the sun lighting up a

countryside awash with different shades of light green. Colours were so various here, Emil thought, and simultaneously tame. Not like Ceylon where the sun was wilder, and the green darker and more aggressive. And yet, the docility of this country and of its countrymen was deceptive. Behind the façade of good manners and low voices there lurked a viciousness. That's what the dreamer, Evelyn, had never understood.

Evelyn, Emil thought, who not only was alive but was also, ironically, in Ceylon. And, he reminded himself, wanting to make contact with her children. What was he going to do, he thought, as he heard Milton's abrasive, 'How did you find out?'

His heart thumping. 'Find out what?'

'That they were going to expel me.'

Slowly Emil let go of his breath. 'They phoned to tell me what you had done.'

'And what did you say?'

'I laughed.' Smiling at the memory before adding hastily, 'Not that I approve, my boy. But still, it showed a certain entrepreneurial get up and go.'

Milton, his face like thunder, grunted.

How odd, Emil thought, and not for the first time. Although he prided himself on his knowledge of human behaviour, when it came to his son he always seemed to get it wrong. Had done, really, from the outset. Or if not from the very outset, from that moment when the young Milton, having set foot in England, had shrunk away from his embrace. Now he said, 'Should I have fought to keep you there?' only to be met by his son's angry, 'Why are you asking me?'

Milton was right. He shouldn't be asking. He already knew the answer. The odds had been too heavily stacked against them – there never was a way to win. This had been Evelyn's blind spot: she had refused to face the fact that no matter how well she behaved or how much she swallowed her own preferences in favour of theirs, nothing would change. And if things wouldn't change for her how much less likely, once she was gone, that they would change for her son?

Sighing, Emil let the silence stretch. He wished he could have found a way to explain matters to Milton. Past effort, however, had taught him there would be no point even in trying.

Was it always like this? he wondered. Did different parents always get on better with different children? Perhaps it was. Perhaps there was something between mothers and their sons. Certainly there never had been any doubt in Emil's mind that, regardless of her apparent affection for Vanessa, Evelyn's heart-strings had been tied around her first-born.

'What am I going to do?' This suddenly from Milton.

Such self-indulgence in that question. It irritated Emil. Not that he didn't feel sorry for the boy and for what had happened. But the sooner Milton learned, as his mother never had, that self-pity would get you nowhere, the better. And so, 'You have a choice,' he said. 'The experience can either make you strong or it can defeat you.'

'My father the philosopher,' Milton jeered.

Before Emil could bark out a suitably sharp retort he heard Vanessa moving. She threw herself, in fact, from one side of the car to the other, there to sit and, via the mirror, direct such a fierce face at him that he was left in no doubt that he must not reply in kind to Milton's provocation.

276

Such a sweet girl. This was such a strain for her. He probably shouldn't have brought her with him but he'd felt he had to, to have them all in the same space while he worked out what he was going to do.

Depending on which child he was thinking about, he had swung this way and that. In Vanessa's case, for example, he knew that if he were to tell her that her mother was alive and that he had lied, she would be shocked. At the same time, and of this he was pretty confident, she would forgive him. Not so Milton.

From the outset when Milton's unbelieving voice had followed Emil all the way out of that cursed school, he had suspected that his son had guessed that everything was not exactly as he had been told, a suspicion that kept repeating although with decreasing intensity in the six years that had followed. And now Milton was adrift from the place that had anchored him. What would it do to him to find out that not only had his father lied, but his mother had readily abandoned him? It would be disastrous, Emil thought: he could not do it.

'You'll be learning the business,' he said. 'Starting at the bottom and working your way up. Don't worry, my boy,' he smiled, trying to display to Milton a confidence he didn't feel, 'you'll soon find a way to enjoy it.'

Milton concentrated his carefully acquired skills on flattening his hair. The trick was to interfere but not so much so as to ruin the geometric line. He paid special attention to the tailored edge around his ears that he mostly kept in trim himself. The bit just to one side of his left ear where he'd lost attention and too brutally hacked away had almost all grown out. In a few days it would be perfect and after that he might wheedle his father into coughing up for another go at the hairdresser's.

There. Much neater. He grazed a comb through, smiling at the effect just as there came a knock on the door and a 'Five minutes,' that set him back to scowling. 'Yippee,' he said, but softly so that his father wouldn't have been able to hear.

'I'm going after that.'

'Well, go,' Milton told the mirror. Not one of his most effective ripostes. No matter. His father wouldn't have been able to hear that either.

He leaned closer to the mirror, lasering his gaze on the pimple that overnight had appeared on the very apex of his chin.

'If you're not down by then,' he heard his father calling, 'I'll leave without you.'

'Leave, you cunt.' Saying this even more softly, Milton pinched the pimple between thumb and forefinger. He squeezed it, at first slowly and then harder and harder until – blast-off – glutinous pus squirted out, clean and straight, splatting against and smearing up the shining glass. The satisfaction was immense. Thinking there must be more to come, he squeezed again, this time overdoing it and so also squeezing out some blood.

'Milton!'

He tore off a piece of toilet paper and stuck it to his chin. That was one bonus of no longer being at school. Slippery Bronco would not have done.

'Come on.'

He stepped back from the mirror so as better to take in the buttoned-down, pointed collar of his shirt, the straight, narrow tie and the tailored lapels of his jacket, and then he quit the bathroom.

His father was waiting at the bottom of the stairs, the sight of Milton's slowly descending hand-made winkle-pickers (a battle over which, with Vanessa's help, Milton had won), causing him to frown.

'So at last, the perfumed rockster.'

'It's Rocker. And that's not what I am.'

'My mistake.' His father was smiling. 'You're a Mod, aren't you? Mod without a cause,' the condescension in his voice making Milton want to reach out and strike him dead.

'What's this?' His father pointed at Milton's chin. 'Have you been shaving?' Reaching over, he flicked off the toilet paper.

Although Milton couldn't help flinching, he did manage to hold back any further visible reaction.

No longer to give the old man the satisfaction of responding was a new resolution taken in furtherance of Milton's single-minded aim to concentrate all energy on saving his meagre salary (this week, he would definitely save some) until he had enough to buy a Vespa, and, more importantly, an exeat from the paternal home. He was resolute. He was going to leave. The day of his departure would surely come, and soon.

He could (in fact he often did) picture it. His father abject as he tried to stop Milton and Vanessa (she'd go with him, of course she would) as Milton, his manly dignity maintained and voice calm, would tell his father that his mind was made up and that he had to go, for what they both knew would be for ever. Oh, the satisfaction of it.

'Beautiful day.' This from his father as they walked towards the car, their feet crunching over gravel and Milton thinking, yes indeed, it would be a beautiful day. A bright, sunny day, his new dawn, with his father unshaven, in that pansy, paisley dressing gown, begging them to stay. And then Vanessa would slip her delicate hand into Milton's, driving home to their father how much he was about to lose, this knowledge dropping his father to his bony knees, his arms flailing, pathetically pleading as Milton kept his resolution. Nothing would distract him from his goal of ridding himself of this tyrant. 'Goodbye,' he'd say. 'Goodbye and good riddance.' In reply to which his father would say—

'Don't you ever stop daydreaming?'

Wrenched back into the present, Milton saw his father already in the car.

'Hurry up.'

Milton hated losing track like this. He felt his face heating up, his eyes smarting, both of which he likewise hated. He had to be on better guard and not let it happen again.

'Come on. Get in.'

I will, you fucker, he thought, and then, meekly, he got in.

'Here we are.' His father, who liked to state the obvious, parked in Golden Square. 'Coming?'

No answer. One of Milton's little victories. He never did answer and his father had actually stopped expecting him to. Now his well trained father exited the car. He was a quick learner, Milton would grant him that.

His eyes focused dead ahead, Milton waited out his father's merciful departure. But, this Tuesday, instead of carrying through with his usual dignified walking away act, his father came round to knock on Milton's window.

What did the bastard want? Still facing forward, Milton mouthed the question, What?

His father knocked again.

Fuck. Milton rolled down the window.

'I am going to take you with me, today,' his father said, 'to an important meeting.'

Oh hooray, Milton mouthed. (Funny how those fashionable expressions, those quirks of language that in school, he never felt entitled to use, would now trip effortlessly off his inaudible tongue.)

'Behave yourself. Listen and learn,' and then having, as always, said, 'Don't forget to lock your side,' his father walked away.

Thank the Lord. Milton twisted the mirror as he also always did, to watch his father's going.

That they never entered the office together was Milton's choice. A pitiable kind of pretence but since it made him feel less like a prisoner, one on which he continued to insist. In his most secret heart, as well, there was something about walking into the office on his own and being greeted by the receptionist, who Emil insisted should acknowledge all new arrivals, even the idiot Milton. When he did this, and not in Emil's presence, Milton felt how it would be to take control of such a fiefdom. Would feel his chest swelling, and would know that he could do it, and do it very well. Except of course, he couldn't. Not with his father breathing down his neck.

He could hear the retreating tap of his father's polished shoes (so small they were hardly men's). This morning, however, there was something about the sound that surprised him. Something about the slow pace of his father's retreating steps. He looked up, and yes, Emil was moving uncharacteristically slowly.

In Milton's imagination, his father was only ever fast and strong. Now this unexpected hint of vulnerability caught him by surprise. To rid himself of the discomfort, he dug into the storehouse of his father's insults, his father shouting at him to hurry up, to pull himself together, to be a man, to learn the business, all that accumulated belittlement summoned up to deny the longing that he might . . .

That he might do what?

. . . That he might roll down the window and call his father, no . . . not that. He wouldn't need to call . . . that his father would come back without Milton having to ask him to . . . Would come to do what?

To sit beside his son not in condemnation but in comfort, the two of them quiet in the knowledge of how much they both had lost. Together as his father and Vanessa seemed to be together. Together as Milton once had been with his mother. This is what, somewhere in his secret heart of hearts, he wished but . . .

Stop, he thought, saying it, 'Stop' out loud. 'Stop it.' None of what he dreamed would come to pass. Instead he would continue to sit here, in the car, as he did every day, and count to thirty-six. An arbitrary number made permanent by the fact that it was the number he had chosen.

'Unus.' Overcome by the pressing need to hear his own voice, he counted out loud. 'Duo. Tres.' Wiping his eyes. 'Quattuor, Quinque.' Better. 'Sex.' His chest relaxing. 'Septem.' His vision clearing, as he slowly ratcheted up the numbers. 'Octo.' And his voice, 'Novem', strengthening. 'Decem. Undecim.' Taking care not to hurry. 'Duodecim. Tredecim.' Each separate number savoured as he climbed up this special numbers ladder, his voice now full of vigour and of strength. 'Quattuordecim. Quindecim.' Slowly up all the way to 'triginta sex', thirty-six, when abruptly he stopped even though he could easily have gone on through sexaginta and nonaginta and all the way up to mille and beyond if he so desired. But thirty-six was the chosen number. Cut-off. He stepped out of the car. Pressed down the latch.

Don't forget to lock your side.' He pulled up the latch and then, with great pleasure, kicked shut the door that he had deliberately left unlocked.

It's not that he meant to sleep at work. It just happened.

If he had asked himself why it happened his knee jerk answer would have been that it was the monotony of the work. Deep down, however, he knew this wasn't true. He actually found the work quite interesting and, he thought, he could get to be good at it.

Perhaps the exhaustion was the stress of always being tied so closely to his father. To be so filled with a longing to be appreciated, and simultaneously fuelled by the desire never to express such longing, could be hugely tiring.

He wasn't anyway actually sleeping, just resting – taking a short break – when the door burst open.

'That busy, are you?' His father scowled. 'The pressure of work presumably being the reason you don't bother answering your telephone?'

What a hilarious card the *pater* was.

'Hurry up, boy. It's time to go.'

Go? Oh yes. He'd forgotten. His big treat. A meeting with an actual client. He got up.

His father was already half out the door. 'Rule number one, do not, no matter what the reason, ever be late.'

When they pulled up in the cul-de-sac off the Strand that was the dropping off point for the Savoy, Milton couldn't entirely damp down his excitement. He'd been here before, of course, to afternoon tea in the foyer after shopping expeditions with his mother, but never as a man in his own right. Now, as his father's Roller rolled up, a frock-coated doorman opened Milton's door while, on the other side, another flunkey was waiting for the keys.

The door half open and his bastard father's, 'Just a moment' stopped Milton from stepping out. He sat there trying to withstand a scrutiny that was hard and frowning before his father reached across to adjust Milton's (already straight) tie and to use his girly hand to smooth Milton's (immaculate) hair. 'Rule number two, always straighten up, smartly, for the clients. Well, you will just have to do.' His father blithely left the car, seeming not to notice that the real effect of this unnecessary tinkering was to transmit to the doorman that Milton was someone not to be respected so that as the doorman moved to shut Milton's door he let loose an insolent snigger.

Full of resentment, Milton followed his father in. Then

once again, and despite his resolution not to drop his guard, he felt himself relax. The genteel hum of conversation wafted through an oasis of polished, inlaid wood and soft, deep furnishings, giving him some of that sense of acceptance and of belonging he so badly craved. And now for once he was proud to be the son of a father who, by the murmurings of the name, Reymundo, was clearly so much a regular that another flunkey was already by his side and saying, 'Your guests are waiting for you, sir', before leading them down a plush corridor and into a private sitting room.

'Emil. How marvellous to see you.' A large man, who by his swarthy skin and long white robe Milton took to be an Arab, enveloped his little father in a long embrace. The man's colleague, another Arab, similarly dressed, hung back, only offering a cool handshake as the first man boomed, 'No Yuri today?' to which his father said, 'No, not today. I am honoured instead to introduce my son, Milton, whom I am inducting into our business.'

'Ah. A great pleasure.' It being Milton's turn to be clasped, he was held close and then at arm's length. He could smell sandalwood and dust, as the Arab looked him up and down before saying, 'What is the phrase the English use? Ah yes, he is a chip off the old block,' which told Milton, who knew that he took after his mother and not his father, all he needed to know about the sincerity of the demonstrative salutation he had just received, a thought confirmed when the Arab said, 'But surely he is rather young for the working life?'

Milton enjoyed the discomfort that flashed visibly (to him perhaps if not to the others) over Emil's expression, but he was also grateful when his father, instead of describing the mortification of his expulsion, said, 'Never too young to learn the family business,' in reply to which came the stranger's, 'That might be true although in our country we prefer our progeny to finish their schooling. But then we are on the fringes and only now finding our voices. For you, at the very centre of the empire, in this great metropolis, it is bound to be different. Welcome, Milton Reymundo. Please do not stand on ceremony, have a seat. Have a seat.'

Obeying the warmth of the voice and the expansive hand gestures that accompanied it, Milton let his bulk sink deep down into one of two plush sofas. Again a sense of rightness. This was his place and here he could be at home. But when he saw his father lowering himself gingerly to place himself at the sofa's edge, he redistributed his own weight until he, too, was leaning slightly forward.

'Your son's a keen learner.' The Arabs took possession of the sofa opposite. 'A source of pride, I am sure of it, to his father,' and then, at a rap on the door, the talking one issued out a regal, 'Come,' getting up to take possession of an ornate silver tray on which was a silver teapot and four small glasses. Having dismissed the waiter with an astonishingly large tip, he poured out the tea. He passed one glass to Milton and one to Emil.

Milton took a sip, the thick, sweet, mint liquid so surprisingly hot it scalded his lip. He couldn't help giving out an involuntary cry.

'I see your son is taken aback by our tea,' the speaker said. 'He has naturally been somewhat anglicised.'

'He came here when he was very young.'

'Ah of course he did and so he has adjusted to English customs. As you have, Mr Reymundo.'

There were some tiny, foil-wrapped chocolates on the tray. For eating. Milton stretched out a hand.

'Or shall we call you by your real name, Mr Raigambandara?'

Real name? Milton's hand froze in mid-air *Mr Rey what?* This had got to be a joke. He looked to his father.

Who was very far from laughing. He wasn't even cracking a smile. His face was, in fact, a mask so ferociously immobile that had Milton been on the receiving end of such an expression he would have thought himself in great peril. Not so the Arabs, who were sitting comfortably back, watching to see what would now unfold.

'You've been checking up on me,' Emil said.

'Of course we have, Mr Raigambandara. You came to us, along with your great friend, Yuri, who was already well known to us. You expect us to trust you with not inconsiderable amounts of our money. If you had been in our place, would you not also have checked?'

'Of course.' This confirmation accompanied by a slight, curt smile.

'So help us with the final part of the validation process, if you would be so kind, and explain this change of surname.'

His father looking straight ahead, waves of tension emanating out. 'Raigambandara,' he said, 'is my family name.' A glance at Milton, so fleeting Milton might have imagined it.

'Our family name. An ancient Sinhalese name and to be venerated.'

'But you decided to alter it once in England?'

'On my wife's suggestion.'

'She didn't like your name?'

'She liked it fine. She merely suggested that we change it so as to live more comfortably amongst the English.'

'How so?'

His father leaned forward. 'I come from a country rich in history,' he said. 'But my wife was right. What do the English care for Sinhalese, Tamil, Moor, Malay, Burgher or Christian? Nothing. To them we all fit one category – the category of foreigner. When they look at us,' his father's voice seemed to rise, 'all they see is the colour of our skin.'

Listening intently and watching his determined father, Milton was reminded of his father's pride and his arrogance that so used to upset the school authorities. For the first time Milton also sensed some of the humiliation that his father must have endured, a thought reinforced by his father's, 'And on the phone, no matter my accent, or my son's accent, when they are told our surname, all they hear is wog. That's why I agreed to the name change.'

A pause that stretched on. Much to Milton's relief. Thanks to it, he had time to make an inner adjustment to his understandings – an awareness that, in relation to the school, his father might not have been so much sinner as sinned against.

'And how does your son feel about this change?' The voice cut through Milton's confusion. 'Shall we hear what he thinks?'

That question crashing in. On Milton Reymundo. No, not Reymundo, another name, Ramabangandarmabum or something unpronounceable. And he hadn't been told.

Comprehension dawning, annihilating sympathy.

Something he had known without really knowing it: that his father was a liar. And now the lie was nailed. His father had lied about his name, not only to the world, but also to his children and in particular to his son, Milton, who wanted more than anything to get up and leave the room and find some lonely corner where he could work out what this also meant and think what other lies his father had up his sleeve. But this wasn't possible. The stranger's voice, although soft, was also insistent. 'So Milton, what do you think of this transformation from Sinhalese to hokey-pokey English?'

His father shifting. Turning. Eyes. Pleading. For what? Forgiveness that he had changed their name and never told? Or that other thing, a plea that Milton should not betray him? Milton's moment had come to . . . to tell them. What?

'Milton?'

It dawned on him that he was enjoying this moment of his starring role. Smiling, as his father could not – no matter how hard he clearly was trying – bring himself to smile. Opening his mouth to say, 'It's not hokey pokey. It's a deliberate bastardisation of the Latin form', oh what joy to hear the uncontrolled release of his father's breath, as he continued. 'Origins, *Rex mundi*. Meaning king of the world. To make it easier for the English, Reymundo. That's us – the kings of our own special world. The fabulous Reymundos. A joke to fool them and it works.' Saying the words and seeing relief washing over his father, and also how that talkative

Arab looked at his companion to be greeted by an almost imperceptible nod that Milton, utterly alert, registered as he then continued to register every other tiny detail. His father taking an over-large gulp of his tea, for example, and almost dropping the glass and the silent Arab leaning back, closing his eyes as the talker said, eagerly, as if he too was relieved, 'Good. And so to business,' and then what followed passed all in a blur.

No need for Milton's further attention. He was already familiar with all those technical terms (forward contracts for crude, and leverage, and hedging funds and flattening positions and more – margin deposits and collateral) that they were using as an excuse, he knew, for the real purpose of this meeting which had been to check that his father was who he said he was. Rather than focusing on this pretence of business talk Milton concentrated his thoughts on much more important things.

The first, that his father had changed their surname and never so confessed. And the second, that he, Milton the hopeless, Milton the expelled, Milton the clumsy had, by his quick response, saved his father's deal, a certainty that strengthened as the morning wore on and afterwards when they didn't head it the car, but went instead to the Grill to celebrate the successful conclusion of their meeting.

A first. Milton and his father sitting companionably together in a restaurant. His father talking to him as if he was really worth talking to. Milton could even show off to his father, revealing how much he had learned about the business, something that his father made a show of listening to although, as they were waiting for Milton's dessert, he could not hold himself back from enumerating another of his stupid rules. 'Rule number three – never betray the company's secrets. Or the family's. That's the most important rule. Back there in that room, you seemed to understand this without needing to dispute it.'

Something in his father's voice made Milton look across in time to see him reaching across the table.

'Time for you to take on increased responsibilities,' his father said as, alarmingly, he actually covered Milton's hand with his. 'And a new office – with its own window, don't you think?'

An odd sensation. A physical connection they usually avoided. As his father took hold of his hand Milton could feel how warm his father was and how soft his skin, a feeling that filled him with longing.

His father's voice even seemed to crack. 'Well done, my boy.'

Embarrassed, Milton used the arrival of a generous slab of gorgeously iced chocolate cake ('and yes, please, cream and plenty of it') to slip his hand from underneath his father's. The intensity with which he then stared down at his pudding was not because of greed but an attempt to buy his father some recovery time. And himself, he thought, as well – his father's unexpected display of sentimentality had made him feel uncomfortable.

A question rose, unbidden, to this throat: So are there any other lies I should know about? It was the sort of thing he had been saying to his father ever since his eviction from school, and now almost again. But no. With new-grown eyes, he saw the question as a childish attempt to re-erect the barriers.

Swallowing his words, he picked up his knife and fork and tucked in. He would bide his time, he thought. Would ask the question only when, and if, he needed to.

1972

It was a beautiful, dappled English summer's day as Milton, Yuri and Emil made their way into Highbury Fields. They were an idiosyncratic looking threesome – the Russian big, bearded and brash, the smaller, coffee-skinned Emil equally ebullient, and the darker, big-padded, quieter figure of Milton. That, in a previous age would have drawn the eye. But this was London, 1972. Rule Britannia was coming to an end. Already the world had begun to turn. British troops were in Northern Ireland, the North Vietnamese had walked out of the peace talks, the Americans had bombed Hanoi and Haiphong, a miners' strike had almost brought down a British government, Bangladesh had become its own country, Ceylon had been renamed Sri Lanka, Nixon had gone to China and his burglars to Watergate . . . and in such an age, this mismatch of three was no longer such a talking point. And besides, the fair they were heading into was thronged with people far more flamboyant than they.

As they walked down a path that led on to a medley of stalls and frenetically trampolining children, Yuri said, 'What's this one in aid of?' in reply to which came Emil's, 'I'm not entirely sure. Concerned ex-students for the Third

World? Urchins against enforced washing? You know what Vanessa's like. An easy target for any worthy cause,' the clear affection in his voice making clear that Vanessa's many involvements were almost as much a source of paternal pride as had been her recent award of a First in geography.

And there she was. She was standing with her back to them, engaged in earnest conversation with a young, bearded man. The sun was shining on her as it always seemed to do, her sheet of straight black hair swinging as, sensing their approach, she turned. At sight of them she broke into a smile that Milton knew was reflected and magnified by his, and those of his two companions'. What a relief, he thought, as she and her friend began to make their way over, that she had finished her degree and would soon be home.

'How wonderful that you came and all of you together. Pete this is . . .'

The man pushed past Milton and Emil to stand in front of Yuri at whom he now thrust out an eager hand. 'Mr Reymundo,' loudly and with confidence, 'I'm very pleased to meet you.'

A beat, Milton almost laughing at Yuri's frozen embarrassment and at Vanessa's, an awkward tableau that was broken by Emil who stepped in front of Yuri to intercept the outstretched hand. 'I'm glad to make your acquaintance, Peter.' Emil's enthusiasm was underlined by an oddly booming, 'Any friend of my daughter's being an immediate friend of mine,' before he let go of the hand and then, to override the man's stuttered, 'I'm . . . I'm . . . I didn't. I mean I didn't realise,' airily said, 'A natural mistake. We Reymundos specialise in the great assortment of our different skin tones,' at which point, to indicate that the mistake was forgotten and the conversation closed he turned his attention to his daughter. 'The fleecing of the capitalist being what you lot aspire to, Vanessa, we hereby present ourselves, cash in overlined pockets, to be fleeced.' Then linked his arm to hers to lead her deeper into the fair.

Following behind, Milton couldn't help thinking that, although the ease with which his ebullient father could eclipse him was sometimes undermining, there was also an attractive side to it. Now he saw Emil put this side on full, flamboyant display. He was game for anything and everything. He bought toffee apples and candyfloss by the bucketful and gave them away to passing children. He let himself be blindfolded to put Ghana on a map of Africa, something, unlike most of the others, he managed on his first attempt. And he insisted that Yuri throw water balloons at a Nixon look-alike in the stocks. He even made the three of them form a team for a tug-of-war.

With Vanessa laughingly refusing to take part, Emil lined the others up. Milton was to act as ballast at the back, Yuri to be the power in front, and the cunning Emil, 'as ever, the meat in the sandwich', between the two. Yuri was by now also in his element. He urged Emil and the protesting Milton into a rugby style huddle, the two older men plotting strategy as if this was one of their large-scale oil investments. And then, 'To battle,' Emil said as he lined them up again.

Their opponents – despite there being more of them – didn't stand a chance. The sheer, confident exuberance of team-Emil (or at least of two-thirds of it) might have been enough to cow the others but as well they had Yuri's hard muscled arms hauling the rope to the accompaniment of his roared out, 'Heave, two, three, heave two, three,' with Emil adding to the din 'The Volga boatman come to Highbury', after which he interspersed Yuri's heave, two, three with his own, 'Come on Castleton, come on Castleton.'

How well Emil and Yuri worked together and how much they liked to win. As the crowd of their spectators swelled, both raised their voices louder – *heave, two, Castleton* – town criers for attention which the crowd – *heave, two, Castleton* – took up, undermining the opposition and, more tellingly, making them laugh. When to plan they shifted gear, the combination of Emil's perfectly timed 'now', Milton's digging in of his feet and Yuri's last-stand heave had them wrenching the rope hard enough to shake off the other team. The abrupt effect of counterweight eradicated sent them flying. They came to land, one on top of the other, on the grass, limbs flailing and the members of the defeated team running over to congratulate and help them up. Milton, the last to rise, a little bruised by the impact of his elders, but laughing as he rose and catching Vanessa's also laughing face, the two of them joined in conspiratorial despair that, in this mêleé of the young, the poor and the politically convinced, Emil and Yuri had somehow managed to make themselves the centre of attention.

Later, having dropped Emil and Yuri back at Bishop's Avenue, Milton and Vanessa walked past the tennis courts in Parliament Hill.

Up the hill they went through a perfect summer's after-noon, the milky light of the waning day blued by a sky that was speckled by bright coloured kites. There were basic diamonds with cheery streamers hauled across the ground by hard-running children, lifting up here and there but mostly diving down to snarl clods of earth. High above these amateur efforts there flew intricate two-stringed box kites, their trajectories so complex and so apparently inde-pendent of any pull on earth that the gaze was drawn down to the place where their operators laboured, with fiercely concentrated and serious straight-armed move-ments, to impress.

There was something in the afternoon – or perhaps it was the tug-of-war – that had relaxed Milton and Vanessa. For a while they stood and watched the kites; and when eventually they did make a move, they did so without first needing to discuss it, silently making their way over to a bench.

Their view was now all the way down the hill, past a long stretch of grass and to the children's playground. With the waning sun still warm, Milton felt himself unwind. He sat vaguely conscious of the reaching up of high waver-ing cries, counterpoint to the lazy strumming of a guitar. He could see a picnic party in the final stages of dissolution, people sprawled on multi-coloured blankets and surrounded by discarded food containers and dirty paper plates and half-drunk bottles of wine. He wishfully wondered what it might be like to be part of such a group and able to laze away a whole summer's afternoon when Vanessa's, 'Did you hear what he was calling?' cut through this reverie.

'What?' He kept his gaze on the picnic party. 'You mean "come on Castleton?" Yep. I heard it.'

'It took me back to the sack race.'

His Waterloo. His moment to understand that, with a father like his, it was always going to be an uphill battle.

'Remember?'

'Yes. I remember.' How could she think he wouldn't have?

'Hearing it again made me realise how much things have changed,' she said. 'Then what all of them, Mummy included, wanted was for him to disappear. Or, if not disappear, at least to keep out of their way. These days, he only has to decide to lead a tug-of-war and everybody ends up telling me what a wonderful father I have.'

True enough, Milton thought, Vanessa did seem to have a wonderful father. Funny, that. He glanced across and saw her smiling, albeit slightly uncomfortably. How long, he thought, had it been since they had sat and talked together? Too long, he thought.

Today, and now, he would find the courage to broach the subject that had been preoccupying him for years, the thought making him so nervous that, to buy himself time he said, 'So was that guy your boyfriend?'

'Who? Pete?' Vanessa laughed. 'No, he's just a friend,' her amusement cut short by her, 'Do you really think a boyfriend of mine wouldn't know what colour my father was?'

In Vanessa's ferocious frown Milton could see some of that same determination that had pushed her to her first-class degree. She was waiting for his reply. (For his apology?) Which he didn't immediately give. Not because he was scared of her – she never had scared him – but because he was sifting through the variety of possible responses. The first, as well as the truest, would be if he were to say that honestly he didn't know what she might or might not have told her friends because, he being so much the darker, had never had to face this dilemma. But she was such a righteous girl. She would hate him saying this.

If this was to be the day when he could talk to her – and by this he meant really talk to her – then he needed her on his side. And so instead of being honest, he threw up his arms in a gesture of mock defeat. 'OK Germaine, climb off your high horse,' winking to take away the sting of his more heartfelt, 'It's not like we ever discuss our different roles – mine as idiot darkie, I mean, in contrast to your golden girl,' although even this turned out to be a step too far. 'Don't be silly, Milton,' came her immediate response. 'You know it's not like that.'

She looked so indignant and, simultaneously, so naïve. And there, in the confusion of this contradiction, she also looked funny. He almost laughed out loud. But instead, 'Sorry sis.' He turned his accent into unadulterated public school: 'It really was an absolutely spiffing day.'

She was accustomed to him playing the buffoon. She smiled.

Silence. Now, he thought, now's the time, and summoning up his courage he said 'Vanessa,' at which exact moment she said 'Milton.'

They laughed. 'You first.'

'No. Please.' Such a relief to be granted this respite. 'Youth before beauty.'

'Well.' Her eyes were shining. 'You know I applied to that course in Boston?'

He nodded. Couldn't speak because he already – his heart sinking – knew what was coming.

'I got in,' she said. 'And with a scholarship.'

'That's great.' He hoped she wouldn't notice his rictus grin and hoped again even more that when he said 'So are you going to go?' she would tell him, no.

She nodded.

'Does Dad know?'

Another nod that, like his question, was unnecessary. Of course she would have told their father first.

'How did he take it?'

'He was pleased. Yes, he was. Delighted. And . . . well you know.'

'Yes, I know,' he said. 'He'll miss you,' adding, at first for politeness sake, 'I will as well,' but then realising that it was true.

'Will you also mind . . . you know . . . being left with . . .' What a loyal daughter she was. She'd never dream of finishing the sentence. No need to, anyway: they both knew she was asking how he felt about being left with their father.

In her roundabout way she was asking his permission. More than anything, he wanted to withhold it. What came to him, in that moment, were the fantasies his younger self had used to weave all of which involved *his* leaving home. Don't go, is what he wanted to say to her. Don't go. Let me.

Her pleading eyes on him. 'No need to worry about me,'

he said. 'I always land on my feet. And if for some reason I end up somersaulting arse backwards and land on my head instead, well then,' rapping his knuckles on his head, three times, and in rapid succession, 'I've got plenty of insulation to keep me safe.'

A more acute observer might have been aware of the edge of desperation that he couldn't entirely conceal. Her answering smile showed just how secure with this jester brother she was.

Never mind. He did love her. He did want her to be happy. 'So when's the big day?'

'Next Monday.'

'Monday?' How long had she known? How long had their father known? 'So soon?'

'I'm sorry I didn't tell you. I had to work out whether I really wanted to go. And . . . and you know how it is.'

He did know. There was so much they each kept to themselves. So much they didn't say. A familial trait.

He looked down the hill. With Vanessa gone, he thought it was more than likely that he'd end up tied to his infuriating father for ever. And even if he wasn't – how unlikely it was that he would ever be mixing with the likes of that light-hearted picnicking crowd.

'So what's yours?'

'What's my what?'

'Your news. You were also going to tell me something.'

'Oh.' How could he? 'Mmmm . . . not sure I can remember.' It was a statement she effortlessly accepted, looking at her watch and then at the darkening sky. 'I should be going.'

'Yes,' He was already on his feet: 'Look at the time,' linking one of his arms to hers, this contact being the best way he could think of to hide his disappointment and his relief at this opportunity lost.

She'd be concentrating on packing up now and thinking about her new life. The last thing she would want to hear was this something that he had never even hinted at – that, try as he might, he'd never been able to shake off the feeling that there was something their father was hiding from them both.

Since his father was going to dine out with Yuri, Milton decided to stay in.

What a treat: the house all to himself. He made himself dinner. He wasn't a bad cook. Nothing fancy but he knew how to rustle up some chips to accompany a thick steak, medium rare. He ate in the kitchen, standing up because that's what he felt like doing, and after that, although he needn't have done, he washed and dried his dishes. There were a couple of honey baked apples in the fridge. Live today. Diet tomorrow. He ate them both with lashings of cream washed down by a can of Courage.

Humming happily, he went to the lounge and put on a record – some Bach that his father had left beside the record player. Then, growing bored with that, he replaced it with his much-loved *Sticky Fingers*. He turned up the music, opened wide the french windows, treating the night to his own loud rendition of 'Brown Sugar', swaggering up and down in passable imitation of Mick Jagger, bawling out the words, his empty beer can standing in for a mike.

As the track came to an end, he thought he saw a flash

of light at the bottom of the garden. Strange – his father's orchid house had fallen into disuse around the time his mother died. With the music still blaring, he took a step into the dark. But no – either he had imagined the light or it was a reflection from some passing car. He shivered – it was getting cold – and stepped back in. No longer in the mood for music, he took a couple more beers upstairs, his footsteps echoing in the quiet.

Such a large house for only two people. He wondered whether he'd be able to bear it. He had money enough: he knew that he could leave. And yet – could he leave his father on his own?

On sudden inspiration he went into Vanessa's room. Surveyed all that old, girlish detritus – dolls and cuddly toys and intricately drawn childish maps – that he was sure she would no longer want. Why not indeed? The more it rose in him, the more brilliant grew his idea of turning Vanessa's room into his sitting room. It was a solution that would keep him at home while giving privacy to both Reymundo men. Pity, with the idea so fresh, he couldn't immediately raise it. Never mind: he'd talk to his father first thing.

He thought about going out to celebrate this inspirational solution to his dilemma. But no – he had promised himself a night in, and a night in was what he would have. Downstairs he fetched more beer. Tried sitting in the sitting room but, having thought of turning Vanessa's room into his, this vast space no longer felt entirely comfortable.

In his bedroom, a reserve of cans to hand, he took down

the Escher book that had been his father's last birthday present to him. Smart of the old man – he really wasn't so bad – to have noticed how Escher fascinated his son. Now, popping open another beer and lying on his bed, Milton turned the pages of the book. Slowly he leafed through that succession of crazy, topsy turvy, mind-bending lithographs he loved so well. As he stared at fish that changed into birds and then changed back again, and at puppet figures marching floppily up and down sets of stairs that, standing on the same plane, were actually in parallel worlds, he thought – tomorrow. At breakfast. Then I'll put my plan to him.

His father, whose weekend routine was to breakfast promptly at eight, was already gone from the table. His head aching from the previous night's over-indulgence, Milton rang the small handbell. The housekeeper appeared – 'Good afternoon, Milton' – bringing a tray and placing it down.

He had meant to start his diet by taking only black coffee and perhaps a teaspoon or two of sugar for stabilisation of his electrolytes. But it was Sunday and all his favourite breakfast foods were there: mangoes and papaya and, even better, thick coconut-rich pol roti he could spread with hard, brown, treacle, jaggery of the *kithul* palm, or else he could add the jaggery to some slabs of kiri bath (his favourite of all time, white rice cooked with coconut cream). His stomach lurched, not from nausea, but because it was so empty. He absolutely had to eat. This, if he was going to be really responsible, was what he should do. Finally a plan. He'd partake of this late breakfast and skip lunch. He layered on the jaggery.

He was nearing the end of an immensely satisfying meal when, glancing up, he saw his father standing, silently, in the doorway. 'You're only taking breakfast now?' His father was immaculate as ever, even on a Sunday, in his suit.

He looked so angry that Milton almost laughed out loud. At his own foolishness. To think that he had planned to share with his father his solution to their living together in harmony. No point. His father would not agree. He was the boss. That was all he'd ever be.

How old was Emil? Forty-eight? Forty-nine? Something close. Almost fifty anyway. And yet, apart from a few tell-tale strands of grey in his otherwise smooth, black hair, he seemed hardly to have aged at all. It's like the picture of Dorian Gray, Milton thought, except his father didn't need a disintegrating portrait in an attic to keep himself fresh. He had Milton's sagging flesh for that.

No point in raising his idea. His father was far too set in his ways. And so persistent. 'Why do you have to eat so late?'

'Because I got up late.'

'Then why not wait for lunch?'

'I'm planning to skip lunch.'

'But your sister is coming.'

Fuck. How could he have forgotten? And not only that.

'It's her farewell meal.'

Double fuck, with a bucket of shit on top.

'She'll want you to be here.'

'Yes and I will be. I just won't eat.'

His father snorted. 'She's due at one. Best be dressed by then. And why not shave as well?'

His father always liked to push out the boat when Vanessa ate with them. Milton ladled spicy beetroot on to his plate, then colour-balanced it with a helping of lentils, a dollop of spiced prawns and, yes, why not, some chicken curry. Better anyway to start a diet at the beginning of the week.

He ate with his hand, an affectation he had copied from his father. He moulded a rice ball using it both as accompaniment and scoop for the different tastes, all the while pushing away from consciousness Vanessa's burbling on about the exciting computer-driven techniques in cartography, that, if truth be told (although he'd never dream of telling her) Milton found dreary beyond belief. Not so, apparently, his father.

'It's such a pleasure that you take your studies seriously,' Emil said, 'not like . . .' me, Milton thought; but he was wrong because his father actually finished the sentence with, 'these hippies who are always on the pots'.

'Not *on* the pots.' Milton dolloped some chicken on his plate. 'They smoke it. And it's pot, singular.'

'There speaks the expert.' This from Emil, mockingly, as if Milton was far too un-hip for drugs.

312

Moulding himself another ball of rice, Milton wondered what his father would say if he was to find out that he had actually experimented with quite a few, well at least a few, different drugs.

'You're too hard on the hippies.' This from Yuri. 'At least they're interested in the project of change.'

'They're hippies,' Emil said. 'They're not interested in changing anything. Only in dropping out.'

Milton mashed some curried prawns into his rice.

'You're wrong, my friend. The whole rationale behind the hippie movement is to question conventional ways of life. An admirable project.'

There, the gauntlet flung down. Now Emil would launch into a trenchant rebuttal of everything Yuri said, thereby needling Yuri into a predictable raising of the stakes. It was ever thus on Sundays, the two locking horns over what was happening in the world or what ought to be happening, the inevitable conclusion being that Yuri would accuse Emil of being an old reactionary and Emil would tell Yuri to go back to Russia, after which they would both laugh and slap each other on the back, secure in a friendship that went far beyond any business arrangement. And all the while Vanessa would continue to happily look on.

Except, Milton told himself, it would soon not be so. How strange that Vanessa, their father's favourite, was to put a continent between herself and her family just as their parents had once done.

He saw how she was smiling. Catching his gaze, she stretched her smile wider. In that moment his jealousy dropped away, its place taken by the love he felt for her. It wasn't her fault she had got things – not least an education – of which he had been deprived. Not her fault that, after their mother had died, she had been at home while he'd been made to stick it out at school. And besides . . . to have been the only child at home with a grief-stricken Emil must have had its drawbacks.

'You're beginning to sound like a die-hard old Trotskyite,' Emil was saying. 'And you know what they did to Trotsky.'

It occurred to Milton how odd it was that Emil, who never talked about their mother, had not found anyone to take her place. Stubborn bugger that he was, he was also charming and he was rich: somebody would have thought him a catch. But as far as Milton knew, his father hadn't even had a girl-friend since his mother's death. He'd had only Milton, who was an annoyance, Yuri, who was his closest friend, and Vanessa, whom he now had to let go.

In that moment, Milton was overcome by a feeling he normally resisted. He felt sorry for his father – for Emil's loneliness – and at the same time he felt a kind of pride in the old codger with his never-say-die attitude and his refusal to conform. Life had dealt Emil many blows. Yet there he still was, a successful businessman in a country that had tried to reject him. A proud peacock who wouldn't let anybody stop him from saying what he wanted to say, and doing what he wanted to do. Perhaps, Milton thought, perhaps Vanessa's going will be a blessing. It might provide the opportunity he and his father needed to make their peace. Perhaps with Vanessa happily in America, Milton and Emil could learn to like each other.

On their way back, separately, from lunch (which in Milton's case had been mostly liquid), father and son met in the street outside the office.

If Milton had known his father was going to be there, he'd have ducked out of sight until the path was clear. But having bought a bag of chips on his way back from the pub he was so busy eating that he didn't see his father until it was too late. By which time he had crumpled the empty bag and let it drop, looking up then to see his father's glowering gaze following the bag's descent.

'Whoops.' Milton picked up the greasy ball of paper. In one unexpectedly smooth and (if he said so himself) brilliantly aimed motion he tossed it straight-armed into the bin that stood on the other side of the pavement. 'Not bad, hey?' He winked at his father who, saying nothing, grimly opened the door.

Milton hoped his father would now just go, leaving him to follow. But his father held the door for him. Well OK. Milton breezed past. 'Good lunch?'

'Yes, thank you.' When his father went out to lunch, he always did dine well.

Employing some considerable concentration to stop himself from lurching, Milton made his way over to the lift. There he slammed his hand (OK, so he misjudged the force of his momentum and hit it a bit too hard) against the call button.

'I was going to walk up,' his father said.

'Good idea.' The lift bell gave a thoroughly satisfying ping before the metal doors slid open. 'See you up there, then.'

'Come with . . . ?'

'Me?' Milton was already halfway into the lift.

'Yes. Unless you think the climb will be too arduous?'

It was the kind of challenge his father always liked to issue. The kind that, instead of diminishing since Vanessa's going (as foolishly he had hoped it would), had increased. Milton must not rise to it. He told himself, *don't*, but the sight of his father grimly daring him was so galling that even as he repeated the thought, he was already out of the lift. 'Come on then.'

Pushing through the double doors, he began to climb the dingy back stairs. Not mincingly as his short-legged, dapper father was doing but in true Milton style, his bulky body leaning forward so with each lunge he could surmount not one, but two steps at a time, and so move far ahead of his father. A triumphant start although, with all that liquid sloshing around his innards, it was foolish too. The first flush of a speedy forward drive gave way to a slowing down that was accompanied by a growing sensation of dizziness.

Weren't you supposed to lower your head when you were dizzy? That's right. You were. Head down, he continued to power forward trying to ignore the sound of his own breathlessness as he listened to his father catching up. Must not let him win.

On did Milton forge, although less rapidly, trimming his stride to one step at a time. Since watching his moving feet was adding to the dizzy factor, he raised his head. One thing he stopped himself from doing was looking back. Even so, he was aware that his steadily moving father would soon draw abreast.

How childish to have risen to his father's provocation to a race that he could not win. Still, he was determined, if not to win, then at least to keep his dignity. If his father insisted on overtaking him, then let him work for it.

His chest was tight as he rounded a landing and began again to climb. He had lost count, couldn't remember how many more flights were to come. Perhaps, he thought, if he pretended to be tying his shoelaces, he could take a break while maintaining his dignity. And then – oh merciful release – he heard footsteps.

He looked up. Saw a stranger – bless his little white cotton socks – heading down. Milton was sweaty, his pores were probably leaking vinegar from the chips and he was, let's face it, rather large. It was, or at least it would look as if it was, thoughtfulness, and not the urgent need to take a breather, that had made him stop and tuck himself into the wall to let the stranger by. Without effect, the bloody man also stood aside. He was, in fact, hugging the wall so tight it was almost as if he was trying to melt into it. In the manner of his adherence to the wall, the stranger was almost comic but it meant that Milton must go on.

It occurred to him that he could still use the opportunity to wait for his laggard father. He stopped. His father, who might have suggested they walk up not as a contest but because there was something he wanted to talk to him about. Yes, that must be it. He looked down.

He was in time to see the stranger come abreast of the thin and always sweet-smelling Emil with whom he easily could have shared a step. But the stranger now mirrored what he had done with Milton, shrinking back against the wall and staying there until Emil had passed by.

So that's how matters stood – Milton and his father were dangerous animals to be avoided. In which case, to give satisfaction, they certainly must act the part. Milton turned to face the retreating stranger. He stretched out his arms, wide and loose, curving, head unnaturally bent and down, until he was almost concave. He formed his lips into a long stretched-out O out of which issued some guttural whoops – *'whoop, whoop, whoop'* – accompanied by a series of clumsy two-footed jumps.

What a great sound, and something about the way it echoed – *'whoop, whoop, whoop'* – against the walls of the enclosed stairwell made it even more satisfying. And what a glorious success. With one anxious backward glance, the stranger went scuttling down the stairs. He was in such a hurry to get away from the malevolent whooping that he tripped over his own feet and only by grabbing the balustrade saved himself from falling. Which sight provoked Milton to laughter as, caught up in the sheer exuberance of his ape dance, he continued to jump but now to growl, rather deliciously filling the air with a guttural *grrrrrrrr* . . . until, that is, his scowling father caught up with him.

'Enough.' So much for wanting to chat. His father having come abreast of Milton overtook him.

Milton's growls abruptly severed and with them the banishment of his victory. Just like his father to spoil his fun. And he had provoked Milton into walking up not to talk to him but only to remake the point on which he continually harped: that Milton should eat less and take more exercise.

Trudging in his father's poker-faced wake Milton had a stab at dispassionately putting his father's disapproval of his monkey act under the microscope. Understood: his father was old school. Direct retaliation had never been his style. Being a grand old reactionary, he wouldn't have noticed that times were changing and that it was the racists now who were on the back foot. Even if Milton had found a way to tell him this, his father, who always had been an egotistic bastard wouldn't have cared.

But would it hurt him to occasionally crack a smile?

His panting breath added to a weighted chest. Serve the bastard right if Milton had a heart attack.

He'd never, the thought surged, he had never asked for much. Certainly not for his father to show him that same strength of love that, when he happened merely to glance in Vanessa's direction, he could not hide. Would it have harmed him, though, if, instead of shrinking away at every point of contact he displayed only every now and then, you understand – some vague fondness for his son?

A flickering of images like a series of rapidly closing doors. His father's head turning – always – away. This same father who couldn't even bear looking at his son and hadn't been able to since (or was it before?) his mother's death. Yes,

Milton had been given increasing work responsibilities but this was because he was good at what he did. And yes, just as with all his other employees, his father always made sure to keep a civil tongue in his head when addressing Milton. But Emil wasn't only Milton's boss. He was his father. A father who didn't care enough to notice how hurtful was his lack of meaningful contact with his son. His drunken, fat, unfit oaf of a son, but nevertheless his son.

His father had now reached the top and opened the door. Milton hoped he would pass through, leaving it to slam behind. But his father didn't seem to feel even that measure of passion for his son. Correct as ever, he held open the door.

Milton was possessed by such a degree of anguish, his body overtaken by it, that it felt as if it might kill him. Only for a moment, though, before realisation dawned. It wasn't so much anguish as beer and chip fat toxically mixed. There was nothing he could do to hold back the gas and so it issued out in a juddering series of explosively pungent farts.

Well at least that got his father's attention. He turned. His fists, Milton saw, were clenched.

Go on, Milton thought. Say it.

His father's prim mouth opening.

Go on. Finally, let it be said.

'You're drunk.' Turning his back on Milton, his father walked away.

By mid-afternoon his anger at his father somehow having served to empty his stomach, Milton went to buy food. Back at his desk, he shoved it in so fast he almost seemed to be inhaling it.

A poem came to mind – one they'd done at school – and it kept repeating on him. '*All hope excluded thus*' – he crammed in another chunk of bread. '*De dum de dum,*' something outcast '*de dum, his new delight*' – biting a tomato. '*Mankind created and* (something about) this *world*,' juice running down his chin, but that didn't matter because the lament of the fallen angel had come back to him, almost in its entirety.

All hope excluded thus,

He said the words out loud:

behold instead
Of us out-cast, exil'd, his new delight,
Mankind created and for him this World.

And now here came the part he and his class had used to shout out, in unison and with gusto '*So farewell hope, with hope . . .*' Something missing. Oh yes, fear,

'*So farewell Hope and with Hope farewell Fear,*

His present tense voice ringing out,

'*Farewell Remorse: all Good to me is lost;*

'*Evil be thou my Good,*' and, reciting it, he seemed to hear those other voices rising up from out of his past.

How great it had been to be part of a riotous gang of boys, chanting along with them in glorious repetition of his namesake's words. And that hilarious moment when a master had come bursting in to order silence but, hearing that they were reciting *Paradise Lost*, had sullenly to withdraw. How glorious and . . .

The adult Milton stopped reciting. He had lost his appetite. He pushed what remained of his food away.

What a stupid delusion. At school, there never had been any belonging. Not then or afterwards. His father's recent disapproval, an echo of all those other and unending disapprovals, was powerful enough to drive him out of his chair. He would, he decided, he would go and face his father, now, once and for all, and say the things that had always needed to be said. And then, his mind was made up, he'd leave both house and office.

He launched himself out of his office and into the corridor.

'Yes?' The receptionist, his father's spy, sitting at the corridor's other end (there to keep a watch on what Milton did?). 'Can I help you, Milton?' They still called him Milton and his father sir.

'Is my father in?'

'No. He's out.'

Out. Still Milton was determined to keep on. Walking fast and straight, he saw panic in the receptionist's eyes. She thought he was going to barge into her. At the last minute, he swerved away from her and into his father's office with her voice pursuing. 'Milton?' A whole question in his name.

A question he didn't bother answering. Having slammed the door, he went to sit behind his father's desk.

A first.

His pathetically tiny father's desk. He had to pump down the chair's pneumatic lever almost to its limit in order to fit in. Here, he decided, he would sit until his father came back. And after that would tell his father how he felt.

He looked around the neatly ordered desk. His father's diary, a leather-bound book was lying there. Taking it up, he flicked through. Friday was easy enough to find. He read down Friday, each of its hours planned out in his father's spidery handwriting, through a working breakfast, and the time when phone calls (enumerated with initials) were to be made, and letters (ditto to initials) to be dictated, until the slot for 1p.m. '*Lunch*', that Milton knew his father had well taken. And afterwards, an afternoon of blank space, his father apparently having planned no further activity worth writing down.

His father could be anywhere. To wait aimlessly would kill impetus. Snapping the diary shut, he jumped up. So fast that the chair toppled over. It never even occurred to him to pick it up.

How was he going to pass the time until his father's return? He saw – yes, good idea – the liquor cabinet. His father had already accused him of being drunk; he might as well go the whole hog and prove his father right. He opened the cabinet.

'Oh!' The receptionist was in the office and calling his name, 'Milton.'

'Yes? What is it?'

'Your father's diary.' She followed through with a hesitant, 'He asked me to change one of his appointments.'

'He asked you' – not for a moment did he believe her – 'to change an appointment?' He knew she'd come to spy.

Her faltering 'Yes' and her eyes cast down confirmed it. She was too embarrassed to look him in the face.

'And when was that?'

'When was what?' Her legs, he saw, were shaking.

'When exactly did my father ask you to change this appointment?'

'A moment ago.'

'He's here?'

'He phoned.'

'Ah. Phoned was it?'

'What?'

'Never mind.'

'Well . . .' She turned before doing a double-take and coming full circle. If she didn't take the diary, her cover would be blown. Scurrying across the room she snatched it up, hesitating then, fear wrestling with slavish attitude to her master, slave mentality winning out as she reached down for the fallen chair.

'Leave it.' His voice was loud enough to make her jump. Stepping away from the chair, she hurried out.

He felt a little bad about scaring her but then he told himself not to. It was time, gone time, for him to start pulling his weight.

What next?

Ah yes. Alcohol. Good plan. He would soak down his sorrows in a mountainful of drink.

Faced by the vast array of bottles that his non-drinking father always kept, he randomly snatched one. Turned out to be an Armagnac and, if its curved, dimpled bottle was to be believed, an expensive one at that. Milton wasn't much of an Armagnac man himself, but needs must.

Next thought: stay or go?

Although his father's office was more comfortable by far, putting up with further incursions by the spy was a major disincentive. And besides, if he stayed he would have to pick up the chair.

Armagnac to hand, he left the room. He waved the bottle high (let her add that to her report) as he passed, going back to his dingy (ex) place of work where, chair tilted, feet on desk, he poured himself a drink. The first of many.

He drank steadily even though nothing seemed to get him drunk. Five o'clock. He poured another finger, well, OK, it was a fat finger, a fat finger and a half, actually, of Armagnac, drank it down and then, picking up the bottle, poured out the next.

His tongue was thick when he awoke. He was also very thirsty. Going for water, he saw the door to his father's office half ajar. If his father had come back at all, he must have gone out again.

It was late. He could hear the other fellows packing up more eagerly than usual because there was a bank holiday to come. Taking a jug of water to his office, he switched off the light, thereafter to sit in the dark as he rehydrated. As he sat, he could hear sequential and fading goodbyes along with the slamming of doors before the last, lone set of footsteps tapped along the corridor and the outer door clicked shut. Silence. The offices must now be empty.

His sleeping had drained away his drunkenness. In its place came a series of remembrances that confirmed the way his father's recent turning away from him was mere repetition of all those other occasions when his father's warm brown eyes, unable fondly to rest on his son, had shifted off.

He felt how alone he was. How unloved.

His mother had loved him but his mother had died. His father hated him. It had been forever thus – this was the secret that had turned out to be no secret – and thus would it always remain. There was no possibility of change.

The place in darkness. Still, he would leave his mark. Let them know that he had been here and that he had gone. He walked along, opening each door he passed and turning on each light. He was leaving, but not quite yet. First he was going to acquire a float on which to launch his freedom.

He'd worked hard enough to build up the business. A pay-off was totally deserved. He wasn't, however, planning to negotiate. He was going to breach his father's citadel – break into his safe – and take what was rightfully his.

There was a picture of a flat-nosed mountain on the wall of his father's office. Unhooking it, Milton exposed the safe. Only one problem with that plan. He didn't know the combination.

The times when Milton had stood witness to his father's furtive fumbling, his father had always been sure to block his view. But even though he hadn't been able to see the actual digits, there'd been nothing to stop him from counting the number of turns and knowing that there were six. Six numbers, therefore, now required.

His father had a proclivity for sentimentality. He was bound to have chosen an anniversary as the basis for any combination. Milton put together a mental list of every anniversary he could think of and afterwards tried each in turn. His father's birthday (day, month, and last two digits of the year), his mother's (as well as the day she had died), his own (didn't expect that to work) and Vanessa's (surprised to find it didn't). No joy. Reversing the numbers so that the year came first, he tried them all again, and then again, this time mixing them up. Still the safe door did not budge. Furious, he backed away and ran at it, delivering a kind of karate kick that, although it hurt his leg, didn't even make the door shiver. Stupid.

Think, he told himself, think.

He would have tried the dog's birthday if, that is, his father had ever permitted a dog into the house. He also thought about Yuri's birthday but he didn't know when it was and he didn't think his father did either. The more he tried and the more he failed, the more convinced did he grow that there would be mounds of cash – his rightful due – inside. He spun the wheel this way and that, racking his brains for other people his father knew well enough to know their birthdays. Again without result. After that, a prolonged and silent brainstorming produced the date of his father's arrival in Britain, and then of Milton and his mother's. No good. Finally, and in exasperation, he chose the six numbers of the date of his expulsion from school.

Such a long shot, but turning to the last number – 3 – and just about to turn away, he heard the snap of a release button. The door swung open.

Bloody hell. The exhilaration he felt at outwitting his father (once and he would do it again. And again. And again) almost outweighed by the shock that not only had his father remembered this date, he had also commemorated it. Proof, if proof were needed, of how much Milton was despised.

Well and good. If that's how things stood Milton would fit himself to the times. He would do what the young everywhere were doing. He would overthrow the old regime. He would wreak his own revenge.

One cursory rifle-through yielded a dollop of cash but nothing like the amount he wanted or deserved. If not cash then, he decided, he would take something else. Some secret to be ransomed for cash that his secretive father (rule number three, or was it three hundred and thirty-three and a third?) was sure to have concealed.

Wasn't his father always telling Milton to be methodical? Well, now he would obey. Two easy armfuls. He put them on the desk. Having clicked on the green desk light he began, methodically, to sort through the pile.

The cash he shoved into his pocket. The red account books, he set to one side. The bond certificates, ditto. The previous years' diaries (was his father planning to write his memoirs?) he flicked through without anything in particular catching his attention (if need be he would read through them later).

Having disposed of the bulk of the pile, he now paid more careful attention to what remained: a handful of legal documents (on the discard pile) and a small packet. Legal documents would be the most tedious to decipher. He picked up the packet.

Did he know already? Certainly it seemed in hindsight to have called to him

It was a brown paper packet, tied with blue string, both of which carefully he removed. Inside he found six airmail letters none of them previously opened. Each was numbered in his father's fastidious hand. On the top left corner. Like an extra stamp.

He turned them over – front to back and front again. No return address and all of them posted from Ceylon. Correction. From Sri Lanka, as it was now known. Double correction. A closer examination told him that all six had been sent in the 1960s long before the country's recent change of name.

329

Letters from Ceylon. His father's mother country. And his own, come to think of it, although he never did think of it like that.

The provenance of this correspondence was not in itself surprising. What made the letters interesting was that, despite not having opened them, his father kept them locked up in his safe.

Blackmail? But no: since his father hadn't even looked inside it could not be blackmail.

Some kind of vendetta, then?

He knew his father didn't get on with his family. That's why they never visited. Perhaps the letters were from one of them?

Only one way to find out. He must open them.

There was no letter numbered one. He picked up number two.

Looking back at himself sitting at his father's desk and about to open this Pandora's box, he would never know whether it was wishful thinking that made his hands tremble. Violently, but not violently enough to stop him from taking the silver letter-opener with its fat, curled-tailed lion and upheld sword and slitting open all three sides of letter number two.

What a mess, was his first reaction on unfolding it. And it certainly was a mess. Poorly written with multiple crossings-out. He laid it down flat, smoothing out its folds. Perhaps this is why his father hadn't bothered with the letters – because his fastidious father already knew that the sender couldn't write well.

Dear Emil,

he read and then he read a series of stuttering first sentences, all of which had been crossed through.

I am sure he read, ~~you were . . . must have been surprised.. shocked.. to hear from me after all this time and from Ceylon!~~

And afterwards he read,

~~I am writing to you from Ceylon.~~

And,

~~I had thought so much about writing to you and no that my last letter might not have be welcome.~~

Which sentence was followed by a different version of the above,

~~I had thought so much about writing to you dear Emil and know that my last letter must have been a shock and a welcome one . . . not be welcomed. You have probably all but forgotten . . . . . .~~

And finally a few randomly blurted out bits of desperation,

~~Dear Emil.. if only~~
~~I know you must want to forget me and the thing I did. but~~

~~I am asking~~
~~I am begging~~.
~~Please Emil~~

All of these in large untidy writing until, at the very bottom of the page, small and cramped because this was all the space permitted, he read,

Dear Emil, I hope you got my letter. when you didn't answer I thought – well you must have been too shock. I know that you will also find this letter odd what with all such crossings-out but I am at a loss to how to write to you after such a long time. Other than to say how sorry I am. I was young. Hardship has since taught me more sense. I told you in my first letter that I was in Ceylon. Without much money but I manage. But I cannot manage, with my great sorrow. A mother should not have to live without her children, Emil – or at least without news of them. Please, write to me and tell me how they are. And perhaps if you could find it in your heart, for me to see them? If they could come only for a visit. Please Emil let them come. Yours who you once loved!!!!!!
Evelyn.

Evelyn. His mother, Evelyn.

Letter still in hand he thought, don't look. Roll back. Hide it away.

Which is what he wanted, more than anything, to do. To seal it up. Put it back in the safe. Lock the door and pretend he had never had his mitts on it. In short, un-think it from existence.

He opened the second letter, otherwise known as letter number three.

No crossings-out this time but not much else either. Only,

> Dear Emil,
> I have still not heard from you. I know this must be difficult. But please, please find it in your heart to reply. Please. Tell me about the children.
> Evelyn.

He set it calmly to one side.

Letter number four was, if the addition of an even greater number of exclamation marks was any clue, more desperate. But five was brief and cold and then, after a gap of some nine months, came letter number six.

How strange. His mother had been dead for fifteen years and alive for only – what exactly had it been – ten minutes? Half an hour at the outset. And here sat her (not) bereaved son, opening letter number six and calmly reading.

Dear Emil, he read, in handwriting that seemed to be, in comparison to the others, uncharacteristically neat:

> Dear Emil,
> I no longer expect you to answer this. It's possible you have not received any of my letters. It's possible you moved and even that you have found happiness with someone else. I hope this is what happened and I hope that, whoever she is, she can love our children as they deserve to be loved.
> I will not write to you again. I too must move on. I must

make my own life, I owe that to myself, and I have found
someone

(someone Milton thought who had either dictated this letter
or had in the meantime helped improve her letter-writing
style . . .)

> *. . . someone who loves me. He is a tea planter and I am*
> *going with him to his estate. The address on the top of this*
> *letter is his, you can reach me there – not, I know, that you*
> *will try. I wish you the best in your continuing life.*
>   *Yours,*
>   *Evelyn.*

And that, it seemed, was all that had ever come from *yours*
Evelyn who, moving on, had left her children in the care of
a mythical woman, his father's second wife, who never had
existed.

He knew it. Had always known it. His father was a liar.

But this? His mother? So shocked was he, he seemed to
feel no shock at all.

His thoughts flitted back to school and to those tedious
hours of speculative maths questions to be answered. Like,
say there are four children on two buses and one has ten
more sweets than the first, and the third ate half the quantity
that the boring fourth would have had if he hadn't forgotten and left them at home . . . well how many sweets will be
left after a vengeful gunman has shot up all the kids? And
now he was facing a similarly bizarre and equally meaningless theoretical question. One day you discover that your

father is a liar and that your dead mother is alive. What do you do?

Take it easy, Milton. Take it easy. Work it out logically. As if it were a school problem.

You pick up the phone, that's what you do – his hand reaching for the receiver – and you dial . . .

Who? You definitely dial somebody. But who?

Your sister. What a great idea. She'll want to know. You need to tell her. Yes. Definitely. Her.

Hold on. Vanessa is in America, her new phone number is not yet committed to memory.

Take it easy. Calm down. Come back to this one later. In the meantime, move on.

Theoretical question number two: say your dead mother apologised to your father, indicating there was something she did wrong. How would you find out what it was?

You could phone your father and ask him. Good idea. Ping the buttons and disconnect the phone. That number, since you live there, you will definitely remember.

The dialling tone. OK. Get going. Which he did, turning the dial round the string of numbers. But before he could complete the call, he slammed down his hand, breaking the connection.

Think, Milton, think.

Your father lied to you and your mother is alive.

Don't phone Vanessa.

Don't phone your father.

Go. Get on a plane. Find your mother.

Sri Lanka

As he pressed on up the hill Milton's breath sounded out. Too loudly, he couldn't help thinking, for such an alien darkness.

It had not been part of the plan to turn up in the dark. It just hadn't dawned on him how long it would take to drive from Colombo to Nuwara Eliya. It wasn't much over a hundred miles but in this dazzling, chaotic country with its twisting, potholed roads, its belching and over-laden trucks, its plodding carts, its wandering cows, its pedestrians who suddenly materialised, and, on top of all of these, its succession of green-painted, sandbagged, barbed wire enclosures from behind which police would saunter to order out passengers and drivers and so set in motion the slow searching of the car . . . well, the journey had been interminable.

The heat had hit him as he soon as he stepped out of the aeroplane. He had stood under a brilliantly clear blue sky, shielding his eyes to take in the sight of the line of palms that edged the runway. He had a distant childhood memory of his mother describing how she had met his father by such a palm. There'd also been one in their first garden under which he had used to play.

Not that this country felt anything like home. The blasting vapour of heat that had bathed him then and ever afterwards in sweat was one reason why. His being the target of countless sideways double glances was another. Even after he had discarded his tie and loosened his shirt, disposed of his jacket and then substituted an entirely new wardrobe of light cotton shirts and loose cotton trousers, still they identified him as the outsider that he was.

Even after the descent of dusk, and though it was much cooler up this high, he was sweating as he trudged. His destination was a mere half-mile away. The driver had wanted to take him all the way but, driven by a determination he didn't entirely understand to arrive alone and on foot, Milton had insisted that he be dropped off.

What he hadn't expected was that it would be quite as dark as this. Or, even worse, as noisy. As he tried his best to stick to the up-winding path, brushing against the sharp points of tea bushes as his corrective, unfamiliar sounds kept cutting through his laboured breaths. The hooting of owls, or the crackling of twigs and, most sinister of all, a snuffling and a sliding that, no matter how he varied his step, seemed to be keeping pace with him, the chaotic syncopation playing on his nerves.

Just as the dank pooling beneath his armpits and the sticking of his cotton shirt to his broad back proclaimed his foreignness, these startling noises of the night made clear how little of this place he understood. He didn't know if there might be fierce animals or poisonous snakes about. He didn't know whether the workforce left the plantation at night. He didn't know whether the insurrection, of which he'd not even previously heard, was over and whether the upheld guns at the checkpoints were just muscle there for show. And . . .

Oh yes. One other thing he didn't know. He didn't know whether he would recognise his mother.

Not his original plan to surprise her. He'd had every intention on arriving in Colombo to phone and warn her that he was on his way. But having located her number and picked up the phone, he couldn't figure out how he was going to tell her who he was.

Better, he had decided, letting the handset drop, to just pitch up. To watch her as she said the things he imagined she would say. Such as how hard she had prayed for this day to come. Or (another of his favourite scenarios) her telling him that she had never stopped mourning the loss of him from her life. Or (a bit syrupy this one) how his being with her made everything OK. All of these responses he had let roam in his imagination. But there was also one other, and he admitted it for the first time as he lumbered up the hill, that had stopped him from phoning. It was the fear that on hearing who he was, she simply would hang up.

It was her letters that gave him the cause for doubt. He had brought them with him and had read them so many times, he knew them off by heart. Not that they told him anything. As he moved ineffably towards the moment of their meeting he was overwhelmed by questions. Like, why she had left. And why it took her almost six years to write and ask about her children. And why she had not written to them direct. And why, although she had apologised, her apology was to his father, not to Milton or Vanessa. And after that last letter, why the silence?

Unless of course, hope flaring, his father had destroyed the

341

ones that followed. But no – hope dying – having kept hold of some, his father would hardly have destroyed the rest. Besides, hadn't she herself announced the cessation of her one-sided correspondence?

No point, he knew, in continuing to ask himself such questions that never could be answered. And yet he continued to let them swirl. They distracted him from having to face his real fear, that the woman who had written those letters would turn out to be nothing like the mother he remembered.

All those years of dreaming of her, to keep hold of her and of her love. His unchanging and precious memory of her as a ravishingly beautiful, loving woman who, unlike his pig-headed father, always knew how to behave. Who had cared for him. This mother, he had nurtured in the deepest recesses of himself. How he had loved her, but what if that woman he had loved no longer existed? What if she never had?

His face was moist, sweat seeping out of every pore as he laboured up the hill. His steps were growing shorter, and slower, and his breathing thick and leaden. He was lost, he was sure he must be, when there – at long last but also far too soon – he saw a glimmering light through the bushes and yes, as he rounded a corner, he found himself surprisingly close to a large and well lit house.

He had not the slightest notion where he was going to find the courage to go forwards.

He stood, hesitating, and then two things happened. The front door of the house burst open to reveal a man centre stage, bathed in warm yellow light. At the same moment, he felt something dig into his back and heard a voice whispering in a language he knew to be Sinhala but could not understand.

'Keep very, very still.' This, in English, from the man in front of the house. 'That's a loaded gun. One false move and my man will not hesitate to pull the trigger.'

Without thinking, Milton turned.

Coming to, he found himself horizontal. A sharp flare of light dazzled and his head was on fire. He groaned, shut his eyes and counted to ten before opening them again.

All he could see was the beam of torchlight and high above and beyond its paltry human reach, a vast darkness. He stretched out a hand to feel about. Felt stones and dirt. Had he been shot? He reached up gently to his head. It was wet at the back but not overly so. Not shot, then. They must have used the gun to knock him out. Another groan issuing involuntarily out and provoking a loud,

'What's the matter with you JVP fanatics? Don't you know when you're beaten?' He saw a trousered leg rising. 'Do you actually want to die?'

The leg was aimed at his stomach. He thought about rolling away but to left and to right were other pairs of legs. He held up a hand to ward off the blow, 'I'm not . . . .I'm not a fanatic.'

The leg withdrew. 'You're English?'

When he attempted a confirmatory nod it hurt so much all he managed was the squeezing out of another groan.

'What were you doing, sneaking up on us like that?'

'I'm looking for . . .'

'Looking for what? Come on, man, spit it out.'

'For Evelyn.'

'Evelyn? Why? What is she to you?'

Flat on his back and looking up into the velvet immensity of the dark sky he said, 'Evelyn is my mother.'

She came running as they helped him into the house. 'Miltie?' Her voice was not soft and mellifluous as he had remembered it but anxiously pitched, especially when she repeated that odd '*Miltie?*' with which he was unfamiliar.

Her halo of hair was as blonde as he remembered. But the countenance it framed was not that calm, kind, smooth-skinned, white Madonna whose fantasy image he had stored in memory. The skin on this face – and of course he should have expected this – was rougher and it was browned by exposure to the sun. There were also frown lines on her forehead that deepened as she said, 'My son?' An uncertain couplet delivered on the edge of such vulnerability that the man who'd been holding Milton had to let go in order to support her. 'Don't worry, Evie. He's only had a little knock, old girl.'

Because of the distraction that attended it, Milton had cause to be grateful for that little knock. A truck was dispatched to fetch a doctor, a cold compress and sweet tea provided and he put to rest in a wicker armchair beneath a churning fan. He sat pretending to be more hurt than actually he was as, out of the corner of his eye, he watched his mother circling. She was keeping out of the way, she said, so that her staff could look after him. He was thankful for her distance. He, too, had no idea what to say to her. And so the bustling in of the doctor and his examination, and his verdict of 'a slight concussion but nothing to cause concern', were appreciatively received.

In a spare bedroom – one of many in this huge planter's house – he undressed.

'Miltie?' Could she be outside his room? Surely not.

In case the sound of her calling was not his imagination, he locked the door. Then he stood in the glorious submersion of a shower hoping, at least for a short while, to make himself forget what he was doing there. Even safely in the shower, however, he seemed to hear her 'Miltie.'

He scrubbed himself. Long and hard. What he wanted more than anything to do was extend this phase of his suspension. Indefinitely, if he could. But in the end he had to leave the shower and put on the clean clothes they had brought to him. He looked with great longing at the bed. He had been dreaming of this moment half his life and all he could think was how much he dreaded it.

'Miltie?' She had been there all along, waiting by his door. 'I thought you might be thirsty.' She handed him an ice cold drink before turning away to lead him down the hall.

For one glorious moment in that low-lit space it was as if the years of their separation had dissolved and he was a little boy walking behind his mother's young self. He seemed to see her shapely legs rising from her elegant high heels and above them her trademark small, wasp waist and the soft white of her swan neck. But when, suddenly, she turned to check that he was still there, he saw a woman aged and disillusioned, whom he didn't know. 'Jeffrey's on the veranda,' she said. 'Drinks before dinner.'

What followed on the porch was an hallucinatory mix of whisky and concussion and exhaustion. He was conscious of vegetation, trees, shrubs, plants, pressing in, shadowy outlines that seemed to shift and turn in sympathy with the fans that stirred the air.

Perhaps he was more concussed than he had thought because the apparition that was his mother kept on shifting. One moment he would see her, the ravages of time and the alcohol that she was rapidly downing inescapable. In the next she seemed to have blended into the shadows only to reappear as that beautiful, loving woman of his dreams.

'Darling . . .' her voice now low and as sweet as he also remembered. She stretched out to touch him. Her touch felt so familiar. As she patted his arm a longing, almost terrible in its intensity, rose up. She must have felt something similar because she looked at him hard, with love and fear, before letting go.

'Darling, you have made me so happy.'

How could he – who no longer knew her – disbelieve her? Yet he couldn't help thinking that she didn't look anything like happy.

'But what a shock out of the blue.' She paused and stared. 'Not that I haven't been longing for this moment. Praying for it. I have, you know.'

Even with that slightly stilted lilt of her sentence end he

did not doubt her words. No matter that she had changed: she still was his mother who loved him. And yet – a further shift as he saw her touching her Jeffrey as delicately as she had just touched him.

Whipped up by encroaching darkness and by the circling of fans he seemed now to see the couple as a portrait of faded Colonials, this picture made complete by the sight of three white-gloved servants who stood to attention behind her chair. Who were so attuned to the needs of their masters that the thought that he was no longer hungry had only to cross his mind and his plate was smoothly replaced by a silver bowl for rinsing his hand.

'Nothing more, darling?' She hadn't even touched her own food.

He shook his head. 'No. Thank you, but no.'

In the silence that descended, he looked across at her. Even through the shadows he could see her eyes were watering.

She turned to snap at one of her servants who had stepped slightly out of line from the others. 'Don't you listen? He doesn't want any more.' She turned back. Her hand that picked up her drink was shaking, although her cheery voice belied it. 'It's lucky you came now,' she said. 'Our time's almost up. It's no longer done, you see, to have Europeans in charge. We'll be gone within the month.'

Would she, he wondered, have bothered to write and tell Emil where she had gone? If the evidence of her long years of silence was anything to go by, she probably would not have.

Another shift and now her voice almost casual as if

speaking to a stranger. 'I don't know how much you follow events in Sri Lanka?'

He couldn't bear it. He got up.

She didn't seem to notice. 'Hasn't been easy,' she said, 'especially last year when there were bodies floating face down in rivers and lying on the road.'

Could she be so detached from what she had done to him that she was actually asking for his sympathy?

'I blame Bandaranaike and his Bhikkhus and their precious Sinhala only policy,' Jeffrey suddenly spoke up. 'I told you they were storing up trouble, didn't I, Evie? And look what happened. Bloody savages.'

She had pushed back her own chair so deep into shadow that Milton could not be sure whether he had imagined that flash of anger that, crossing her face, brought back the beautiful young woman she once had been. But he must have imagined it because when she spoke it was only mildly to say, 'It's not for us to judge, Jeffrey.' She looked old, he thought, and tired, her gaze unfocused.

She seemed caught up in reverie to which he had no access. 'We are the foreigners here,' he heard her saying. 'I have always, always believed – I really always have – that the onus must be on the newcomer to tailor his behaviour to fit his new country. Don't you think?'

Looking expectantly across the table, she was surprised to find him on his feet. But that wasn't all. He had a feeling as she raised her eyes up to his face that she had been half expecting someone else. Or maybe this was just imagination. Maybe she, like him, was just having trouble adjusting to the way he'd changed. She smiled brightly.

'That's enough of me and my opinions.' A forced burst of laughter accompanied her outstretched hand.

'Now darling,' she said. 'Tell me everything that has happened since last we were together.'

Once Evelyn had left her son. Now he had left her.

He had run away, in fact. Rudely from her table.

She stepped off the veranda, stumbling out into a darkness that soon wound itself around her. She moved aimlessly and without intention over the uneven ground until at last, tripping on a particularly thick root and reaching out to steady herself, she happened to grab hold of a stem that, slick and wet from the humid night, broke off. She let it drop.

All around was so very dark. Neither moon nor stars visible. She must be under a dense canopy of leaves. It was also very still. As if her world had stopped.

She stood with the memory of the dreams she had kept on dreaming washing over her. They had all been wish fulfilment. Reunions, not always happy, with her children. Many were the times when, as she was about to hold their dream shapes in her arms, they would simply disappear. Yet even those bad dreams had offered consolation, the yearning she had felt on awakening having, for one elusive moment, brought the children close.

How often had she promised herself that if ever she were lucky enough to get them back, she would hold them and never let them go? And now that her beloved son had sought her out, what did she go and do? By her drunken, boorish behaviour she promptly drove him away.

She could hear a faint crying out. Distantly, in the still, hot night. Not her conscience at what she'd done or who she had become, but a high pleading repetition of her name. *Evie*. And then again. *Eveeeeeee*. Must be Jeffrey who, fearful she was going to do something stupid, had organised a search party. And yes, she could see darted threads of torchlight weaving through the undergrowth.

Dear, well meaning, useless Jeffrey. Didn't he know that her criminally stupid deed had been committed many years ago? Not the affair with Charles – although that had been stupid – but the voluntary relinquishing of her children.

'Evie . . .'

She didn't want to be found like this but she had no energy for moving on. Looking straight up she saw that the tree under which she was standing had a branch low enough for her to reach. Grabbing hold of it with both hands, she braced her feet against the trunk and then began to glide them up, that way hauling herself on to the lowest branch from which she could climb on to the second, and then the third.

There – not bad for an old dog – she was safely out of sight. She was also now partly above the canopy of leaves. She could see tiny light pulses of distant stars breaking up the pitch of sky.

That immensity almost unbalanced her. She settled herself closer to the trunk.

As she did, a memory – the kind she usually kept at bay – washed over her. Another tree and another time and the girl she once had been, caught up in the first glimmerings of the passion that would eventually destroy her. That flighty, rebellious, exceptional girl who at her mother's table had blithely rebutted some of those very same, awful, chauvinistic sentiments that Jeffrey so often expressed and, worse than that, that sometimes rose up in her own throat.

'Eveeee . . .!' There was an edge of desperation to Jeffrey's cry.

Poor Jeffrey. He had never shown her anything but kindness. It wasn't fair of her to hide from him. Not his fault that she had got so drunk. Not his fault either that, every now and then, coming across him unawares, she couldn't help thinking that he was the kind of man that the girl she once had been would certainly have mocked. And neither could she hold back the thought that, if in those early days of her ebullient confidence, someone had told her she was going to end up with a Jeffrey, well she would have laughed right in their face.

That girl she once had been had thought herself invulnerable. Had thought, in fact, that all she had to do was wish for something and she could make it happen.

What was it her mother had used to say? 'If wishes were horses' – that was it – 'then beggars would ride,' her mother's way of trying to shake her younger daughter out of fantasy. And her mother had been proved right. Dreams were useless when it came to living.

Even so, and especially now, Evelyn couldn't help thinking that the girl she once had been was much more likeable than the parody of a woman she had become.

She had tried on explanations like clothes. Had blamed

herself and Emil separately and then together. But no amount of blame could drown out the question – *why did you desert your children?* – that was always accompanied by its more terrible subsidiary, *and after you deserted them, why when you were feeling better, did you not get back in touch?*

The loss of her hopeful self had been nothing compared to the loss of her son and daughter, and especially the loss of her son for whom she still felt a passion that went beyond all other passions. Yet when he had come and found her, what had she gone and done? She had talked and talked, that's what. And all to stop him asking, why did you go?

Her letters. At least, she told herself, she had written them.

Yes, but even knowing how proud Emil was, and how badly he must be hurting, she had addressed her letters to him. How could she ever have expected him to smooth her path back to her children?

It was her fault, not his. It was she who had made no proper effort to get back in touch. Her fault. She did not deserve her children or their love. That's what she continually had told herself. One glimpse of her grown-up son, however, had made her understand something that she also always should have known – that the scourge she had so lavishly inflicted on herself had hurt those very children whose happiness she had pretended to herself to be protecting.

Now, almost fifteen years later, she sat in a tree and she thought,

What did we do Emil?

We loved each other so much and we loved the children more.

What did we do?

Heart pounding, Emil made his way slowly through the office.

He had started at one end by checking the toilets. Then he had gone down the lighted corridor, opening each door he passed. Having looked inside each separate room, he then switched out each separate light. The proof that Milton had definitely been here was that he, alone, amongst all other staff, would extravagantly dare to leave on all the lights, knowing that, because of the bank holiday, they would be on until the cleaners arrived early on Tuesday morning.

This was a Milton-style carelessness that normally would have provoked Emil to the heights of irritation. But not on this Monday night. In fact if Milton suddenly were to appear with some loutish drinking bout as explanation for his vanishing act, well even in that instance, it would be only with a great effort that Emil would be able to stop himself from hugging the boy so hard that an embarrassed Milton would be bound to force out further exhibitions of the flatulence that annoyed his father.

There was something wrong.

From the very beginning, on Friday, when his son had failed to come home, Emil had known that there was. He had tried, lightly, to indicate as much to Vanessa on the phone but Vanessa, who always could sense what he was really saying, had laughed off his concern. He had pretended to himself that she was right – that he should be more worried if the twenty-five-year-old Milton never let down his hair by staying out – but in his heart of hearts, he had known that there was something wrong.

He had even known this when he had been standing at the top of the stairs and looking down on his son. Had sensed in the fury of Milton's answering stare something not breaking but already broken. Milton's four-day disappearance had confirmed it.

Heart beating more rapidly, he opened Milton's office door. The relief he felt at not finding the prone body of his son was immense. Old bits of food and crumpled papers were strewn on the floor, the sight of which previously would have angered him. Now it merely seemed to confirm his boy's distress. Switching off the light, he carefully withdrew.

On he went and down the corridor.

What could he have done, what should he have said, on Friday?

Odd to be so tongue-tied in the presence of your son with whom, after all, you have lived and worked. And yet it wasn't that odd. Emil had grown accustomed to standing mute in the face of his son's silent accusations. And he knew he had not talked, and could not talk, to Milton because the words he had needed to say, and the truth he had needed to expose, were too hurtful. Not to Milton but to himself.

Once, he remembered, when he still had the heart for breeding plants, he had gone to great trouble to import a rare black orchid, only soon afterwards to uproot and destroy it. He had done something similar to his son. He should have told him the truth. Should have borne the costs of his anger, and asked for his forgiveness.

Past the receptionist's desk he went and into his office.

Had he left this room to the last because he knew? Had he? Even if he hadn't, as soon as he opened the door to see his picture of Adam's Peak on the floor, then he did know.

The moment he had long been anticipating. Had waited for, while simultaneously deceiving himself into believing it would never happen.

The safe was empty, its contents scattered on his desk. All of them, as far as he could see, present and correct save for some cash. And the packet of letters. Those letters that, even though he had never even opened them, he could not bring himself to throw away. So there they had been kept, snug in the safe, waiting for their moment of betrayal.

Sinking down into his chair, Emil thought, what have I done? For the first time in his life, he began to cry.

A cry and Milton awoke. Sat bolt upright in bed although he couldn't, at first, work out whose bed it was. Then he remembered, he was in the hotel to which he had insisted that they bring him.

Breathe out, he told himself, relax.

His mother, whose voice had followed him into sleep, wasn't there. He was safe, breathing in and out and this despite the way that the dark blades of a swirling ceiling fan reminded him of that other turning fan, and of his mother's face.

I must have been dreaming about her, he thought, thinking it must also have been his own distressed crying out that had wrenched him from sleep. But then it came again, that same blaring out of sound. Like a peacock call, but uglier and more mechanical.

Over at the window pushing aside the heavy drapes he saw a sky misty with a yellowing dawn and, beneath it, a manicured lawn, its edges lined with neat rose bushes. How strange to find such an English garden so far from home and, as the first glow of a clear light began to bleach away the dawn, to see how it lay under such an utterly un-English sky.

It came again. That eerie sound.

Pulling on the open-necked shirt and the sarong that he had, late the previous night, borrowed from reception so he wouldn't have to wear Jeffrey's clothes, he made his way along the wood-lined hall. He passed under gilt-framed portraits of stern, frock-coated men and fading photographs of white-clad cricket teams, all of them dating from a time when this building had been the headquarters of an English-only club. His father would, he knew, by virtue of his race, once have been prohibited from coming here. And, because her family could not have afforded the fees, his mother would also have been kept out. While here came their son, clad in a stranger's sarong, slowly and with an air of belonging, down the ornate stairs, under the glazed eyes of mounted animal heads.

He pushed through the double doors.

'Good morning, sir.' The receptionist looked up and frowned. 'You didn't sleep well?'

'I slept well enough. But that sound?'

'The muster horn, sir, calling to the estate workers.' Pushing aside the wooden counter, the receptionist said, 'Let me show you to the dining room.'

'I'm not hungry.'

'But sir. She is waiting for you there.'

'She?'

'The lady. She has been there most of the long night. She said not to disturb you. She said that she would wait.'

She was the only person in the empty dining room. She was sitting at a table that was as far away from the door as it could get and tucked into a corner almost as if she were hoping not to be spotted. No sooner did she see him, however, than she was on her feet.

She looked different, partly a result of his being prepared for the sight of her and partly because, in contrast to last night's loose and flowing frock, she was now all buttoned up. Literally, in a beige dress with a high collar and, he saw as she made her way over, a tight waist. Such a picture of respectability and yet, he thought, somehow odd.

He was not the only one doing a wardrobe check. Her eyes flared as she took in the sight of his sarong. Remembering the venom of her new husband, he half expected her to accuse him of going native, a thought whose singular lack of generosity was underscored by her actual, 'Milton, I am so sorry.' Her blue eyes were limpid and large.

He felt the sudden lurching of his heart and afterwards his aching chest, physical confirmation of how much he loved her. But the years of her desertion still stood between them.

'I was terribly shaken when you turned up like that out of the blue,' she said. 'I probably drank too much.'

By the look of the broken skin around her eyes, he thought, she probably often drank too much. 'Shall we sit?'

He saw the effort it cost her to hold back the words she had been waiting all night to deliver, but 'Good idea,' is what she said, going then to the table he chose and sitting down and waiting until he was seated opposite, before she leaned forward to launch in, 'Milton . . .'

'How about some tea?'

'No.' She blinked.' Or . . . yes. OK. Yes. Certainly. If you would like some.'

The ordering of the tea bought him precious time, especially when the waiter bustled around flicking imaginary crumbs off spotless linen tablecloths before laying out cups and saucers and bringing in a tray.

She poured out tea, adding milk and sugar to fit his requirements before handing him the cup. 'I loved your father,' she said.

He picked up his teaspoon and began to stir.

'Emil was so handsome.'

His stirring dug out an inverted tornado that, as he continued to stir, disappeared, soon however to return

'And he loved me.'

The tea waves kept on building. Lifting out the teaspoon, he waited for the swell to die before beginning again to stir, varying the circuit of the spoon, his mind preoccupied with the differential equations that once had been drummed into him. Something about amplitudes and oscillations and harmonic wave resonances, he remembered, these words filling his head as he heard her saying,

'. . . I was . . . well I was such a nonconformist. Once I had made up my mind, nobody could sway me from my chosen path. Not even my mother. Who tried but I wouldn't listen . . .'

. . . and he, realising that once she had launched herself into speech there could be no interrupting her.

'I thought I was special.' She stretched out a hand to cover his. 'That's quite enough, darling.'

She was right, tea had begun to slop over the rim. He watched its brown stain spreading across the starched white of the tablecloth.

She lifted off her hand. 'If only I hadn't been so proud.'

Some strange vagueness in her tone of voice made him look at her. She was half-turned away from him and staring, with concentrated intensity, out of the window as if there was something fascinating there. Following the direction of her gaze, all he could see was a stiff and silent garden.

She turned, abruptly, to look at him. The smile she delivered offered him a glimpse of the mother he thought he had remembered. 'I had you, of course,' she said, 'and I loved you very much. But then,' it was more of a grimace than a smile, 'after you went away to school, I was very lonely.'

She was lonely? *You?* he wanted to shout. *You?*

'In this country,' he heard her saying, 'people don't get married until they have cast a horoscope to see which day to choose . . .'

Stop it, he thought.

'. . . Emil and I should have done this,' she said, 'because, you know, on the day we met, a man died . . .'

Stop it.

'. . . which should have been our warning . . .'

Stop it . . .

'But we were both so very headstrong, we thought we could break the rules. We thought . . .'

All those dreams he'd had of the perfect mother he had lost, well, now he knew that dreams were all they ever had been. How sad. He pushed his cup away. He had spent half his life idolising someone who never had existed. The thought was almost unbearable. He also pushed back his chair.

It scraped against the wooden floor so loudly it seemed to

shake his mother out of herself. She shivered. Looked across at him. 'I'm so sorry, darling,' she said. 'It's a habit when I'm nervous. I'll stop. I promise you I will.' Seeing his gaze on her, she looked away.

Sideways on, she looked much younger. Almost like she used to.

He thought of the two of them, in another country and at another table. Both caught up in the delicious naughtiness of his having skipped school, the intimacy of this conspiracy, he now realised, a sign that things were already wrong between his mother and his father.

'It was a terrible thing to do. I am sorry, Miltie . . .'

He flinched.

'I never used to call you that, did I?'

He shook his head.

'I am so sorry, Milton.'

It came to him then why she looked so odd. It was the way she had dressed herself almost as if to summon up the mother, and the woman, she once had been. As if she could ever call that woman back.

Once, and he was sure that this was not just his imagination, she had been so full of life. So beautiful. So full of love. Determindly he had held tight to that memory of his wondrous, his unfailingly tender, mother.

Now, in the face of his new reality, that memory had faded. In its place there came this image of her as she truly was; a woman who could not bear the weight that she had been asked to carry.

Silence in the empty wood-lined splendour of a dining room that had seen better days. All around were tables starched and laid, and polished cutlery that shone hopefully under artificial light for colonial patrons who would never again frequent this place. And the two of them, driven into speechlessness by the things that could not be talked about until suddenly she said, 'Stand up.'

'I beg your pardon?'

'I'm sorry, that was rude of me. Please, Milton, would you mind doing me a favour. Would you mind standing up?'

How odd, but he found himself obeying her request.

He rose, slowly to his feet, and strangely it felt good to be standing and seeing her push back her own chair so as to better take in the sight of him. And then she said, and although she said it quietly, he could not have missed the unmistakable love in her voice, 'Look at you,' she said, 'My handsome son. What a wonderful man you have become.'

He was in the car. Going and perhaps for ever. They had left behind the town and were driving along a high and narrow road. Such a vista. He leaned forward. 'Stop here.'

The driver drew up.

'I won't be long.'

'And then we are to travel on to Colombo?'

'I don't know. I just don't know.'

Slowly, in the musky heat, he began to walk. On he walked and on, following the road, around the corner and still on. Trudging at first without even looking around, but when eventually he happened upon another sharp bend he realised that what he was doing might be dangerous. He went over to stand at the edge of the road.

He could see rolling peaks blued by the morning light, and running in a narrow band along the foot of the peaks, what remained of the jungle that had once covered the whole island. Even from this great distance he could see a gentle wind ruffling the topmost leaves. In front of this alien, impenetrable green, running from there right up to his road lay the astonishment of the new, cleared jungle now entirely given over to tea. The bushes were packed so evenly together that from a distance they seemed to form the unbroken surface of a raised and undulating green sea; closer in, they made a patchwork quilt of green, each plant its own neatened embroidery that added to the whole.

He turned to look across the road and up another, lesser hill on which tea had also been planted. It curved around the hill like a spreading crinoline. Amongst these bright-tipped bushes was a dotting of electric pylons each ringed by its own circle of green, tea worshipping the progress of electricity.

He had thought he was there alone but, as he continued to look, he began to notice that the hill was in fact full of women who were picking tea. Sacks banded to their heads and flowing down their backs, they were like a flock of birds, their fingers pecking off the topmost leaves that they then tossed back into their sacks while forward they moved, from dawn, he knew, until dusk.

No traffic to interrupt the calm. And it was so very calm. So quiet that he seemed to hear the whispering of the tea pickers' fingers as they moved on. He was gripped by an urge he didn't quite understand to join them.

Crossing the road, he began to weave his way through the plants, slowly climbing up the hill. Before long, however, he saw that although she neither looked up nor did anything else to acknowledge his presence, a nearby tea picker had shifted almost imperceptibly away from him. Not fair, he thought, he was disturbing her. In an attempt to demonstrate that he had no ill intention, he turned away to look past the road and to the wide valley that lay between it and the distant line of peaks.

He was conscious of the sound of her fingers dancing against the top of the bushes, like a quiet wind against a field of grass. He could also hear the soft fall of flowing water while, from the rich brown pendulous sacks of beehives hanging from high branches, came a busy hum. So much of nature, he thought, and so little here of man – only a few green tin roofs in the distance, and they were dwarfed by the towering trees.

It's paradise, he thought. No wonder his mother had found herself pulled back to this place. And he began to cry.

The thought of his mother had opened him to grief that, as it came spilling out, seemed almost to dissolve him. Softly at first he cried but gradually more loudly until he was standing and crying openly as he had never, ever cried. Not when his father had come to tell him that his mother was dead. Not when he had gone to see her grave. Not when he had been expelled. Only at school and at night, but furtively so that nobody would ever know. And now, in this place to which he was so foreign, he didn't mind that a stranger was standing, and staring, open mouthed as he continued crying.

He was crying for the mother he had dreamed of and who, if she ever had existed, was now entirely gone. For the father he couldn't talk to and who had entrapped himself in defiance and in lies. For the sister who had travelled thousands of miles so as – and he knew this was why, even if she didn't – to get away from the things that could not be said. Crying, not silently as he had taught himself to do, and not caring what anybody thought of him, but crying, on and on, because there was nothing he could have done to stop his tears.

'Colombo?'

'No. Into town,' and then, in response to his driver's crest-fallen face, 'I'll pay you extra in compensation.'

As they drove back into town, he felt strangely calm. And also hungry. He contemplated going back to the hotel, up the neat gravelled driveway, past those well weeded and constrained flowerbeds and into the plush dark of the dining room with its starched tablecloths and obsequious waiters, and he said, 'Stop here. I'll make my own way back.'

He stood for a moment to get his bearings. He looked at the vast, over-decorated red construction that was the post office. He would go in there soon, he decided, and ring Vanessa and tell her what had happened. He might even, instead of heading back to England, travel in the opposite direction around the world to visit her.

The post office dwarfed the other low and makeshift buildings that were crammed, one beside the other, along the side of the road. He went in. It was very crowded, queues snaking round the huge room.

Not the time to phone, he thought. Not yet. But he could write.

He'd already taken a postcard from his hotel room. Leaning against the wall he addressed it to his father. What next? Oblivious to the people swirling around and about him, he stood and he thought. First he thought, I found her, and he wrote it, *I found her*, adding his name, *Milton*. Then another thought – no, not enough. And so, underneath his name he wrote, *We have a lot to talk about*.

The queue was far too long. He put the postcard in his pocket. He would get the hotel to send it.

Out he went.

There were people everywhere including in a road that was dusty and full of potholes and old cars parked at odd angles. Groups of men chatting softly as sari-clad women went about their shopping.

From a roadside kiosk he bought two hoppers. He took the hot parchment-thin folded dough into which a dollop of curry and sambol had been wrapped over to a makeshift seat outside the post office. There he bit into the first, his taste buds revelling in that combination of sharp spices and coconut and hot, hot chilli. As he ate, he looked up. He could see the dusty, hanging shredded leaves of a banana tree and, beyond them, the vestiges of the jungle that was waiting, he knew, for its moment of return.

Still he continued to eat and, as he did, it dawned on him that something was different. It was the way people were looking at him. No. Scrap that. It was the way they were not looking at him. Wearing, as he was, a sarong, he was no longer a walking advertisement of his own foreignness.

While he wore it and while he made sure not to open his mouth, they would take him for one of them.

So did Milton continue to sit, slowly finishing his hopper, feeling, for once, that truly he belonged.

Acknowledgements

Thanks to Sita Abeyasekara, Neil Austin, Craig Brough, Bill and June Goodings, Ayisha de Lanerolle, Indra de Lanerolle, Vijay de Lanerolle, Bryan Logan, Steve Morell, Gloria Paul, Kumar Paul, Shehan Paul, Boniface Rajaratnam, Sue Shakespeare, Johnny Wild, Julian Wilson and Keith Writer, many of them strangers who opened their homes and their lives and their knowledge, to me.

Elise Dillsworth, Sarah Dunant, Linda Grant, Maria Margaronis, Fiona McMorrough, Gwen Metcalf, Susie Orbach, Elaine Proctor, Sally Riley and Ronald Segal were generous with their reading time, their thoughts and their encouragement.

My agent, Clare Alexander was unfailingly good tempered and on my side throughout this sometimes tortuous process. Robyn Slovo's kindness and flashes of brilliance dug me out of many a deep hole. Coming up on the inside track, Cassie Metcalf-Slovo proved herself to be the most perspicacious of readers. My editor, Lennie Goodings put the whole force of her considerable abilities into helping me find and write the book I wanted to write. And, finally, although his role has changed, Andy Metcalf still walked with me every step of the way. Thanks to you all.